Claire,

If you go to
L.A. Don'T
Bring your
Morality.

Sleeping with Snakes
Notes from the Los Angeles Underbelly

Ron Sievers [anthologist]

Cover Art: Marcellus Hall // www.marcellushall.com
Layout & Design: Descamino Art & Design // www.descamino.com

Sleeping with Snakes
Notes from the Los Angeles Underbelly

www.sleepingwithsnakes.com

:[The Orange Labs]:
www.orangerecordings.com
www.orangepublishings.com
www.orangeaudiolabs.com

Thank You
The Edendale
Joe Muran
Gwyneth Asdorian
Valerie Aiello
Jennifer Pillsbury
All of the authors that made this possible

CONTENTS

Charles Bukowski

From A Letter to Mike Golden at Smoke Signals Magazine

Volume 2, Numbers 2 & 3, 1981

//

Sleeping with Snakes

To encourage bad writers to continue writing in spite of rejection doesn't matter: they're going to do it anyhow. The little mags print about 15% of material that is fair writing; the larger mags, perhaps 20.

Sad things happen in the little mag field. I knew a writer who was writing fairly live stuff for the littles. He got published here and there, there and here. He had 2 or 3 chapbooks published by little press editors, say issues of 200. This writer had a terrible job and he came home each night, his guts stamped and dangling, and he wrote it down, A chapbook or 2 more, many appearances in the littles - - every time you opened a mag, here was his name. He decided he was a writer, came west with wife and kids, wife got job and he sat over the typer and punched at it, His bookcase was full of little mags and chapbooks and he gave poetry readings to crowds of 9 or 11, where they passed the hat. His poetry gradually softened but his bookcase was behind him. Of course it couldn't pay the electric bill, but since he was a genius there was the wife to do that, get that bill and all the others and the rent and so forth. I hope he's working again. Maybe it's time for his wife to sit down to the typer. This is one case but I believe it could be multiplied by 50 or 1,000.

It's confusing as to what's real or what isn't real, I remember when I was in my early twenties, living on one candy bar a day so I could have time to write, I was writing 5 or 6 short stories a week and they were all coming back. But when I read the New Yorker, Harper's, the Atlantic, I couldn't detect anything in there but 19th century literature, careful and contrived, worked out tediously, inch by inch of boredom crawling across the pages, name writers, fakers, yawing me into imbecility. I had an idea I was a pretty good writer but there was no way of knowing. I couldn't spell and my grammar was crap (they still are) but I felt I was doing something better than they were: I was: I was starving excellently.

Because you're not accepted doesn't necessarily mean you're a genius. Maybe you just write badly. I know of some who publish their own books who point to the 2 or 3 examples of great writers of the past who also did that. Ow. They also point to guys who weren't recognized in their lifetime (Van Gogh and co.), and that means, of course, that .... Ow.

The rejects from the big mags are usually printed and therefore soulless. But I've gotten some things from little mag editors who thought they were gods. One I remember: "Just what the fuck is this shit?" No signature, just the large ink scrawl across the page. Much more than once, things of this nature. How do I know it's not from some 17 year old kid with acne, hooked on Yeats, using his father's discarded mimeo machine in his garage? I know: read the mag. Who wants to? When you're writing 30 poems a month there's no time to read: If there's time, and some money, you drink.

Very successful writers are like presidents: they get the vote because the madding crowd recognizes something of itself in them. It's confusing, Mike, I don't know what to tell you. I'm getting ready to go out and play the quarter horses.

yes, yrs, Buk

Notes from the Los Angeles Underbelly

Brandon D. Christopher
The Mortuary Driver
2004

//

Brandon D. Christopher was born in Los Angeles, California, where he acquired his taste for the odd and macabre at an early age. A fan of both vice and virtue, he believes nothing in this world is as savory as a passport, a pair of boots, and a good cup of coffee. His first novel, *Household Gods*, is soon to be released.

Spending two months in your apartment without a job is like visiting another country without a camera. It's great while you're there, but a couple of months later when you're back home, you start forgetting about all of those good times and those great, picturesque views, and you now only vaguely recall those magnificent sights in dreams and nostalgic moments during foreign films on cable.

My two-month vacation had burned through all $3,000 that I had saved up, and since I had quit my previous position as a full-time chauffeur and part-time artist, I was unable to get unemployment assistance.

Come Monday morning, I was awake and ready with my Starbucks coffee and *LA Times* classifieds section. I made a little breakfast and started circling ads that I thought might be of some interest. I called several positions that I was qualified for and faxed my first onslaught of resumes.

There were no callbacks by lunchtime. There were still no callbacks by 2:00. I checked my bank account online, hoping some money had been accidentally transferred to me. It was still at $110. $110 is a lot like having $10 when you need $800 for rent. I was determined not to borrow money. I had thirteen days to make rent.

By 4:00 in the afternoon, I was frantically calling every ad in the classifieds section. I added several new variations of my resume to the fax file, equipping myself with working knowledge of almost any position available. I was now a qualified accountant, a landscape technician, and a personal assistant. Still no calls. I checked the phone line and the fax machine again. I was just about to give up for the day and make a martini when my eyes caught a big ad in the classifieds. It read:

MORTUARY DRIVER NEEDED. GOOD MONEY,
GREAT HOURS- CALL 323-555-0856 NEED ASAP.

What luck, I thought to myself. I called the number, and the woman on the line set up an interview for that night, and I thanked her graciously. The way I figured it, I had two kinds of experience in the mortuary field: I was once a limo driver, and I was once arrested for breaking into a cemetery. Although I would omit the latter part of my experience, the limo driver bit would come in handy. Throw in a few past sales positions and maybe a summer job at a cemetery in, say, Colorado or Phoenix. Perfect.

I drove out to the small building in East Los Angeles for the interview, arriving seventeen minutes early. Phil, the owner of the mortuary company, alongside his portly wife, sat me down in a leather chair in a perfectly rectangular room and casually explained the position to me.

"Basically, we pick up "expired" bodies and take them to different morgues. Now, sometimes these expired bodies are messed up, okay? Sometimes they're decomposed, sometimes they're infants or children, and that's the worst! And sometimes they're just parts of bodies, okay? Hands or legs, but you have to remember, they're just empty shells now, they're just bodies," Phil explained to me.

"Hmmmm," I nodded, thinking about the show *Six Feet Under*.

"I'm not trying to scare you, okay? I just want you to know what you're in for. Sometimes when you pick them up, the pressure will push out body juices from their nose and mouth, and you don't want to get any of that on you, okay?" Phil further explained.

"Okay," I replied, "don't want to get it on me." I felt like saying 'surreptitious' for some reason.

"You a religious man, Brandon?" He asked me.

"Oh, I was a catholic when I was a kid, but now, you know, now I read too much to be religious." I said.

Phil looked at me, slightly confused by my answer. "Well, good then. So, you don't believe in ghosts?"

"I've never seen one," I replied.

Both Phil and his wife chuckled to one another, and I knew I was in for a ghost story or two.

"Now, I ain't no religious man myself, but I've seen things that would freak even Geraldo Rivera out," Phil said, and I wondered just how out-of-the-zeitgeist-loop they both were. I haven't even heard Geraldo's name mentioned since the chair hit him in the nose.

"This one time, when I was dropping off a body at a mortuary in the early AM, when no one was around, I kept hearing laughter coming from this closed casket, then something took my keys from my belt and threw them across the floor, right in front of me! Right in front of me!"

I wondered if Phil drank. Pausing there, nodding my head, I deliberated on just how much I needed this job. $110 kept flashing in my head.

"How does this sound to you, Brandon? Would you like something like this?"

"What's the position pay?" I asked.

"See, that's the tricky part," Phil replied. "You get paid per body, about eleven dollars per body. So, you pick up ten a day, you made about a hundred bucks!"

Eleven dollars per body! Eleven dollars. The sanctity of death worth a mere eleven dollars.

"Sounds real good, Phil," I said. "Real good."

"Great! Why don't you come in tomorrow and we'll get you started. We'll send you out with Matt for the day, he's about your age," Phil said after we shook hands. I thanked him and drove home, thinking, this could either have been the coolest job in the world or the second stupidest thing I've ever done.

I awoke early, showered, and arrived back at the small building in Los Angeles just as Matt, my new coworker, pulled up in the confidential, white, mortuary van and parked beside my Volvo. We shook hands as I got into the van, and we made our way to Northridge for our first pick-up: Richard Fowler, a residential death.

"Residentials are when someone dies in their house," Matt explained. "That's a good bulk of the business we get - like old people and stuff."

It was a large house, and Matt backed the van into the driveway. He organized his clipboard of paperwork for the third time before we walked to the front door and were greeted by a young woman with a cried-out voice and red eyes. She welcomed us inside and escorted us to the master bathroom, where her 70 year-old father, the aforementioned Mr. Fowler, had collapsed on the floor and died in a fetal position. Matt told me to bring the gurney around through the back of the house while he took care of the paperwork.

I returned with the gurney and pulled the blanket off of Mr. Fowler, and I was quite surprised to see both of his eyes wide open. They seemed to follow me wherever I walked, like a creepy doll's eyes.

Matt returned to the bathroom and found me in a trance, staring down at the deceased. He nodded to the white sheet on the gurney, and I grabbed it and laid it length-wise beside the corpse. We pushed the body onto its side, and everything moved in one big motion, with his its eyes still following me, then slid the sheet beneath him.

"Now, using the sheet, we'll lift him and put him on the gurney on one, two... THREE!" Matt said, and we lifted Mr. Fowler and walked him the five feet to the table on wheels outside the door.

The corpse had a serious case of rigor mortis, making it difficult to attach the gurney's safety belts around his crimped arms and bent knees. The white sheet ballooned out atop the gurney, like we had covered a large tree branch. I kind-of knew what was coming next.

"We're going to have to straighten him out," Matt explained. "Just pull down on his legs and I'll get the arms." Mr. Fowler's cold ankle felt like a thawing turkey in a sink. I pulled hard and pressed down on the knee, and the sound of breaking twigs erupted. My stomach began to turn. Matt finished the other leg for me.

We easily fastened the safety belts this time and wheeled Mr. Fowler around the side of the house to the back of the van in the driveway. "I want you to slide the gurney into the van now. Remember to pull up on that lever there as his head reaches the bumper," Matt said.

"Sure, Matt, I can handle this," I replied.

Mr. Fowler weighed about 150 pounds, so I was going to need to pull back a bit and shove the gurney forward to the bumper with some might. As I pulled it back about three feet, the daughter of the deceased appeared beside us with two steaming cups of coffee. I was startled by her presence and released the lever too soon. The sound was the most frightening part as Mr. Fowler's head smashed into the bumper, and the gurney dropped to the ground. The sheet had flown back, and Mr. Fowler's eyes now watched us all from under the back of the van.

"Oh Jesus," I sighed, as Matt quickly kneeled down and lifted the gurney back to its wheels and into the van.

We both turned around to apologize to the daughter for what just happened, but all that remained of her was the sound of a slamming door and two splashes on the driveway where the cups of coffee had spilt.

We drove back to the main office, where I explained to Phil and his wife that I just wasn't up for this type of job. Again, Phil and his wife chuckled. He gave me the eleven dollars I had earned for my one gig, patted me on the back and said, "Yea, we kinda figured that."

Notes from the Los Angeles Underbelly

Marc Shapiro

Voiceover

Sometime around 1985 (the memory is the first thing to go)

//

Husband. Father. Wife. Daughter. One dog. Two cats. No secrets.
Except one. Film rights available.

God! How he hated doing this shit!

Bob vented his frustration by banging his head twice on the steering wheel of a car so old it was new again. Not hard enough to do damage but hard enough to shock him back to reality. Reality driven home when his third head strike hit the horn.

Bob was a forty something actor. Too old for leading man roles. To unusual looking, at least according to his last agent, for character parts. He couldn't buy a bit part in a direct to video slasher movie.

But Bob smiled. A cruel, sad, ironic smile. Because Bob could moan and
groan with the best of them.

And that was why he was here.

At midnight. In a gravel parking lot. Next to a dark, windowless black hole of a bunker...On the wrong side of town.

He took the parking lot in twenty steps and found the building's only door around back. Bob looked down as he reached for the knob. A welcome mat stared back at him. Somebody's idea of a joke. Bob had to hand it to them. It was funny. He gingerly wiped off his feet and entered.

Down a long, deserted corridor. To a large circular alcove.

"Evening Jane."

To an elderly woman, sitting behind a cluttered desk, her nose buried in *The National Enquirer*. She did not look up.

"Dubbing Stage four. A one reeler. *The Lusty Ninjas*," she droned in monotone.

Bob blew Jane a kiss, turned on his heels and shuffled off in the direction of Dubbing Stage 4, mulling the title of this gig over and over in his mind. And having a laugh at all the uptight third world countries who churn out this low grade porn like so much summer sausage and yet were so hung up on religion that their actors couldn't bring themselves to make the pleasure noises that accompanied their acts.

But hey! Who was he to complain? These mindless voiceover exercises were a quick and dirty way to pay the rent. And, he sighed, given his luck with women lately, *The Lusty Ninjas* was probably the closest he was going to get to getting laid in this lifetime.

He rounded a corner just in time to see Fred, an over the hill Hippie who was in a seemingly perpetual state of bliss, walking into the projection booth with a can of film under his arm.

"Hey Fred. What's shakin'?"

"The leaves on the trees."

It was Fred's stock greeting and it had long since ceased being funny. But Bob did not feel like raining all over Fred's karma and so he chuckled at the cliché one more time.

"You're going to love this one Bob. It's a period piece. Period piece. Get it?"

Bob got it.

"So, who's my voice babe tonight?"

"Don't know. Helen was supposed to do it but her agent called at the last minute with a legit gig."

Bob's insides turned green. Even his porn partners were getting decent jobs.

"Her replacement's inside. Jane says she got here a while ago."

Fred disappeared into the projection booth as Bob started for the dubbing stage door. He hesitated, mentally masturbating with the mystery of who was on the other side. These looping actresses were inevitably stone foxes. Maybe he'd get a boner. Maybe he'd get lucky. Maybe...

He stepped through the door.

"Ann!"

His heart sank. Across the room, sitting on a stool. So did Ann's.

"Hello Bob," she said icily.

He crossed to the stool next to hers, picked up the headphones sitting on it and sat down uneasily next to her.

"I'm sorry about this," he stammered, not really sure that he was. "If I had known it was you I would have canceled."

Ann shifted her blue jeaned legs. His eyes instinctively went from them to her white T shirt that was not leaving anything to the imagination. She said nothing. She's not making this easy. It was just like her.

"So," he said. "How's it been going?"

"Not too good. That's why I'm here."

Ouch! She could not have cut deeper if she had used a chainsaw. But wasn't it her wit, not to mention her body, her great personality, the way she balanced her check book and her body that had attracted him to her in the first place?

They should still be together today.

If only he had been more of a man.

They sat in silence for what seemed like eons. He making a big deal of adjusting his headphones. She of reading the trades. Bob's heart and brain beat a double drum solo. He was ready to bolt. But this was not a business that suffered fools and the lovelorn lightly.

I've got it! I can't read these lines! Time out for a rewrite. Yeah, sure. The absurdity of the thought broke a smile on his face. He glanced across at Ann. Her smile mirrored his and then quickly turned upside down and returned to the safety of *Variety*.

"Okay kiddies!," bellowed Fred from the projection booth. "This is pretty simple stuff. A few moans, some heavy breathing and a couple of 'yes oh yes's' and we'll be home free."

They slipped on their headphones as the room lights faded to black. White
light appeared against a screen on the far wall. The projector began its click clack and some scratchy leader film created instant abstract art. *The Lusty Ninjas* title shimmered onto the screen and off in a wash of tacky optical effects.

A bright orange sun appeared on screen backed by some tinny Oriental muzak. Good no credits. No Johnny Wad, Sally Twats and all that other porn bullshit. This would be slam bam thank you mam. That's what Bob thought. What Ann thought, outlined next to him in the flickering light, was anybody's guess.

On screen a young Oriental girl ran into frame and away, fear on her face, head turning to that fear closing in. The sound of hoof-beats as a Ninja, dressed in full fighting getup, rides after her. He leaps from his horse and tackles the frightened girl. She fights him as he ravages her with kisses. Finally she relents.

"Oh! Mmmm! Oh!"

Ann was right on cue, admired Bob. What a pro.

Bob worked his mouth muscles in method warmup as the Ninja tore open her kimono and, of course, found her naked underneath. Bob started with some heavy, labored breathing as the warrior tongued her silicon enhanced breasts and flat stomach. He was joined with low moans by Ann as the screen lover found that hot, wet space between her legs.

"Oh my God!," roared Ann taking the lead. "Oh yes, yes."

"Yeah," purred Bob adding some unintelligible animal grunts for good measure.

Foreplay over. The Ninja disrobed, spread his conquest's legs wide and sank the pink deep inside her. Ann marked the occasion with...

"Yes! Oh yes! That feels sooo good!"

Ann was on a roll. Her expression said she was reading a laundry list. Her voice said she was in orgasm heaven.

"Yeah! Oh yeah! Uh! Uh! Uh!," rallied Bob as the action on the screen headed into the home stretch.

"Oh my God! You're so good," chimed in Ann with a straight face.

Their passionate looping reached climax in time to the final thrusts and shudders on the screen. The screen couple collapsed in a heap. Ann and Bob sat back, awaiting further instructions. The screen went momentarily dark. Fred's voice came, jokingly, through their headphones.

"Okay folks, it's time to get real hot and nasty. Groans, yells, pots banging. Just use your imagination."

Bob turned in the dark to where Ann was sitting. He was using his imagination. Remembering the good times.

The projector flashed back to life and into a three ring circus of lust. The stud and the hot babe were going balls out on some throw pillows while two hand maidens had a third spreadeagled and were working a dildo in and out of her.

Bob and Ann were off and running.

"Oh! Ah! Yes! Oh give it to me! Oh yeah, you're so wet!"

Their erotic tirades were rocketing in the darkened room. Bob found his enthusiasm growing at the insanity of it all. He was laughing to himself as he made coupling noises. What a joke. What a laugh.

Ann's hand crept into his.

His "oh yeah, oh God yeah" skipped an audible beat. His insides stopped laughing. This wasn't part of the drill. He looked in Ann's direction. Her eyes, in the shifting light, were half closed, a drop dead look that told a tale of their own. Ann's hand tightened in his. And he heard…

"God! You feel so good inside me! Oh yes! Give me all you've got!"

This too sounded very real. Bob knew because he remembered when what had been between them had been that way. And the memory of that made him grow hard as he roared…

"Oh yeah! Does it feel good? You're so hot!… I'm so hot!"

He meant every word of it.

"Uh! Uh! Yes! Yes!" Their passion count jumped a level, matching and eclipsing the seemingly puny efforts of the porn images to keep up. Bob and Ann eyed the screen in a hypnotic gaze, mentally getting each other off as the screen banging neared its climax.

"Yes! Yes!," roared Ann as she shuddered, a charge of orgasm that shot up Bob's arm and bucked his body. He was close but not there yet and he was convinced that he could get Ann off one more time. His hand dropped hers and found her thigh. He squeezed, moved his hand up and found her spreading dampness.

"My God!," exploded Ann in one final surge of ecstasy. Bob's loins responded with a jump and an explosion of their own.
Just as the screen faded to black and the lights came up. They looked at each other, fighting for composure and breath as the sweat

beaded on their brows.

"Have fun folks?" It was Fred's best, all knowing, understated voice in their ears. Bob and Ann's hands instinctively moved to cover their damp areas. Embarrassment replaced satiated lust. But a longing look between them, shooting love daggers, quickly dispelled that feeling.

Fred had been around the porn racket long enough to see the signs. Voiceover types, especially those on the rebound, often got carried away with the heat of the moment and well..shit happened. And so he was cool as he watched the pair pulling their disheveled mental selves back together.

"One take and we're in the can. Thanks folks. The key's in the lobby. Lock up when you're finished. I'm out of here."

He quickly rewound the film and set it in motion again, turning down the lights as he slipped out the door. Fred loved playing Cupid.

"I can't believe we're doing this," Ann whispered as she wrapped her arms around Bob's neck. His hands trembled as he sought out her waist.
"Neither can I."

Their mouths found each other in an electric kiss that held as they slipped to the dubbing stage floor. Groping and thrashing in the shadows of *The Lusty Ninja* which was once again unspooling to their sex dance. Ann's mouth moved from Bob's lips to his neck, offering small, pecking kisses. Bob's eyes glazed, an animal something eyeing her trim body. He pushed her advances away and ripped her shirt off, exposing taut, firm breasts.

Ann's face reflected her own heat, picturing her former lover and now lover again caressing her nipples to the point of insanity and the first of many foreplay orgasms. Her face turned to concern when Bob ignored her obvious desires and, instead, unbuckled her jeans and tugged them savagely to her ankles. Her panties followed in shreds. Bob, in a primordial rage, forced her legs open. Ann's mind flashed fear and frustration as Bob attempted to thrust his angry beast into her.

Nothing had changed.

"Bob! Stop! Stop it now!"

His ardor came to a stumbling halt. He looked down at her and saw the disappointment in her eyes. His erection fell flat.

"You haven't changed," she half screamed-half sobbed. "You still don't know how to make love."

His mind mentally backtracked. She was right. Never had, never would. He was selfish that way. His total lack of consideration had been a turn on when they first met. She got off on it, literally and figuratively. But when she discovered that was all he had to offer and, more importantly, was not willing to learn new tricks, she had left. And now a year later...Was she really expecting anything else?

They stared, one sad last moment. Ann pulled away and began putting her clothes back on.

"You pud pulling asshole! Don't you know anything?"

They froze. The attack had not been hers. Or his. But rather a smooth, reptilian bit of ghostly air.

"Up here! On the screen!"

They turned to the porn film. Their mouths fell silently open.

Lusty Ninjas had ground to a freeze frame right in the middle of the orgy sequence with all the principles frozen in their coitus poses. Except for the Ninja, who now stood naked, hands on hips, in nightmarish relief. He looked out at them with a look of disgust and disappointment that easily surpassed Ann's.
"You cowboys just don't get it, do you," the Ninja growled. "We lay it out for you all the time. It was in *Debbie's Desires*, *The Red*

Garter Diaries. Hell, it was even in *Virgins Get Drunk And Disorderly.* All you had to do was look!"

Bob rubbed his eyes. Ann continued her zombie stare. The Lusty Ninja took two giant steps out of the screen and onto the floor.

"We made love to our women in all of those films. L.O.V.E. Love! We were serious about it. That's why part of us stays with the project when it's over. That's why I'm in your face. Sure we're all hung like horses but we got the gigs because we know how to please a woman."

He cast a particularly accusing glare at Bob.

"And what do you rain coat freaks do? You ignore us. Oh sure, you're out there in those sticky seats, playing pocket pool. But what do you do when you go home to your wives and girlfriends? You forget everything we've taught you and just pop your corks."

He turned to Ann. Understanding replacing contempt. Then back to Bob.

"Get out your notebook chump! I'm going to show you want to do."

He stepped up and back into the frozen tableau. One arm reached out toward Ann. She was transfixed, a look of fear, confusion and that deadliest of emotions, curiosity, playing out across her face. She looked at Bob whose own face offered no answer. Her jeans once again fell to her ankles. She kicked them away. Ann took a hesitant step forward, then another. A third brought her to the Ninja's outstretched hand. She looked at Bob.

There was nothing to keep her in this world.

She put her hand in his, pulled back slightly and finally settled into the spectre's firm grip. She felt electric lightness lancing through her body. Ann looked down at the floor. Her feet were not touching.

Bob found his voice. It was a cry of anguish at the sight of Ann floating through space and into the screen. The air around Ann crackled and sparked as she left her world and entered his. Ann found herself in the middle of the throw pillows and the dildo wielding trio. She stood facing the strong, compassionate and, yes, manly features of the Ninja. She was not afraid.

Bob ran to the screen and banged on the flat, unyielding surface with his fists. Ann and her new suitor looked out at him. The Ninja turned to Bob, screen face to his real world face.

"This is how it's done."

The Ninja turned to Ann and pulled her close. Ann shuddered but did not fight him. For there was no threat or brutishness in his embrace. He kissed her full on the mouth, forcefully but with tenderness, his tongue entwining hers. Then to her neck where nips of love sent shivers up her spine. He moved to her breasts, showering attention on each, bringing her nipples to hardness.

"Oh yes!," moaned Ann. "That feels so good!" Her body spasmed as she climaxed slow and long.

Bob stood, his mind fogged, as Ann and this residue of a two bit porn actor did the long, hard and nasty. There was fear. There was madness. But, when he finally laid his mental cards on the table, there was the reality, mixed with jealousy, that celluloid come to life was giving Ann something he never could.

Pure love and lust.

The spirit brought Ann gently to the pillows and, after a few cautionary nips at the insides of her thighs, probed her vagina with his tongue.

"Ohhh! Godd!," she screamed as she came once again. "God! What are you doing to me!"
The porn ghost worked his way around her body, probing spots and emotions, working his magic. Almost as an afterthought he mounted her and, in a series of long, short and intermediate strokes,

grew and exploded inside her. They lay together in exhausted silence. The Ninja turned to Bob.

"That's how it's done."

Ann rolled over, still in her lover's arms, and smiled at Bob. The smile told it all. Bob had to admit he had never been that good.

"Ann I can do those things," he pleaded, his face flush with the screen. "I've learned my lesson. I know what it takes. I can be the man you want."

"Just give me another chance."

Ann's expression softened. She looked from Bob to the Ninja laying next to her. He said nothing but rose, helping her to her feet.

"Please come back to me," whimpered Bob. "You won't be sorry."

"Maybe you won't be sorry," the Ninja boomed in. "Maybe you will. You can go back to this man or you can stay here with me."

Ann looked to Bob, to her new love and back again.

"Ann come out," yelled Bob, bound and determined to not make her decision easy. "You know what it was like before (oops wrongo)... well imagine what it will be like now that I've learned how a real man loves. Please just give me one more chance."

She hesitated, swallowed deeply. Ann took a cautious step forward and then stopped. She looked back. The Ninja's look made it plain that the decision was hers.

She stepped back.
"Ann I love you," pleaded Bob.

Ann took a step forward. The Ninja let go of her hand. She took another step and another. The air crackled and broke around her ankle as her foot sizzled back onto the dubbing stage floor.

Bob smiled. He had won.

"No!," yelled Ann as she stepped back into the film. "Yes! No! Yes! I don't know what to do!"

Bob cringed at her indecision and watched, helpless, as she stepped back and forth between the two worlds half a dozen times. Finally she moaned a low, pitiful cry and collapsed at the feet of the Ninja.

"I love you," wailed Bob, clearly on the verge of a breakdown. "I love you."

The screen image began to flicker as the projector clicked once again into motion. The Ninja returned to his copulating country-woman and the hand maidens were once again working their dildo. Ann's face suddenly grew to fill the screen. Sprocket marks and the graininess of the final feet of film crisscrossed her tortured features. A crudely scrawled The End flashed briefly across her face.

"I love you Bob," she cried. A cry cut short as the last few feet of film was gobbled up by the pick up reel.

Bob cried and stumbled in the darkness. He suddenly became logical in the face of the horror of it all. He raced to the projection booth, rewound the film and played it through. The porn film was just that. Missing was the footage of his lover in a multi dimensional tryst. He watched the film a dozen more times.

Until he finally gave up and went home.

"It's that guy again," the usher reported to the night manager of The Cat House Theater. "He's back again."

The manager followed the usher back into the darkened theater where about a dozen men sat scattered as *The Lusty Ninja* played out for the tenth time that day.

"The day guy told me he's been here since the theater opened at noon. He just sits there in the front row, looking up at the screen."

"Pretty much like it's been all week," responded the manager as the returned to the lobby. "He maybe trouble. But there's been no complaints, no wienie wagging. Hey, you know it could be he's a normal Joe with a thing for Chink sex. Leave him be."

The usher shrugged his shoulders and swished the lobby door shut, plunging the theater once again into total darkness.

Down front. Center seat. Bob. Stubbled, wrinkled, bleary eyed. Looking straight up at the orgy scene playing out once again. Once again he strained, hoping against hope that Ann was in there somewhere and that she had changed her mind and was ready to come back to him.

But the only bodies he saw humping and bumping were yellow. He slouched
back in his chair. Maybe the next showing. Or the next theater. Or the next town. He knew she would come back to him eventually. Because he had been taught a lesson in love.

And now he knew what to do.

The End

Gordon Basichis
Spook
Completed in the summer of 2004
//

Gordon Basichis is the author of *Spook*. This first chapter is excerpted from his roman a' clef about about his own adventures working for the man responsible for detecting Chinese espionage operations within the United States. The novel was completed this past summer. Basichis has authored two other books as well as produced screenplays and television episodes. He is a longtime resident of Southern California and sees Los Angeles as an evolving character in much of his work.

CHAPTER ONE

It was winter in Van Nuys. Winter in Southern California could never evoke the frosty bleakness of the northern states, but on the right night it was still capable of creating an ambience of urban drear and desolation. The streets were empty; traffic was sparse. Gusts of wind blew leaves and trash. I was sitting in the shadows inside Noah Brown's ancient Chevy El Camino, sipping bad coffee from a Styrofoam cup, my eyes cast toward a dumpster ridden alleyway that divided the tacky shops on Van Nuys Boulevard from the tacky apartments two and three stories above the street.

"That's it." Noah pointed to one ugly apartment building that was nearly indistinguishable from the next. "He lives in the back."

I nodded and studied the dark windows in the second floor rear. A creepy feeling swept over me as I focused on the older, cheaper vehicles parked in the carport on the street level just underneath the building.

"You sure he's not there?" It was less a question and more a plea for reassurance.

Noah gestured. "See the empty space, the last space on the last row? That's where he parks his car."

I nodded, catching the sounds of blue-collar din-a dish clattering in some unknown kitchen, violence from an overloud TV. The smell of a hundred microwave dinners mingled with the garbage odor spiraling from a couple dozen dumpsters. It was bleak and banal, and it stood in sharp contrast to the pre-conceived glamour of cloak-and-dagger romance. But, in fact, it was the banality itself that heightened the danger that lay just a few yards away.

"He may be a contract player, working for Louie's friends. He may be here on his own, it's too early to tell."

I nodded, turning to look at my companion. Noah Brown. Noah was a one of a kind, a government spook with a social and scientific pedigree. Having traveled with Noah for more than a year, I knew all too well about the many times and many places Noah had sat waiting in the darkness. Waiting for his prey. Noah's gray hair and angular face were appropriately noirish in the shadows of his faded beige El Camino. Despite his age, Noah remained the ever-faithful adventure junkie, seeking his own peculiar gratifications, which he sometimes cloaked in the guise of patriotic ideology. The El Camino, like the aging and seemingly fragile Noah, was deceptively virile, filled with spy gear, weapons and a powerhouse engine.

"Either way, I don't want him around causing a ruckus," Noah went on. "The last thing I need is to go chasing him all over the country. Not with all this other business on my plate."

"How did he get into the country?" I asked.

"Slipped in," Noah shrugged matter-of-factly. "Happens all the time. They're in and out of here. Sometimes we catch them, sometimes we don't. But Yomiya, he's one of their big chief muckety mucks. He gets loose and..." Noah let his voice trail off.

I nodded in understanding. I looked to the apartment where Dennis Yomiya was living. Yomiya, a native Japanese, was a high-ranking member of the old Red Brigade who was rumored to be selling his skills to the highest bidder. Surely, he was worth his price. Yomiya was a solid professional who reportedly specialized in terrorist bombings and political assassinations. For years he had eluded law enforcement and intelligence agencies, in Europe, especially. He was a former college professor who had embraced the radical vision a little too tightly, and now he was stuck with the habit of killing and mayhem. Yomiya was a rogue without legitimacy, and without a country to call his own.

"So what do you want me to do?" I asked.

"Find his mailbox," Noah said, handing me a key. "And take whatever mail's inside. It'll help us establish his current network. Remember, he's going under the name Katayama."

"This key will work?" I asked, holding up the key he had given me. "You're sure?"

Noah barely smiled. I knew that miserly smile was all the assurance I was getting.

"And be careful. This guy is a pro. I mean he's marquee material. He spooks easily, and he can put a knife through your eye at twenty yards."

"Any other words of encouragement?"

"Look around. But don't dawdle up there."

I got out of the car hoping I was ready for the unthinkable and the unexpected. I was frightened. I knew I was no match for a renowned terrorist, and my youthful sense of immortality had, a few precious years before, left for parts unknown. I made my way through the rear walkway and into the spare and modest courtyard where the tenants entered their apartments. There were several doors facing the spare concrete courtyard, with a stairwell leading to the second floor of apartments. Yellow lamplight from inside the apartments slipped out through the cheap drapes and aluminum frame windows, casting shadows against the lone banana tree on the weathered stucco wall. I found the mailbox marked Katayama, Yomiya's cover name, and slipped the key into the lock. I opened the mailbox just as I heard a car pull up in the driveway.

It was one of those moments frozen in time, when you realize you just committed to a single foolish action that could actually end your life. I stifled the shakes, pulled the single letter out of the mailbox and stuffed it inside my jacket. Reaching into my pocket, I felt for the .25 automatic I had stashed there. It was a cheapo Saturday night special, the kind the anti-gun lobbyists vilify for its predominance in gang marauding and drunken shootouts. If anything, at that particular moment, the .25 was puny and inadequate, more of an ornament than decent protection. I remembered how old gun nuts I knew used to joke that shooting someone with a .25 caliber would only piss him off. I hoped I wouldn't have to disprove that theory.

Yomiya appeared in the mouth of the courtyard, blocking my exit. He was momentarily startled by my presence, but since I made no move toward him, he feigned indifference, barely looking up as I started past him on my way out of the courtyard. He was wearing wire rim glasses, a short leather jacket and his trademark woolen newsboy's cap. At first glance he wasn't threatening at all, more like the college professor of old, lost in his thoughts. But looking closer, there was no denying his wary movement and the deadly aura he projected from deep within.

Either my sixth sense was in tune that night, or I actually did hear his rubber sole sliding every so slightly on the courtyard's surface grit. I'm still not sure. I turned suddenly, drawing my gun, and found him facing me, his hand inside his jacket pocket. Before I dared think about it, I fired twice. The first bullet caught him flush in the cheekbone, just under the eye, and the other skimmed the side of his face.

Instinctively, he grabbed at his face, grumbling what I was sure was "Shit," in English, before muttering and cursing in what sounded like Japanese. He staggered like a drunk, desperately reaching into his jacket. I sensed it was no knife he was going for, but his gun. Sheer fear compelled me to step in to point blank range and fire three times in rapid succession, putting small, bloody holes in his temple. It was like a dream. Echoes and flashes in the tiny courtyard. He was gasping for breath, still weaving and muttering, making vain attempts to pull his gun. The blood pooled in his ear and ran down his neck. He dropped hard to his knees, like his feet had been chopped out from under him. I nearly shit when his nine-millimeter pistol spilled out of his jacket and clattered on the concrete. Yomiya muttered something again, in a softer, barely audible tone and then pitched forward on his face. I shot him one more time through the back of his head.

As I walked quickly toward the car, I thought my heart would leap out of my chest. My knees were locked and buckling; my legs were rubber. Somehow I found the presence of mind to stash the hot and smoking pistol into my jacket. When I reached the end of the driveway, I found Noah hobbling toward me on his semi-crippled legs. From the look on his face, he had been afraid for me, and now the creased and worried brow was showing visible signs of relief that I was the one still walking.

"Better get the fuck out of here," I uttered through clenched teeth.

He nodded and started back to the car, moving remarkably fast for a guy with legs the width of cue sticks. As I climbed inside, Noah pulled away slowly. He turned up Van Nuys Boulevard at traffic speed, and a few blocks later he entered the freeway. Moving north on the 101, Noah picked up speed, maneuvering discretely in and out of lanes, checking to see if we were being followed.

"No one on our tail," he said with a fair degree of relief and satisfaction.

I didn't respond.

"You were only supposed to get the mail," he admonished. The fear and concern were still in his voice. It was his way of covering up for sticking me in a dangerous situation.

"Well, what the fuck," I gritted. "There was a sudden change in plans."

"I know," he relented. "Is he dead?"

I stared. "I sure fucking hope so."

"You did good then," Noah acknowledged, lighting up a cigarette. Just what I needed, second hand smoke.

I sat in silence while Noah covered miles on the freeways, making sure we weren't being followed. When he was satisfied we were safe, he drove to his house, where Noah, the scientist, prepared a glass vat of sulfuric acid and tossed in the gun. We watched in meditative silence while the .25 caliber pistol dissolved like an Alka Seltzer, providing us both with a bit of relief. Dissolve the evidence. Clearly, Noah was used to the drill.

I had a lot on my mind. I had just killed somebody, and I realized it wasn't enough to rationalize he intended to kill me. I was so scared I acted first, and by acting first I got lucky. In the flash of understanding I realized two significant precepts. The first was fear could be the overwhelming guiding force in a time of crisis, and it could produce better results than professional skills. The second was that, to my good fortune, when people hear gunshots, they do not run outside to see what's going on.

In my head I replayed my shooting of Yomiya, my watching him die awkwardly and ugly, like a puppet cut suddenly from its strings. Killing him was not an act to be taken lightly, and any show of nonchalance would be pure bravado, denying the feelings I grappled with inside. Killing was wrong for the usual reasons. I knew that. A momentary wave of nausea overcame me as I wrestled my conscience. I recognized Yomiya was the terrorist sonofabitch responsible for the murders of a number of innocent people and that the planet wouldn't be missing him. I glanced at Noah; he was already whispering to someone on the telephone, making sure Yomiya's body vanished without a trace, like some dead alley cat swept up by the animal regulations people and dumped in an unmarked grave.

I soon dispelled the nausea, and I found the struggle with my conscience was inexplicably transplanted by a life confirming rush. I had faced death and I had survived. I wondered if I would ever be forced to kill again. And could I ever get so used to killing that my conscience no longer affected me? Like Noah. I sensed in the darker, more manipulative recesses of Noah's brain, he certainly hoped I'd become more like him. I looked over to where he was sitting, puffing on his cigarette, working out our next set of moves. I smiled the secret smile of irony and watched the last bits of gunmetal dissolve in the acid. And in the silence of the canyons, punctuated briefly by howling coyotes and the occasional rustle of sage, I wondered how in the hell I had ended up here.

Michael DiGregorio
Heat Stroke Bound:
A Rollicking and Pervy Sexscapade Across the American Sahara
2002

//

A high-lowbrow nugget, Michael DiGregorio's *Heat Stroke Bound* symbolizes a supercharged return to the men's adventure pulps of Argosy and Sir. After a stint at Larry and Althea Flynt's *Hustler* empire, DiGregorio went freelance to pursue magazine, newspaper and TV features about the West and its vestigial wild places, high among them Death Valley. In '99 the Los Angeles native won Canada's Northern Lights Award for travel journalism.

Not since director Michael Angelo Antonioni evoked a trance-like orgiastic scene in his 1970 film, *Zabriskie Point* has Death Valley been so sexed-up. *Heat Stroke Bound: A Rollicking and Pervy Sexscapade Across the American Sahara* was written in 2002 - albeit with one hand on the wheel.

Sleeping with Snakes

Before us Highway 190 stretched out gloriously desolate. Just as the supine and sexed-up redhead to my right did.

Undulating 60-foot high waves of golden sand edged the capillary-thin road, the western approach to what is undoubtedly North America's most extreme environ: Death Valley.

And as we closed in on the hottest place on Earth my thirty-something traveling companion was about to find her own hot spot. Framed against the stupendous dunes, Lynn was no less a staggering sight. Her dramatically pronounced topography, reposed across tawny leather, beckoned for exploration.

As whirling sand drifted across the highway, so eventually did my reach. My slow advance began at her alabaster midriff, which was showcased between a tight top and low-rise jeans.

Now southpaws may be advantageous at Yankee Stadium, but at least in an American-made vehicle-a DWI (Driving while Intimate) demands a rightie such as myself.

From soft caresses of Lynn's flawless pierced tummy my dexterous hand went to her fly, then into her panties.

Yet unlike the 49ers of yore, who'd burrowed below ground and into these broad ferruginous mountainsides 150-years ago, I sought a precious gem that lay beneath gold. Following a sluice of sweat my fingers came to arrive at Lynn's gold clitoral piercing. With a strike at paydirt, that unmistakable and exquisite acoustic called deep arousal filled the car.

The next move belonged to Lynn.

Up tantalizingly slow came her top. Her erect, terra-cotta nipples were the exalted matches of the upswept sand dunes.

With gnawing urgency she began to cup and knead her heavy, buoyant tits. Lynn's emerald-aqua eyes had all but lolled back beneath lids nearly folded in soporific ecstasy, while her tongue dabbed languid circles at lips that could seep only fevered groans.

All of a sudden the dun 270-degree panorama around our rental dissolved into a seamless blur. Autoerotic abandon reigned. Asphalt morphed into lava, and New Car Smell-fueled by a whole different type of lava-was lapped by Heady Sensuous Musk. As the stripped down landscape whirred by, my fingers let loose an orgasmic flash flood. Call it Climax ecology.

A 19th century newspaper headline sensationalized Death Valley as "the loneliest, hottest, most deadly spot in the United States. Where the dead do not decompose, but are baked, blistered and embalmed."

By 3:00 p.m. we would get a taste of that stark hyperbole. Arriving with all the subtlety as a summons from hell, a fierce afternoon wind pushed the temperature toward 129, only five degrees short of the highest ever recorded.

On the lee side of an 11,000-foot high, 80-mile long granite fortress known as the Panamint Mountains a scape flared open that wasn't content to just pervert terrestrial nature, but strongly hinted at another far off desert: Mars. That fact wasn't lost on filmmaker George Lucas. Drawn by the mother lode of striking austerity and phantasmagoria, he shot some *Star Wars* scenes here.

Midway across the 175-mile long valley we came upon our destination: a 1930s inn of Old Western luxury and cool grace; all inlayed stone and stucco coexisting peacefully alongside a vibrant spring.

And when she's bad she's really bad

Without question survival in the desert, especially the Mojave, is reduced to the level of a catchy marketing slogan: "Hydrate or die!" Left severely parched I reached out to a nearby oasis.

Yet this one loomed, not amidst the angular palms or shorter Mesquite surrounding the inn, but in the form of a welcome amenity; Left outside our door was an oversized plate of lengthy thin-sliced pineapple, honeydew, cantaloupe and grapes.

Lynn, a 'la the raw sweep of mountains sprawled languorously behind the inn, had struck a classic pinup pose on the beds edge, resting sideways on her elbow, nude. I drew my cinnamon girl in tight, to an upholstered bench at the foot of the bed. Then, after a lengthy spell of lavishing Lynn's sex with my tongue and lips, I canvassed the brimming plate of fruit.

Our ode to Bacchus began by my drawing a long, curving slice of melon slowly across Lynn's swollen lips. Initially the cool wetness caused her to gasp slightly. With her head fully reclined in deep pleasure, I then pushed citrullus vulgaris ever so slowly inside her.

Back and forth I sawed with the green and orange crescents. When any one of the dozen or so pseudo-dildos foundered, I simply decanted the now marinated sustenance with my tongue and ate it. Long into the afternoon, evoking the mountainside aquifer that feeds the Furnace Creek spring below our room, Lynn flowed into my mouth. Relishing her twat turned tart, I exhausted the deliciously decadent melons.

Midnight at the Oasis

The sun had finally quit. Not so the action, which raged against the dying light, although the theme had certainly switched gears: from free flowing pulp sex to fetish.

My harem of one faced an expansive brassy headboard.

If the antique playpen my companion kneeled atop had been a song, it would have been Shirley Bassey circa 1970s.

Lynn exhibited extraordinary detachment. She turned sideways. Maintaining perfect slave obedience, she kept her eyes lowered- the liquid-filled gaze of a consummate submissive never to make contact with the master. A moment later she offered her already inter-linked wrists.

Producing a pair of stone-cold law enforcement handcuffs I shackled the mirage lady to the headboard. Before my eyes she had metamorphosed into a martyr to Eros. Her pure white flesh was about to be sacrificed to the desert. Lynn arched her back, raising her flaring lilac moneymaker to accommodate my entry. My cock rose Phoenix-like. From behind I reached around to grope her fleshy succulents.

Henceforth there were no ifs or ands. Just butt. Long into the dead calm of night I rode roughshod over Lynn's virgin outback. Only by throttling down, from full-tilt pneumatic to staccato to the short and slow tease was I able to stave off the mother of all climaxes.

Once Lynn was handcuffed I'd placed at her left knee a 20-inch black paddle made of fine English leather and shaped like a cricket bat. With no hint of trepidation she smiled devilishly upon seeing the formidable CP implement at all the ritual symbolism it implied.

I reached between the wicked vixen's legs. Blithely I draped the tapered switch across her lips, first flat, then sideways as a knife through butter. That was followed by a series of slight slaps at her twat. What made for an even greater turn-on was that Lynn seemed to crave corporal punishment as much as I thrilled administering it.

A dull crimson-colored antique ceiling fan above the bed helped keep the air moving. The drone left in the wake of the large, whirring blades also helped muffle the repeated lashings across Lynn's taut bottom, and with them the ancillary groans of pain and cries of pleasure.

My mind went on its own space odyssey. Free-floating into some transcendental and primal nethersphere, nothing whatsoever-save for the furious, all devouring gust of our lovemaking-registered. Time had melted away like some long-off point of reference. Our torrid union through pleasure and pain surged as powerful as a religious experience.

From soft caress to dirty talk we would traverse, only to revert back to the thick lash all over again. One delicious and discernible welt after another creased Lynn's glorious ass-cheeks, which she swiveled seductively in response to each slap of the paddle.

Drawing out the pervy disciplinarian within bore fruit. The sense of control combined with the erotic punishment unleashed a huge endorphin rush, shooting me into a euphoric stratosphere.

Fade to White

That fiery hedonism, I came to realize, would carry over to the ride home. On an utterly desiccated inland sea south of Death Valley I outed Lynn's now raw ass. Leaving California 127, a truly lost highway, we drove off-road onto Silurian dry lake. From a dark zone of lust, Lynn and I emerged at the other end of the spectrum.

The ochre-colored playa stretched out akin to a five-mile long kidney. A major stack called the Avawatz Mountains all but erased the western horizon. Halfway across the crusty bog and beneath a strident, plasmic sun I bent my sexy redhead over the Lincoln's front fender.

The imagery-a lithe, creamy skinned bare-bottomed babe, khaki hiking shorts and white panties pulled down round battered hiking boots-proved immensely provocative. Even from miles up. I can honestlysay this because it was enough to bring swooping down a supersonic F-16 fighter jet down for a closer look.

My thrusts were the equal of the unrelenting landscape, a wilderness now valued mostly by thick-set gentlemen in flash track-suits searching for ad hoc gravesites.

If the million-year old playa symbolized the end of history, than this blistering brutal rut was the end of romance. The white-hot fusion our bodies generated lent new meaning to this world-class wasteland so bereft of seduction.

Perhaps Lynn and I had been conditioned by all the hard sharp angles, the heavy atmospherics and powerful magnetism. But whereas countless other souls had staggered across North America's apocalyptic blast furnace at its pique and cursed its fury, the all-too-real valley called Death had only stoked our passion.

-XXX-

Sari Domash

Jap in Jail

2004

//

Sari Domash has written a book *From New Jerks to Hollyweirdos* and is currently seeking a publisher. This is an except from that book. She moved from New York to Los Angeles 20 years ago and has been a struggling writer, business owner, masseuse and wino for 20 years.

We were called "fresh fish" inside that dark blue bus with those fence-like metal windows you see prisoners being hauled away in. There was so much yelling on the bus. Then men in the back sounding like animals and the women (off course a door had to be between us) sounding like yapping hyenas. I sat next to a nice, young, white real estate agent who knew how to talk without yelling.

For our mug shots, we lined up. A black nurse I talked to who was also in here for a DUI, but her first one, so she was only in for 48 hours (lucky!) asked if she could keep in her ponytail band since it wasn't a real rubber band. The female cops\guards ripped it out of her hair. "It's contraband!" She said "Ouch, that hurt. I would have taken it out." One mean redhead pushed her against the wall causing her head to hit the wall hard! "Don't you talk back to me!" The nurse rubbed her head. Everyone took out anything they had in their hair and threw it in the garbage. She was next in line for her mug shot. I thought she was going to burst out crying. The cops looked satisfied at the good job they had done. I was up next. I stood in front of the camera and gave it my best ditsy blond smile. "*What are you doing?*" "Having my picture taken," I replied doing my best Reese Witherspoon in "Legally Blond." They were so angry, but what could they do? I glanced at the nurse and gave her a slight smile. She acknowledged it with a slight nod back at me. Cops 1 -- Prisoners 1.

Then we were separated. After eight hours of picking up different inmates, being let out to pee at different holding cells, given a day old ham sandwich and an apple with a wormhole, (which I ate) I was handed my wardrobe and accoutrement: two unflattering knee-length "gowns," a towel and toothbrush and toothpaste in a little baggy. We put what money we had (forty dollars was the most we could hold) in our baggy. I put in forty dollars. Friends would have to deliver more to me later. We had to line up, undress -- completely naked and turn around. I saw the female guard put on surgical gloves. This was the moment I was dreading. I had no idea I would be strip searched. You'd think after eight hours whatever was up there would have come down by now. We had to bend over, spreading our butt-cheeks apart and cough. Down the line I noticed the coughs got weaker and weaker. So did the spreading of one's cheeks. By the time it was my turn, I thought, I was going to hardly cough and barely spread my butt. Except for this -- when the woman next to me bent over, maybe they saw something in there, but the guard put a finger in her butt and swished it around. It was hard to look away, so no one did. "Next!" That meant me. Well, now I had to be as congenial as the first girl in line!

We were lead with our stuff to a huge bunker, very dark - the windows were very high up and it was sometime at night. This "dorm" must've held over 500 inmates. We were to spend the first night here. This was ridiculous. The real estate agent and I were given beds three yards apart. So, with nothing better to do, I went over and jumped on the top bunk with her. It was like this humungous slumber party. Anyway, her back was killing her and I was still a great masseuse, so I offered to give her a back massage. She couldn't thank me enough. I must have been doing a good job because she was moaning. No one moans with pleasure in jail, I guess, I looked around and felt like I was EF in the EF Hutton commercial. Someone finally broke the silent stares and said, "Can I have one too? My back is killing me." Another gal, "I'm kickin', can you do me after her?" "I'm kickin' too! Can I be after that girl?" I had my work cut out for me. But had to ask, "What is this kickin'? What are you all kicking?" "Heroin. Aren't you?"

The next day we were divided again and I was dropped off at my final destination. It could only be described as the snakepit. The huge steel green door slammed behind me. In front of me were 250 women running around howling with the noise bouncing off the 40 foot ceilings. It was like an airplane hanger, only much noisier. Bunk beds lined up in rows like the last place. Home sweet home. I couldn't hear myself think. I put my stuff down on my bunk. I took a shower. Thank god they had shower curtains and doors on the toilet stalls. It was even relatively clean. There was even and abundance of Tampax and Kotex in every stall and I was so worried about getting my period here!

The first hour there, I bought a cigarette for two dollars (actually, I was only given two hits of someone else's, so I got ripped off), a valium for three dollars, a candy bar for one dollar, and then we were taken to the commissary, wherein I bought a candy bar for

fifty-cents, a newspaper, cocoa butter, more toothpaste and sham-
poo. It was best to keep your money in your underwear -- the only
safe place for it. A crazy-eyed white young girl walked up to me
with a finger pointed at my face, much like a gun. "You just bought
a valium for three dollars! She ripped you off! You should only pay
one dollar! They just *give* them to you here! Get your two dollars
back!" "Really, it's okay." "No, it's *not*! She's *showing off*!" "Okay,
I'll try, thanks." Her eyes went even crazier when she turned to go.
I felt so alone. Where was my white real estate agent friend? I felt
like screaming "SHUT UP!" but didn't want to make any enemies.

This is how you get drugs in jail: the doctor visits each dorm
about once a week. The doctor sits in a chair at the front of the
room. Everyone with an ailment stands single file in line. If you
have headaches and can't sleep or just feel like you might go crazy,
the doctor will give you valiums. You then make money selling
them to them to fresh fish, like me.

If you were in here for a certain time and showed good behavior, you could be selected to work as a "Trustee." You are actually
unpaid help. From working in the kitchens to doing office work.
The Trustess are given more freedom to walk around without anyone watching them. The Trustees are the ones who find new and
used cigarettes, steal them and sell them. You can't really trust a
Trustee.

While we were waiting to dine, we were told to "line up." This
place reminded me of a bad camp. I mean, *they* had the guns.
What's the difference if my shoulder wasn't against the cold concrete wall? So, it wasn't and I was shoved into the wall by a male
guard. What kind of job was this for anyone anyway? Did this guy
flunk out of Hamburger U? I'd rather shovel shit out of a dog ken-
nel than work here. I told everyone at lunch my protest. That we
are not children, that it was oppressive to be told to line up. We
were doing time as adults and should be treated as such.

Lining up for dinner, I got even madder. I said, "I'm sure we
don't all belong in here anyway, I know I don't." Some big Latino
girl got really mad at me. "You think you are too good to be here?!"
I replied that she was also too good, not just me. And most every-

one else in here. She got very mad. "You think you're are too good to be in here with us!" "I said the opposite." Another woman chimed in, "You don't wanna get *her* mad at you. You don't." Great. We lined up in single file, of course, my shoulder was not touching the cold wall. A little pregnant girl behind me said this must be my first time here. I said, "Isn't it yours?" "Of course not. We've all been in here a lot. You get to know the rules. You don't know the rules, you don't know what they can do to you. I'll protect you, but you have to do what I say." My body guard stood under five feet tall and was seven months pregnant. I looked down at her and told her I would. We sat down to my first meal of the day. We were given those trays you get in elementary school (or mess hall at camp) and while you went down the line, oatmeal was dripped into one, a 7-11 burrito in another and a cup of brown bug juice called "coffee" was in another. "What is this garbage?!" I cried out as we all sat down. A big African-American prisoner across from me said, "Excuse me! Do you mind if I enjoy my breakfast?!" My body guard slowly shook her head. I was not to impose my opinion of the cuisine onto others.

When we got back to the dorm, I noticed my towel was taken. So I had to use my other gown as a towel. We walked around in these blue sacks during the day and were supposed to sleep in the white ones. Because I couldn't get a guard to give me another towel, I slept in my underwear. I can't believe how shy these women were about nudity. I never expected that. Also, I washed my underwear by hand and hung up my undies on the bed railing behind me, carefully guarding them until they dried. There was a laundry machine which had a line of 25 women and girls waiting all day to use it. There was another one but it was broken. The laundry room was also the tv room. There was one table with seven chairs and one bunk bed for seats. Fifty screaming women were watching I Love Lucy as if they could hear it. If the dorm was the snakepit, this was the rattlesnake pit. I ran out of there. No T.V. and hand washing were fine with me.

White Pink

A little later, I'm on lower bunk reading the newspaper when a bunch of African-American cell mates wanted to know if they could sit on the end of my bed to talk to their friends whose bed was across from mine. "Yes, ladies, but no yelling, please." After five minutes they forgot my rule. I hoisted up my long skinny gown so I could sit cross-legged and enjoy my newspaper on my lap. Hopefully this would all become background "noise." One girl screamed out. "Oh now, you are not wearing underwear, girlfriend! You have to put them on!" I told her, "We're all girls, here. And they're drying. Don't look!." Another gal answered her correctly: "Don't worry about it. No one here wants white pink anyway." I got under my covers. I must have told the "white-pink" story to everyone I know but my family members. It never fails to get a laugh.

Anyway, they kept talking/yelling at each other and perhaps I was taken far away, mesmerized by the screech level so much that I was day-dreaming of long ago. I was reminded of old slave movies where they whoop it up after master goes to bed. For some reason I said this: "I just realized why they had slaves. It was in Vogue. I mean if all your friends had some, you'd have to own a few too, you know?" Suddenly, one of them was on top of me and my neck had two hands around it. "My gramma was a slave!" "I didn't mean anything by it. Really. I mean, it just occurred to me - they couldn't all be evil back then - you know, Scarlett O'hara, she wasn't mean. She was just keeping up with the Joneses." Her friends pried her away from me. I think the "in Vogue" thing might have made sense to them. But I felt ten glaring on me as I crept away. Good thing my bodyguard was taking a nap. She wouldn't have liked to witness this scene and I would have been reprimanded. How in the hell was I going to get through this? Here I was alone - with enemies close by my side.

That night, we had to sit up in our beds and all be quiet. If we were all quiet, they'd let us go to bed. Very bad camp. We could not do it. There were at least four gals who kept shushing everyone. Then it got to be: "You shush. I *was* quiet." "No, you weren't! Now shush!" "No, *you* shush!" Someone else said, "Everyone shush!" "No, you shush, girl!" Oh god. Finally the guard banged a baseball bat on a metal bed post. "QUIET." Then someone said. "Shush." and then "No, *you* shush!" The cops finally gave up. The valium didn't do a thing and I had trouble getting to sleep. Seriously, you cannot have 250 women sharing a bedroom.

The next day, we were taken to the commissary. My five favorite enemies scrambled to get ahead of me in line. Geesh! They pooled their change together. Miss Hostility took charge. "I'm going to be a Avon Lady some day. I knows about makeup. I'll pick out what we need." "Shit! This doesn't go far enough for nothing. How am I gonna do makeup now?" She decided on one lipstick. I guess they would share it. I felt bad. I felt rich. Here she wanted to know about make up and would never - well not any time soon, be able to afford to play with it - and I could afford to buy the whole lot for each of them. I had a plan. When they left, I bought all the make up I thought would look good on dark skin. Just as we were lining up for lunch, when Miss Hostility jumped up to beat me for a place in line, I put the baggy of make-up on her bed so she'd see it first thing when we came back.

When they returned, I watched from a few bunks away. They all kept asking each other who bought all this stuff? She found me looking at them and came over to me. "It was you, wasn't it?" I nodded. "Thank you." She said. "Okay." "No, really, thank you so much." She ran back to her friends and they all started grabbing eye shadow, blush, mascara and going to town. I really enjoyed that. I made friends out of enemies.

And, my body guard even had an idea. "You have money --" "-- How does everyone know I have money?" "They *know*." "Listen, do you want to start a little business - make some more?" "In here?" "No, we'll get jobs and come back for the free rent and great food." "What do you have in mind?" "We buy all the candy bars we can at the commissary. They cost fifty cents. I'll sell them on the weekend when no one can get candy bars cause the commissary's closed and we'll charge $1.00 each. I'll give you back your investment and we'll split the profit. Ya in or out?" "But since everyone knows the commissary is closed on weekends, won't they just stock up on candy bars they're going to want anyway?" "No." "I'm in." I handed her my money.

Just before lunch, I knocked on this huge window the guards sit in front of to watch us do whatever we do. The female guard ignored me, but was talking to another inmate. She wouldn't listen to me. I yelled out. "Someone stole my towels. I need one towel. Please! Listen to me! Over here!" She gave me a furious look. I should never have made this move without proper consultation, damn it! A male guard stepped out suddenly and threw a towel at me. I said thank you to deaf ears. Why was I treated this way?

It occurred to me later that, of course, there were microphones. We were being listened to. On the way back from lunch, I signed up for tile laying, psychology and to be a Trustee. Then I noticed they had a library. Not one book did I see anywhere in the dorm. I signed up to check out books.

Miss _____ (I dropped hostility from her title) was an expert at crocheting slippers, and thong underwear. She was in here so long they trusted her with a crochet needle, even though it was contraband. She held up a sweet pair of perfectly crocheted pink thong underwear. I knew it was my size. She wanted $7.00 for it. I started giving it to her and she told me I couldn't take them out. That they wouldn't let me take anything out. So I didn't buy them. I asked her how long she had to go. "Five years." I would have hung myself with the yarn.

Suddenly I heard my name on the loud speaker to "come upstairs." The guards let me out and let me walk alone to find the room. I could have jumped out a window! Everyone else went to lunch at this time. I found the door and sat in front of a desk. The female cop/guard was absolutely *pleasant* to me. What did I do right? "Nikki, as you can see, some gals live here, they decorate their beds, make little homes. They're going to be here a long time and have gotten use to the rules and it's sad, but it's free food and rent for them. We don't feel you belong in here. Do you?" "Well, I signed up for tile laying and to see the shrink. Isn't that good? Oh, and the library? Also, I'm helping a pregnant gal make some money, but maybe I've said too much." "Just stop now." "We want you to leave, if you'd like to. We're offering you eight hours of community service in exchange for the rest of your time here. Would you like to leave today?" "Yes." "Good. Good-bye." "That's it?" "That's it."

I went down the dorm. It was unlocked. Everyone was at lunch. What was going on here? Everything looked different. I felt light on my feet. This feeling - what was it? Oh, it was joy! I made a collect call to a friend who would come over right away to pick me up and couldn't wait to hear what jail was like. I went over to the bunk of the girl who crochets the pink underwear, the one who tried strangling me. I gave her my new comb and brush. One of her five friends I noticed earlier had burnt finger tips. I can't imagine how she grew up, but my heart went out to her. I left her my cocoa butter. Maybe that would help with the scars. I gave my newspaper to my bodyguard and walked away knowing she really had earned the 30 dollars plus all profits - she would be glad too.

Down the hall, I opened another door. Then I was to be buzzed into a room. This was the way out. The only other door said, "EXIT." They gave me my clothes and no one watched me change. I could have taken out anything from jail - like the thong I should have bought. I put on my jeans and T-shirt and opened up the "EXIT" door. It was sunny outside. I had this silly smile as I stared at the sun and looked around waiting to be picked up. I don't know what's wrong with trying to make jail a nicer place to live, but it must be against the rules -- because -- truly, I must be the only person ever to get kicked out of jail.

.

Brian C. Weed

Leaving and Longing on a Bus from Montgomery

2004

//

Brian originally hails from a small farm in the southeastern corner of Alabama, where he spent most of his time devising clever ways of skipping town and leaving the state without anyone noticing. Eventually he just walked out, and no one said a word.

I barely gave her half a chance, even though she continuously sought me out. I rather liked her, too. She had a pretty face and a slender body, not to mention an overt sexuality that she never seemed concerned about hiding around me. Christy was her name, though I think she spelled it "Kristi". Funny how I remember that, but for the life of me can't recall her last name.

My friends hated her. All of them did; I heard their sneers and insults, the laughter at her expense. I can only assume she had a more awkward middle school term, the remnants of which transferred over to high school. I never knew her in middle school, so I had no preformed opinion. I had recently moved, and my new friends all had histories that I was blissfully ignorant of. So the only tool I had to judge people with was the present, which I found, oddly enough, allowed me to judge in a much more generous light.

It was my insecurities that proved to be my ultimate downfall with what could have been my first foray into the sexual wilderness. My friendships were new and fragile; the slightest of missteps could have cost a fortune in acceptance. In retrospect, the price would probably have been fair. Young minds are fickle, but they are also fleeting.

Once she slipped a scrap of paper with her phone number on it into my locker. No one saw when I found it, and I quickly stuffed it into my pocket. That night, I called her, and we talked briefly about school, before the subject turned quickly to sex through awkward joking laced with physical longing and curiosity. She told me she wrote poetry about it, which I found to be at once inappropriate and seductive. From church and family, I knew thoughts on sex were not to be talked about, much less committed to paper. I asked her to read them, and masturbated while she did. I didn't call her anymore after that because she might have realized that I wanted her. I think she knew, though. She understood sexual desire in a way I never thought a fourteen-year-old virgin could.

On the way back from school bus trip to see a play in Montgomery, she sat across the aisle from me. When the sun set, as we drove through the night, she laid her head innocently on my lap in the dark, while I pretended to be asleep. Her hand rested on my thigh, and I could feel myself becoming aroused. I wondered if she could too, and partly hoped she didn't, but partly hoped she did. She knew how taboo it was for me to be seen with her, how my friends would comment and judge. She wouldn't tell anyone if I was aroused, and would probably have touched me in the most clandestine manner. I prayed that she would.

I laid frozen, afraid that the slightest movement would bring attention to our comfort. I wanted her to move her hand farther up my thigh. I wanted the night to be darker, pitch black so that only her and I would be close enough to see each other. I wanted the world to disappear for the rest of the night.

Instead, Jesse noticed our suggestive position, and shouted "OH MY GOD!!" loud enough to bring the entire bus to our attention. He was much too boisterous to ignore. I jerked upright, flicking my knee in the process and catapulting Kristi out of my lap. I played dumb, and pretended I had been asleep and clueless. Kristi turned and stared out her window at the passing cars while some kids made fun of her, calling her a "twig."

When the excitement had settled, I felt her looking at me. I turned to her before I could stop myself, and our eyes met. In a fraction of second I felt her sorrow, and she felt my guilt, and we both looked to the ground. We never looked at each other again after that.

Notes from the Los Angeles Underbelly

Melissa Rosen

My Heart Will Go On

2004

//

Melissa Rosen was born and raised in the heart of Chicago. She has a dog named Luna who sort of looks like Bambi and sometimes acts like Cujo. They now call Venice Beach home. When not working on her three point shot, she can be found smiling and staring vacantly into the distance. A graduate of Northwestern University's Radio/TV/Film program, Melissa is now obtaining her Master of Professional Writing from USC.

It was raining outside the day I opened my father's safe. Inside, under the bonds my mother's father had given him to hold until they, my brother and myself had reached maturity and beside the 9mm handgun I'd seen him handle once, but never actually use for protection, were the pictures. Three pictures of him. Three pictures of my father, naked on a bed, my parent's bed, having another man suck him off. Except for athletic socks, the guy wasn't dressed either. His olive body was hairy and toned; his face, covered in stubble and oily, was smiling at the camera, despite my dad's dick shoved in his mouth.

He seemed truly tickled to be in these photographs. This stallion of Greek, Turkish or quite possibly Latin descent clutched my begetter's balls as if they were some gold miner's *Eureka* discovery. This beau hunk was going to town on my old man while propping himself up, palms firmly planted, on Dad's new hips. He'd just undergone that double replacement and the doctors had instructed him not to apply undue pressure. What the hell was my father thinking?

I could hardly fathom which one disgusted me most: this Adonis with his silly, self-satisfied exhibitionism, or my father, who had the identical expression in every picture. An expression with which I was long familiar. It was the way he looked passed out on the family room couch after a heavy meal and his usual bottle of Chianti. Above the neck, there was no difference and that, of course, was frightening, but not as revolting as the sinking realization my dad and I shared not only DNA, but the same taste in men.

Yes, I was a freshmen girl with braces on my teeth and a palate spreader which had to be turned once a month with a miniature key. This condition, understandably and up until now, self-consciously prevented me from engaging in oral activities with other Homo sapiens. But this didn't mean I wasn't a sexual being. While boys, my brother's age, seniors at Wheaton Military Academy, gave weekend recess rides home and free weed to a number of underclassman girls, who performed road head and let them play tonsil hockey, I took the bus. The Greyhound and it wasn't pretty. But it gave me time to fantasize and the weekly six-hour commutes flew by with my reverie.

"Someday I'll be a middle aged divorcee or have a husband conveniently away on business," I'd whisper this to myself quietly as not to wake the elderly degenerate who'd dosed off on my shoulder. Then looking into the window's reflection of my blackhead speckled face shrouded by my mouse brown bowl cut, I would imagine my braces gone. I'd envision my teeth overly bleached, with leather tan skin and ample crow's feet. I saw the wide brim hat and sarong I'd wear over my neon hued string bikini while sporting the type of heels manufactured for lounging, high society ladies. Resting by the poolside of my second home, waiting for another Mai Tai, I'd sigh and remember Tolstoy. The man whose works I'd wrestled with in Ms. Mackenzie's English class.

"Boredom is the desire for desires," I'd say, "He was so true...so very true."

Then remembering my cocktail, I'd rail against the summer breeze, "Ernesto! Ernesto! Mama wants her sauce! Chop! Chop!"

"Coming, Missus," Ernesto would bellow from the patio bar around the corner, trying to hide the quiver in his voice brought on by my repeated hand clapping.

He would approach. His shirt sleeves ripped off to reveal biceps bulging from carrying my order of libations and illegally prescribed painkillers on the silver tray above his head. Our eyes would lock. Within seconds, we would be intertwined on the chaise. Head to toe sticky from all the sweet and sour mix spilled in the careless heat of passion.

That's when the fantasy would end. The very moment when body intersected body. Sure I knew the slang. I played along with the other truants gossiping as we did poppers in the girl's bathroom before ditching class. Yet, up until now, in front of my father's unlocked safe on a rainy Sunday afternoon and shortly before I'd have to leave for the bus depot to travel back to school, I didn't have a clue as to what actually occurred when people did the nasty.

My mother had never explained the birds and bees to me. She was far too busy with her latest hobby - preparing and sending baked goods to her various pen pals. They consisted of certain telemarketing employees she'd developed a connection with over the course of a twenty-minute phone survey and several prison inmates serving at the local minimum security facility for white collar crimes against humanity.

"They need love, too," she said lighting her cigarette off the pilot light next to the warming pot of her infamous candy corn icing.

"Yeah, but what about me? I'm a juvenile delinquent. Shouldn't that count for something," I whined, watching her drip the sugar coating over cupcakes bound for call centers in New Delhi.

"Didn't we just celebrate your birthday? You get plenty of love. Too much," she said.

If a package of tube socks is an adequate expression of affection towards your only daughter on the anniversary of her entrance into the universe, then I was a spoiled, rotten brat. I'd gotten two packs. White with three red bands around the top. Remembering them and looking closer at the pictures, I suddenly felt dizzy. This guy, I was gradually falling in love with; this greasy, olive man blowing my father was wearing the same exact model of socks. Could this be a coincidence or was my mother somehow involved in these sordid shenanigans?

She had her quirks, but I never realized she was so kinky. These pictures. Did she take them? There was no way. My mother didn't know how to operate the microwave, let alone our digital camera and she was so overwhelmingly modest. She kept her eyes shut when she did her own bathing.

Wait, my brother was a computer freak. Did my dad somehow cajole him with promises of a newfangled keyboard, if he'd act as paparazzi? Impossible. He never left his room since deciding to take over his own home schooling.

Ah, the tripod! My parent's kept it folded in their bedroom next to the unused Nordic Track®, food dehydrator and various other infomercial items purchased on a whim which they were planning to someday return. My father and Guido must have used it to help document their activities. But how long had this been going on? Did Mom know Dad was into this sort of thing?

It wasn't a secret to me. I had always suspected he preferred men to women. Not just because he favored my older brother over me and only showed the bare minimum of platonic fondness towards my mother. It was his sob. When he cried, it sounded so gay.

But it's not like my dad cried all the time. Actually, I'd never seen him cry until I was nine and that was the first and last time. The *Titanic* came out and we all went to see it as a family. After, once we'd piled into our Cutlass and pulled from the multiplex's parking lot, my old man set into a crying jag more melodramatic than the movie.

"Barry, please, it's not like the ending was a surprise," my mother said taking a drag from her Parliament.

I had assumed his continually streaming tears were caused by his hemorrhoids flaring after three hours of sitting in the movies. But my brother knew better. He stopped picking the scab on his knee and gave me a look that told me: "Idiot, roll down your window now, so we can breath," and "Oh, boy, Dad's swishy."

When we returned home from picking up the film's soundtrack at his weepy behest, my father ran with it. He stumbled to his study where he kept his safe and hidden stash of *Playgirl* magazines. I'd found those when I was four, but he'd explained they were medical journals on the male anatomy he needed for his homeowner's insurance company. It sounded reasonably convincing and so I never told anyone, but the memory stuck with me.

When I watched my mother blast obscenities at the door as she passed from doing laundry, I prayed that the three days my dad had spent locked in his office devastated by the depiction of this at sea tragedy and playing track 14, the chart topping Celine Dion ballad, in continual repeat, didn't mean my parents were getting a divorce. My dad could dole out three-dollar bills all he wanted, but I needed my nuclear family. I kept a vigil outside.

"For strength," I said, sliding slices of cheese under the door.

"For snot," I said, pushing individual squares of toilet paper next to the cheddar.

But there was no response. When his high pitched weeping gave way to guttural snoring, I felt secure enough to make a speedy dash to my bedroom in the garage and grab my latest TeenBeat® magazine. I ripped the centerfold of a pouting, soaking wet Leo (portraying Jack Dawson, the fictitious third-class passenger and penniless artist who'd won a voyage on the ship that would end up as the most notorious maritime tragedy) from the glossy rag and stuck it carefully under the study's bolted entry. Merely seconds later, most surprisingly, my father emerged with his comb over flipped in the opposite direction, revealing his dermatitis stricken baldness. His face was bloated and red from days of bawling. He patted me on the head and gave me back the image of Di Caprio, crumpled into a ball.

"Who's up for Parchessi?" he asked.

The rest of my family followed his lead, setting up the game on the basement card table and partaking in our routine of Chex Mix and RC Colas (the adults using it to chase Jim Beam) as if nothing had happened. But it continued to bug me. While my father was out driving my mother to her macramé class or away at a daylong Landmark® personal development retreat, I'd sneak into his office to investigate what he was doing. Until today, the day he accidentally left his safe unlocked, the only semi-juicy items I'd found in all these years were a tub of Crisco and a brochure for a Miami circuit party. Now I finally had direct evidence, nudie pictures blackmail material, that would enable me to get away with whatever my heart desired.

Unfortunately, I loved my father far too much to shake him down for special privileges or stacks of cash. I could have used these tattered snapshots to force him to disown my brother and leave his highly appraised collection of LPs from Broadway's bygone era to me, but I was genuinely concerned as to the damage he might be doing to his recent arthroplasty.

Letting a hunk of meat (like my guy in those pictures) do pushups on his pelvis could only eventually cause one or both of his hips to become irreversibly dislocated. He'd be left wheelchair bound and potentially forced to give up bowling. I felt like a little girl again whose only concern was to see her daddy happy. After I'd done the last of my geometry homework and packed my tote bag for school, I went to the kitchen where my mom was making her chocolate caviar cookies and flicking ashes into the just used mixing bowl as she watched NASCAR on TV.

"Where's Dad?" I asked.

"Barry took your brother to Best Buy for something," she said without glancing up from the screen.

I took the pictures I'd removed from the safe out of my back pocket and with a sweaty palm placed them in front of her.

"Your father gave you these," she said suspiciously, glancing over the photographs and flipping them face down on the counter.

"No. The safe was open and---"

"And you wonder why we sent you to military school! You shouldn't covet other people's property. It's quite unbecoming of a lady. When I was your age---"

"But Mom... Is Dad gay?" I blurted out.

She laughed for what seemed like an eon and then an eternity.

"Believe you and me...if your father was a homo, don't you think I'd know. You give him way too much credit. The man has no fashion sense and his sense of humor doesn't even come close to witty. He just likes to have sex with men... occasionally," she said lighting two smokes with a match and handing one to me.

We sat there puffing away without speaking.

"These are Kools," I said looking at the pack before me.

"That's what life's about...changing and evolving. You gotta try new things. Otherwise, there's no point in being."

"Is that why Daddy let that gorgeous man do things to him?"

"No, no. Barry was into that way before he snagged me."

"Then why'd you marry him?" I asked, dizzy from confusion.

"When you're single and over thirty-five and you find a guy who'll open the door for you, wants kids and a commitment, and can dance without the white man's over bite, you feel like you've struck the jackpot. You'll see. Mark my words."

With those pearls of wisdom, the phone rang and my mother pressed the talk button on the cordless as she motioned for me to lower the volume on the television.

"Namaste Pratik!" she said, "I got your e-mail...Yes...such a shame about your daughter's dowry...How awful...well, tell your wife and Apurna to be expecting goodies coming...No, you're welcome. They should arrive in Mumbai by a week from Monday."

As my mother proceeded to provide comfort to one of her headset-wearing friends she's never met on the other side of the globe, I snuck the pictures back into my possession. After taking one last peak, I placed them in my father's safe almost exactly the way I'd found them. I'd let them stay a secret, but I still had loads of questions to continue pondering.

Like what would happen if someday I ran into this olive man wearing my identical tube socks and we fell in love and got married. Would Dad be understanding? If their relationship was purely sexual, as Mom claimed, I couldn't see why not. There would always be a bit of awkwardness and maybe continued erotic tension between them. But if they didn't spend extended, quality time together (at the elaborate family gatherings I'd orchestrate on my yacht in the Florida Keys), I saw no foreseeable problem. I'd just buy my brother a scanner or some other high tech gadget. Yep, he'd make sure everybody remembered to mind their "P's and Q's" and that the boat stayed its course, so we wouldn't end up sinking.

Sleeping with Snakes

.

Notes from the Los Angeles Underbelly

Darin Bennett

Kill William Baxter

2003

//

Darin Bennett is a musician and writer who was born, raised, lives and plans to die in Los Angeles. For a complimentary copy of his Social Security Card and Driver's License, please visit www.darinbennett.com.

It must have been at least five in the morning as the sun was beginning its familiar ascent towards the center of my filthy bedroom window, when I decided to kill William Baxter. I was no less pleased with the fact that the smell of freshly brewed coffee was seeping through the vent above the broken door that lead to my washroom. The aroma was a daily invitation to the morning breakfast ritual where I would most assuredly be entertained by the bliss of my father's ignorance regarding international relations, accompanied by the gaze of his blind right eye that fell beneath a shock of white hair that was, by no mere coincidence, positioned routinely at forty-five degrees downward from the center of his head. This may seem to lean on the verge of nitpicking if I were not to inform you that this miraculous patch of growth was the only hair remaining on his body after a freak accident with the chemical known as Minoxidil. This highlight could only be outdone by the thought of the two mounding slopes of perfectly symmetrical flesh rolls that bunched up within the confines of my stepmother's aged brassiere. I rolled out of bed and into the only slipper I could find and was lead towards the kitchen by an untouched morning hard-on.

My father curled his legs into a pretzel within the framework of one of two chairs that were positioned at opposite ends of a three-legged table and perused a week-old copy of the *New York Times*. The sight of this was a matter of conditioning that never seemed to amaze me, despite the fact that we lived in Los Angeles and that he could not read. I set myself deep in the back of my chair in a continued attempt to be as far away from him as possible while still being able to reach the food on the table. I was never allowed to bring food outside the perimeter of the kitchen area and was once severely beaten when my father followed a trail of, what must have been, microscopic breadcrumbs into my room.

Not a word was spoken in the following moments with the exception of an audible grunt by my stepmother as she sniffed a weathered carton containing two somewhat beige eggs. For a woman of fifty she was a perfect sex heifer to my widowed father. She had no formal education, tattooed-on eye makeup, and an ass that could crack a walnut. My stepmother placed on the table a wide array of unprepared food items that were meant to resemble an ample supply of the necessary daily nutrients; the majority of which were sucked down my father's throat without the slightest hint of his chewing any of it. I focused on the only half-decent items placed in front of me - a cup of mildly warm instant coffee and a stale croissant. After admiring my stepmother's bulbous nipples through the lace of her nightgown, I excused myself without a word back to the confines of my bedroom retreat where I pleasured myself for approximately thirty-seven seconds until ejaculation and then began planning the manner in which I would kill William Baxter.

My first order of business would be to quit my job. No self-respecting killer would or could maintain an occupation and simultaneously remain focused on the task at hand. I walked the three and a half blocks from my father's home to Dell's Taco Hut and, without any advanced warning, notified Terrance the manager, an oil producing well of spots who was prematurely bald at fifteen, that I would not be able to work on any future occasions. Without any further explanation or specification, I promptly handed in my nametag and demanded my final paycheck.

Three hours later I found myself in an alley behind the Taft building on Hollywood Boulevard at Highland Avenue in a rendezvous with Rafael Perez, a past acquaintance of my stepmother. He was a notoriously rambunctious fellow who wore a knit beanie that was pulled down low on his brow and a parka that was emblazoned with the words "Hustla Fo Life" on the rear. The lurid scent of expensive marijuana wafted from his pores like a Jamaican air freshener, but was a welcome change from the trash piles heated by the summer blaze that attacked my senses in the hour spent waiting for Rafael to arrive. I could almost see his eyes beneath the cap as he counted the handful of cash I had just given over to him in exchange for a 357 Magnum loaded with one bullet, as that was all I had accounted for in my plan of action. He briskly assured me that the weapon was clean, in terms of any past "legal ramblings". He also made note that I looked nothing like my stepmother - a logical detail that seemed to escape him at the moment. As I secured the weapon in the underside of my shirt and between my pants and belt, Rafael commented that I was committing a crime by wearing a brown belt with black shoes, especially after January. I was all business as he walked away and told me to say hello to his favorite piece of street ass.

The hours of the day seemed to grow longer in anticipation of the felony I was about to commit - what would be my first actual crime, I might add, despite a minor penalty for failure to pay a parking ticket the previous year. For the most part, I was a model citizen. I had, up until a few hours earlier, held a reputable job and paid annual income taxes (several weeks before April fifteenth, I would like to humbly add). I bathed semi-regularly and, on occasion, was known to assist an elderly neighbor with her weekly grocery shopping. Mrs. McDougal would always pay me with a fresh apple and a few coins for my trouble, which I would promptly throw in the trash and piss away on my favorite candy bar (the Look bar), respectively. It may seem odd, but I blame her for a persistent boil on my rear end that I cannot seem to find the courage to have lanced. I would have continued to help the old lady if she had not taken a bad fall down the stairs several weeks earlier. It was suspected by the other tenants that my father pushed her on his way to cash in a winning five-dollar lottery ticket. The funeral was a quiet affair of which I attended from a distance.

Sweat poured down my head, arms, and legs ultimately ending up in an overflowing pool between my legs. I ran a checklist of events through my head and tried to remember the ultimate focus of the day. Kill William Baxter.

If there was ever a time for a nap it was after hiking up the fifteen flights of urine-drenched stairs to the top of my apartment building. I had planned to make a short stop in my father's unit to confess my proposed mission statement for the day. But I new he would not listen, or rather, he was unable to, as he was legally deaf and generally more inclined to blurt out mostly monotone diatribes about the world outside his confined perimeter. Introspection was a concept I had learned in school, not at home. I could have been a writer, they said, or even a politician. I left school after two years abroad studying at Oxford on an academic scholarship. The funds were cut off after the university administration learned of my birth mother's tremendous family fortune. She was a class "A" blue blood and a specimen of perfection. After giving birth to me from the seed of a rather unfortunate one-night stand, she jumped ship and ran back into the arms of her ever-understanding parents. When I notified her of my academic financial problems due to her wealth, she wished me luck and placed me on a mailing list for her charity to help impoverished children in America. She promised that she would be in touch. She never called.

Reaching the last flight of a barrage of steps, I stumbled through the fence that made up the door to the roof and collapsed down towards the broken tiles sectioned off into a patio. Kill William Baxter. The words ran through my head from one ear to the other and sometimes seeped through my dry, dehydrated lips. Without any proper energy to stand, I crawled over to a hose next to an empty planter and moistened my dry lips with water. It was a welcome relief and helped me focus my attention back to its original intention. Looking over the ledge of the roof I had a perfect three hundred and sixty degree view of the city of my birth - a place that I left without any intention of returning to, only to be shamed into a return engagement. Dusk slowly crept over the skyline, burying the sun in a cascade of concrete and lopsided palm trees. I glanced down and noticed that a small ladder lead down to a tiny resting spot aside the fire escape adjacent to my bedroom window. Lowering myself down, I could feel the gun pressing into my back.

Once on the ledge outside my bedroom, I finally rested in a comfortable position to watch the final moments of daylight creep away. I pulled the gun from my belt and set it between my legs. A cool awareness of self-realization overcame me as the matter at hand became deafeningly present. From inside I could hear my father attempting to hump the life out of my stepmother and, I have to admit, I was envious. Had I ever had the opportunity of a discreet liaison with her, I most definitely would have jumped at the chance. She was a professional and I admired her gusto. Why she settled on a man like my father was beyond me. As I raised the gun upwards, I heard the ring of my telephone in a chorus with my father's mumbling groans. The answering machine picked up and I heard my outgoing message proclaim, "Hi. This is Billy B. You know what to do." I carefully pulled back the trigger and for a short second I felt the sharp tip of the bullet weld its way into my temple. My body slumped down, hanging half off of the ledge while a spurt of blood transformed into a steady steam, pouring down like a waterfall on the city I had grown to loath. As consciousness began to steadily wane, I heard a voice call out from the speaker of my answering machine: "William, this is your mother".

Matt Dukes Jordan

Sunset Boulevard Escort Services

Summer 2003

//

Matt Dukes Jordan has published fiction, poetry, and lots of journalism on both coasts. He has lived in Los Angeles on and off since 1990. His book *Weirdo Deluxe: The Wild World of Pop Surrealism and Lowbrow Art* was published by Chronicle Books in April 2005.

He was standing at the intersection of Franklin and Winona trying to decide where to go-east for some sushi and beer on Vermont Avenue, or south for beer and strippers at Jumbo's on Hollywood Boulevard.

A large luxury car rounded the corner and paused. The window on the passenger side went down silently. The interior of the car was dark. Paul could see a female inside, but not her features. A refined-sounding woman said, "Are you Andre?"

He walked over to the car, leaned down, looked in. The woman pointed and smiled. "Andre?" She looked beautiful.

Paul nodded.

"Get in," she said.

He opened the door and slid onto a very comfortable leather seat. It had been months since he'd been in a car with a leather interior. His own car's seats were covered with a synthetic fabric scarred from minor accidents with flammables-cigarettes, joints, or matches he had dropped while waiting for deep fried nourishment in the drive-through lane at Jack in the Box or Krispy Kreme.

The woman's face was in shadow. She had on a short dress made out of a silvery, silky fabric. She had nice-looking thighs and they were parted slightly. He wanted to lean over and bury his head in the softness.

He didn't know if, as Andre, he was supposed to say something. But he knew no matter what, it would be best to remain silent.

He smelled the faint odor of some flowery perfume and perhaps a hint of smoke-cigar or cigarette, he wasn't sure. He wanted to light one of his cigarettes, but held back. Possibly Andre didn't smoke. Anyway, he liked her perfume and the smell of the leather seats in the car. That was enough.

She drove into the hills to a gated driveway. The gate opened. They went around a fountain and she parked in front of the house, which was a mansion with a red tile roof. He followed her inside, past a heavy dark wooden door like something from a California Mission church.

"Would you like a drink?" she asked in the Spanish-tiled foyer.

"Yes, please. Whatever you're having."

"I'm having a glass of wine."

"Sounds good."

He waited in the foyer for a moment. She said, "Sit down in the living room. It's to the left. I'll be right in."

The living room was more like a big library with dark wood paneling and bookcases and deeply cushioned leather chairs and couches. At the far end of the room was a beautiful wooden desk with a green leather surface on top. He walked over and looked closely. He guessed that the desk was made of walnut. Whatever it was, it was very smooth when he touched it.

She came in and held out a large glass of wine. He took it and thanked her. She said, "Do you have something for me?"

He felt queasy, a little dizzy. What might that be, he wondered. Drugs? Money?

A good strategy was always to turn the question around. "Do you have something for me?"

She said, "I paid by credit card over the phone. I guess if we hit it off I might tip you, but that remains to be seen. Did you bring some of your short stories?"

"I'm sorry, no. I goofed. I was running late." He took a gulp of wine, sat on a soft burgundy-red leather sofa. She sat in an armchair nearby. She was still quite pretty looking, but he noticed that her face was a little weary, not deeply lined, but, well, tired and sad. Yet the sorrowful air suggested someone who was sympathetic to the suffering of others.

"No problem. I only wanted to see some proof that you're a published author," she said. "I've never used Sunset Boulevard Escort Service before. Or any escort service for that matter. How did you get into this line of work?"

"Just supplementing my income." The less said, the better. So he was an escort who was a writer too. That was funny. He'd once sold a treatment for a film to a producer who never paid him and later made a film with a story much like the one he'd written, only some elements had been changed, along with the names of the characters.

She had a slight tone of amusement in her voice as she said, "It's such a unique concept for an escort service. A night of interesting talk with a highly educated writer. Todd said you've published several novels."

Paul took a swig of wine, smiled. "Yes. Small press only though. New York doesn't appreciate my sensibility."

"I'm working on something special now. I'm trying to tell my mother's story. She was a friend of Paul Bowles. I'm writing it as a novel."

"Interesting."

"Yes. She visited him in Tangier and ended up staying for several years. She had amazing adventures which are recounted in her diary, which I have."

"Is she still alive?"

"No, she died three years ago. Left me this house and a sizable fortune. I'd been just getting by for years, running a small flower shop and writing on the side. I recently sold the business and I'm going to write full-time."

Paul smiled. "God, that sounds wonderful. This is a beautiful house. Must be nice to sit at that desk and write."

"It was built in the twenties for a film star of that era. I love this Spanish Colonial style. The arches, the wrought iron, the red tiles. My mother was married to a television producer. He ran off with an actress and she got the house and lot of money. It was her second marriage. My real father was a shoe salesman for Bass shoes. He made a nice living, but we weren't wealthy."

"Where's he?"

"Well, as Tennessee Williams said about the father in *The Glass Managerie*, he fell in love with long distances and left us. I don't know where he is."

The phone rang and Paul felt queasy again. What if the guy she was supposed to have picked up was calling to ask where she was? Or the escort service? "I'm going to ignore that," she said.

"Good. I haven't gotten your name," Paul said.

"I'm Lisa," she said.

"Nice to meet you."

"You too. You know, I expected someone all snooty and arrogant and sort of damaged who would go on endlessly about literature. You seem like a regular guy."

"I tried the starving-artist-in-the-garret routine, the torment and the terror, but give me a cheeseburger and a squeaky toy and I'm happy for hours."

She laughed and the phone rang again.

"Darn it," she said. "I'm having such a good time. Who is it?" She picked up the phone. "Hello."

A beat. Paul drank some more wine. Well, this was the end of the charade. He might as well finish off the wine. He took another gulp. It was delicious. Really good stuff. He'd forgotten how good wine could be. It was better with a meal though. His stomach grumbled. He remembered that he'd been considering going for some sushi before this whole adventure started.

Lisa spoke into the phone: "Hi. Yes, I found him. In fact, he's here now."

Paul smiled at her. She really was attractive, if a little world-weary. Much like himself. If they'd met at a party, he would've tried to score her phone number at least.

"Really?" Lisa said, and stared at Paul, then reconsidered and looked away.

Well, it had been fun. The wine, the nice house, and all the books. He stood up and went to the bookshelves, scanned the titles. He noticed some of his favorite authors: Borges, Cervantes, Hammett. What great books.

"Really?" Lisa said again. "We'll work something out. I have to sort things out here first. Let me call you later."

She hung up the phone. "That was the escort service. Andre is waiting at the corner of Franklin and Normandie. He's quite upset. I guess I went to the wrong corner. I'm terrible with street names."

"Don't jump to the conclusion that you made a mistake. For your information, Andre is a three-hundred-pound guy who was in a white gangsta rap group and now writes infantile poems and claims he's a serious writer. He's very peevish and has serious body odor."

Lisa laughed. She was beautiful when she laughed. He liked her more and more. He couldn't really think about it with any sense of genuine hope, but she might just turn his life around.

"So who are you, and what's your name?" she asked softly, a little timidly.

"My name is Paul and I'm a recovering alcoholic," Paul said. He laughed.

She smiled. "Like another glass of wine?"

"Great."

He handed Lisa his glass and their hands touched. He noticed her perfume again. He sat on the comfortable leather sofa and watched her as she walked out of the room. Very graceful. Nice figure. Maybe they would end up between her expensive cotton sheets later, sweaty and pressing their warm flesh together. This was going to be a whole new beginning.

A moment later, Lisa appeared in the doorway with a gun in her hand. "You impostor. You lied to me and I don't trust you. You haven't even written a novel, I bet."

He stared, aghast. "Lisa-"

"You're an intruder. I'll tell the police that you tricked me and got in here and then went crazy on me and I had to shoot you. We have no history. We have no connection. The police would side with me."

"But we were getting along so well. What's crazy about our conversation?"

"Nothing, except it's all a lie. You pretended to be someone else."

"True. And if you shoot me, the police will eventually find out that you called an escort service tonight. It will taint you, undermine your story. You hired some poor starving Hollywood writer for sex. You were prepared to exploit him just as the producers and agents and other Hollywood vampires have. Doesn't anyone in this town have a heart?"

Somehow he'd managed to put a sobbing sound into his voice. It was so easy to feel sorry for yourself in Hollywood, to feel that you were riding your own personal Slip-N-Slide to ruin and there was no one there to pull you off.

He said, "I saw a woman the other night. She was covered with grime, wearing rags, sleeping on a sheet of cardboard in the doorway of an empty shop at Western and Franklin. Cars and buses roared by a few feet away. Once people had loved her, cared about her. Now she was trash in a doorway. I started to weep. I wondered what happened to our sense of compassion in this city."

She kept the gun pointed at him, but her face softened.

He said, "I'll be honest. I'm down on my luck right now. A job I had lined up fell through. I'm almost broke. That's why I got in your car. I wanted to escape to another world for a few minutes."

She seemed genuinely concerned. "I'm sorry. I wanted some help with my novel. And maybe a little fun on the side. Can you forgive me for my crazy outburst?"

"Sure. What fun is a relationship without some occasional drama like guns being waved around and threats of death? You get the wine and we'll pretend that I'm Scott Fitzgerald and you're Zelda, who, by the way, wrote a novel called *Save the Last Waltz for Me*. She wrote it while in an insane asylum." He regretted the last comment as soon as he'd said it.

Lisa nodded. "Have you read it?"

"No, but none of the critics liked it."

"They like so few books," she said. "I'll get the wine."

He felt pretty good. He'd taken charge of the situation, proven that he knew something about literature, and talked her out of shooting him. It was all going to be fine, maybe.

He leaned back, studied the intricate geometric border painted around the edges of the ceiling in deep reds and blues and gold. Someone really knew how to make things look nice back in the twenties. Movie stars knew how to live.

Lisa walked in, handed him a glass of wine. He took a sip. She looked a little strange. She was staring at him and not drinking any wine.

"Drink up, baby. Then I'll help you with your novel and give you a foot massage." He gave her what he felt was a rakish grin.

She shook her head. "You men and your posturing. You've never written a book. I have. In fact, I've written several novels, all unpublished. But it's hard to make anything happen with fiction unless you're already famous or you do something to draw attention to yourself."

The way she was staring at him made him uneasy. He tried to smile. "I know. Writing is a hard game. Many are called and few are chosen."

"Exactly. Do you realize how much better my odds of selling a book will be if I'm involved in a scandal and a homicide? I can't lose. At worst I'll get manslaughter for killing you. How could premeditation be involved in killing someone I didn't know? The escort service issue will work for me. I'll explain what happened. I picked up the wrong person, a stranger on the street who lied to me. I brought him home, and then he tried to assault and rob me. I'll act contrite and it will be a morality tale warning women about using escort services and looking for sex from sleazy guys. It's a great story. A movie maybe."

She pulled out the gun again, which she had tucked into the back of her dress.

"Oh, please. Not again," Paul said, now deeply annoyed. He shook his head. "I can't believe it. And I'd already forgiven you and was ready to move on."

"To what?" she asked. "More of your lies?"

He stared at her, trying to see something human or alive or kind in her face. Nothing. Fuck it. His life sucked and so did hers. She was miserable in her own way. She was lonely and worn out and desperate for the love and attention she thought that having a novel published would bring. What utter folly. He was so tired of everything. What did he care if she shot him? He was miserable anyway. He smiled bitterly, shook his head again, and took a gulp of wine. Now that everything had turned to ashes and he was about to be murdered, the wine didn't taste so special anymore. Or maybe once she realized who he really was, she'd poured him a glass of some crappy table wine she used for cooking. Who cared, anyway? Wine was wine. Only phonies worried about the vintage and where it was made and how old it was. You drank it to get drunk or high at least. He took another gulp.

She was hesitating about shooting him. Maybe she wasn't that ambitious after all. Maybe she had a heart. Or maybe she was just another weak, average, boring zero of a person who'd been cowed by life into a submissive, scared, hopeless, protective stance, like someone waiting to be slapped and afraid to fight back.

His annoyance surfaced again. "Go ahead. Shoot me. You and your fucking novels. Who gives a shit about literature, or fame, or celebrity? You think that publishing your little stories will bring you love and attention and you'll be treated well. That's bullshit. You're right, if you want attention, you need to get in the papers. A shooting is good. Come on, shoot me. You'd be doing me a favor."

He felt pissed off as he thought about the disappointments of his life in L.A. His weakness and excessive use of alcohol and cigarettes left him with a feeling of disgust for himself. It was all so ugly and pathetic.

He leaned forward and tossed the wine in his glass into her face. She pulled the trigger. There was a loud noise. He reached forward and knocked the gun out of her hand as she blinked and tried to wipe the wine out of her eyes. He stood up and raised his right hand to slap her. She looked up with wet, blinking, pleading eyes, and cowered. He'd never hit a woman. He moved his hand back like he was winding up to give her a real good smack.

She covered her face and began crying, saying, "Oh, God, oh, God, don't hurt me," and sobbed loudly.

Paul remembered that she'd fired a round. He looked down, felt his body. There was no blood. She'd missed. Unconsciously, she had no urge to kill him, just as he had no urge to hit her.

"That's a good one, given that you were just about to kill me."

He walked out of the house and down the long driveway to the gate. He was shaky again, but the cool night air felt good. Walking briskly and occasionally throwing a few hard punches at the air helped release his anger somewhat.

In fifteen minutes he found himself at the corner of Winona and Franklin. He paused. He could go east to Vermont for sushi and beer, or south to Jumbo's for beer and strippers.

He hesitated. He wanted cigarettes and beer and naked women. He wanted to escape from life. The violence and nastiness he'd just experienced was disturbing. He knew that in some way he'd brought it on himself. He was passive, self-destructive. He'd lied and pretended to be someone else to see where it would take him. It took him to a weird place.

He headed down to Jumbo's. When he walked in, a familiar pudgy Latina was on the small stage in a white bikini. One day he'd tipped her repeatedly as he sat near the stage and she danced just for him. He was excited by her then. Now he wasn't interested. There was a very tall, very skinny blonde with very pale skin sitting at the bar, waiting to go on stage. She seemed more sexy. She looked at him and smiled as he walked to an empty seat at the bar.

Paul ordered a Newcastle. It was $4.50. He left the fifty cents on the bar and looked over at a few guys who were always there, sitting at the bar, talking. Jumbo's was as much a neighborhood bar as a strip joint. Half of the time the place was boring. He drank some cold beer and walked to the door, looked outside at Hollywood Boulevard for a moment, then gazed back to the stage. The skinny girl walked out and began dancing awkwardly to some heavy metal music that she'd selected on the juke box.

Now that she was on stage, her long leanness was no longer attractive. She couldn't move in rounded, feminine ways. Her movements were skeletal, stick-like, mechanical. Like a giraffe with knocking knees, the skinny woman didn't move in fluid ways. He felt good that he'd gotten out of Lisa's place alive, but he still felt jittery and a little sick too. He smoked a cigarette. There wasn't much of a buzz. He threw it down. A homeless guy came over and picked it up, asked for money. Paul handed him the pack of cigarettes and the few dollars that were in his pocket, then walked away from the night club.

In his studio apartment he checked his email while eating some leftover Thai noodles that he'd heated in the microwave. He saw an update from a friend traveling in Europe. Other than that, all he had was spam from various companies trying to sell him porn and drugs and mortgage refinancing.

He stretched out on the bed. He pictured himself lying on a beach with his ex-girlfriend. It turned into a sexual scenario. He started to get turned on, but then he just felt sad and the fantasy just didn't seem that sexy after all.

He imagined being back in Lisa's living room. Now he had the time to think of things to say and do that hadn't occurred to him when he was there, under pressure, in the midst of a crazy situation. Maybe he'd feel better now if he'd pulled down some of the books, or smashed some of her belongings. He could've picked up the gun and fired it into the couch to make her feel the fear he'd felt at the moment the gun went off and just after. He could've said something clever when he walked out. He could've stolen her car, or robbed her. She was rich, and he barely had enough to get by.

None of it really appealed to him. What good would it have done to hurt her? She was already fucked up enough in her own way.

He got up and opened a beer and poured it into a glass and walked to the windows that faced the Hollywood hills in Los Feliz. He could see a few stars in the sky and some softly glowing lights in houses. Maybe one of them was Lisa's.

She was in a mansion and he was in a small apartment in a run-down 1920s building. Almost a century ago, a movie star had lived in her place. Maybe that same movie star had lived in Paul's apartment before becoming a star and moving to a house in the hills.

It was best to let go of things. It was best not to accumulate things, or pain, or needs. Now if only he could let go of feeling assaulted. He knew that if he waited, the bad feelings would go away or fade out. But what to do in the meantime?

He stared at the hills. The sound of a train's whistle drifted over in the night air as a train moved along the tracks that ran beside the L.A. river. He took a drink of beer and thought about trains in the night. They moved under the stars and the people on them went to other places, far away. He began to feel a little better.

Andrew Charles Bloy
Meat Puppet
2003

//

An actor by trade, Andrew Charles Bloy began writing monologues in the mid-nineties for himself and other actors to use in the auditioning process. He had found writing in first-person narrative fiction to be so inspiring that within a few years' time, he had written several hundred short but biting pieces. Nine of which were performed by Bloy in a staged collection called *One Man's Pages* in Los Angeles in May of 2003. The main charactor in *Meat Puppet*, the darkly comical 'Scarab' appears in many other monologues. In two more main stream works, *Writer's Bloc*, a sit-com that demonstrates how what we buy gets sold and *Lemon Fight*, a feature film, we see life through the self-professed "evil scribe" Bloy's some what 'tweeked' sensibilities. Andrew Charles Bloy and his dog Luckyboy live in Toluca Lake, California.

God-damn dog, shut the fuck up! Oh, jesus kryste! Fucking
heroin to me.I am the meat that sits out an hour too long. I can taste
it. My god-damn teeth are rotting out of my mouth. How am I supposed to justify paying some dentist five hundred dollars when I
feel like this? I miss that smell: the sweet scent of decay. My mom
smelled like that way before I knew what it was.

Ten forty three am. Great, no students today. Mr and Mrs Blah
blahson trust me with shaping the musically intuitive minds of their
spawn."Cello? (I'm a fucking guitarist.) How much? Oh,okay every
monday and thursday? Fantastic!" I don't know cello so I'm slowly
convincing Babs Blah blahson the little scamp's retarded.
Hey,175.00 an hour means I get the same junk as Weiland with out
the press.

Get me coffee and Luckyboy can run like a mad dog thru the
park scaring all the sweet little yuppie families and darling children. Coffee:the only thing easier to digest than my current diet.

I'm not a junkie, I have a lot of responsibilities. You can catch
a pretty decent buzz just standing next to Ted Kennedy and he still
gets to be senator.I guess with the history involved every body looks
at something shiny if the topic is broached.

Luckyboy's got the life of fucking Riley, whoever that is. I did-
n't even want him when Life Sucking Hole found him at Runyon.
Two years gone and I'd see you bleed before anything happend to
him.

Coffee: the final legal drug. Anyone can get it,any
age,color,sex,size. Truly worth all that I go through to get it. I would
bet anyone all I have they don't walk two miles to get coffee. In Los
Angeles? I do.

Even when I know I'm going to be behind one of these fucking
sheep with the double frappa-cappa soy extra foofie no foam on and
on. It's just coffee, health nut. Ease up just a tweek. You might actually enjoy the eight bucks you just blew on bean.

Things could be worse. I could live in the valley.

Josh Gloer
Except from "The Carpool"
Spring 2003

//

Josh is currently a freelance writer based in Los Angeles, where he writes for a variety of music and film publications and literary magazines. In his spare time, he is working on several screenplays, two novels and a comic book. www.joshgloer.com.

I wasn't sure what to expect when I answered the ad. I just needed to get home. I hadn't been able to hold down a job that year, so a plane ticket was out of the question, but I needed that summer vacation away from the books, parties and everything else that went with college. I had grown increasingly tired of the superficial fraternities and arrogant jocks as they knocked books out of my hands or took my seat in classes. I hated them. I hated the way they treated me; like I wasn't a person.

I needed that summer job I had been promised manning the dock at Jim's in the Ozarks. While filling up boat gas tanks might not sound like a very desirable job, it definitely had its perks. I got free gas for my boat, I met plenty of girls spending their summers at the family cabins, and most importantly, I got to work outside. I refused to work a job that kept me from the summer air, and Jim had always guaranteed me a spot at the dock, so I needed to get home.

Walking through the school bookstore, I briefly paused at the bulletin board that was usually decorated sporadically with strips of paper advertising everything from free marijuana to kidney donors, when something caught my eye.

Carpool Needed
Must Have Valid License
Must be willing to Drive
Call Tony
573-555-9380

Upon completing an initial phone interview, I learned that Tony was, in fact, going my way. He was headed to Lawrence, KS, and offered to pay my bus fair back to the Ozarks in Missouri if I would drive him all the way. I agreed, and he wanted to meet in person.

A little nervous, I got to the diner a few minutes early. Fidgeting with the plastic yellow ashtray, I sat with my back to the wall attempting to gain the best vantage point in seeing Tony before he saw me. While I didn't really want to back out at the sight of whomever it would be that walked through that glass door, I wanted to leave myself the option.

He was late, and I was getting antsy. As they walked through the door, each diner patron became less desirable then the last, ranging from bikers to bums, none of which the man I imagined Tony to be. I don't know what I expected.

"Jason?"

I spun a little in my seat as he managed to sneak up on me despite my clever vantage point. Turning slightly, I saw something that I never expected. Slightly unkempt, Tony looked a little disheveled. His hair was messed up, his shoes untied, and I suddenly realized why I had failed to see his approach. Some physical handicap or accident had left Tony confined to a wheelchair. My surprise must have been obvious through my speechless stare.

"Hey, I'm Tony," he said with a slight smile. "Forgive me if I don't shake hands." He wheeled himself to the edge of the booth using a straw tightly clenched in his teeth. I didn't know much about the handicapped, but it was obvious that he was completely paralyzed as he used his remaining motor skills to suck and blow himself forward and backwards.

"Yeah…no, it's cool." My complete ignorance of the situation left me dumbfounded. What was the proper etiquette here? I stood and awkwardly put my hand on his shoulder.

"Jason Murch." I spoke a little too loudly in an idiotic attempt to compensate for his condition. I quickly removed my hand, realizing that I just made a complete ass of myself as Tony eyed my hand, and probably my motives for physical contact. I thought it might make him think I was completely comfortable with this, as if I deal with handicapped people all the time, a coping mechanism I have readily adapted. When I meet gay men, I am overly friendly. When I meet people with deformity, I stare at it. I try to make them think, "Wow, this guy really is cool with my condition," but instead I am really showcasing my ignorance.

The waitress came by, an older woman too tall for her waitress skirt, a feature that would have been attractive if it weren't for her obvious age, something she tried to cover up with a clown quantity of make-up and several cans of Aqua Net. The curves of her buttocks were clearly visible below her hemline.

"What'll ya have?" Her evident apathy served as an additional turn off, as if that were necessary.

"Can we get some menus?" Tony asked not being able to turn in order to take in this full picture of beauty that stood before us. Tossing a few menus down on the center of the table sending the salt shaker toppling into my lap, she walked off toward the kitchen.

I was about halfway through the first page deep in an indecisive quandary as to which would be less horrible, the Super Sunshine Scrambler or the Mega Morning Mania, when I realized something wasn't right. Tony, unable to pickup his menu was squinting his eyes trying to translate what he could from the menu as he attempted to read it upside down.

Again, my ignorance of such situations left my mind full of questions. Was this a situation in which I helped him? I had seen on television so many of such similar occurrences in which the receiver of erroneous help didn't really want assistance. My simple misguided act might make Tony feel inferior or like I pitied him, but he obviously couldn't read the menus from its arbitrarily tossed position, and he certainly couldn't move it himself.

Picking up the menu, his eyes shot to me. Oh God, he's going to reject what I thought to be a kind gesture and see right through my façade, knowing that I wasn't comfortable with this disability which was suddenly thrust upon me. Should I drop it? Should I go on? What the hell should I do? In an attempt at what, in my mind, would be a compromise, I simply turned the plastic menu so it was facing him, a nonchalant, and hopefully non-threatening gesture.

"Do you mind putting that in my hands?" A slight look of worry crossed his face. He didn't know me. I could be anyone, but I guess he dug deep, testing me as he was looking for someone he could trust. "I like to appear as normal as possible." My brief silence betrayed my indecision, and his acknowledgement of my hesitation came through clearly in a look of true disappointment.

"Umm, yeah." I picked up the menu. It was three pages. "No problem." It was a problem. Should I open it? What page would he want it open to? It was so simple, yet I didn't know how to handle this situation. Here I was engaging in physical contact with another male who less than five minutes before was a complete and total stranger, and the brief introduction that we had moments ago barely rectified that fact.

"Here you go." The feel of his flesh was nauseating. I had shaken hundreds if not thousands of hands before, but this was different. In one hand I held a laminated menu, and in the other hand I held an object that didn't feel much different. As a human hand that was basically dead it still had a normal sense of warmth, but I knew he couldn't feel my flesh on his. There was no reaction from his skin, no gentle squeeze one would expect to receive from a handshake. These hands were simply lifeless.

Stupidly, I chose to leave the menu closed. He was stuck looking at a picture of the restaurant with its "World Famous Staff" waving a friendly hello. "Open me," they said. "Look inside at what wonderful things we can prepare for you." Only Tony couldn't. He couldn't move his pinky, let alone turn the page of this oversized menu.

And then the panic hit me. He might ask me to open it for him! What had I gotten myself into? The mere thought of returning back to those soulless lumps of flesh that seemed to drain the life out of my own hands was terrifying. I couldn't do it.

But Tony wasn't even looking at the menu. He must have been here before because he didn't seem to possess the slightest curiosity as to the contents of the inner pages, and our waitress was on her way back to the table expecting us to have made our selection.

"Y'all ready?" Was Tony ready? I had no idea. Having spent the entire time I was to be perusing the massive selection of hash brown varieties worrying about Tony's ability to see his menu, I had to arbitrarily choose something.

"Yes, I'll have the Pig in the Poke." It was the first thing I saw.

"That's from the Kountry Kids Korner, hon." Oh, my God. I realized that I was looking at the back of Tony's menu, where the children's menu was located. Damn.

"Yes, I understand that." I had found that portraying a false sense of confidence got me through many of such embarrassing situations in life, but such a portrayal was unnecessary in this particular instance as our whorish looking waitress couldn't care less if we burned the building down, customers and all.

"Son?" She was looking at Tony now.

"I'd like a vanilla shake please." While the request seemed a little odd at first, it didn't talk me too long to realize that had he ordered the Heart Attack Special or one of the other fine selections on the menu, someone would have to feed him, and after a quick survey, I didn't see any qualified nurses coming in the diner to his aide. Suddenly, a vanilla shake seemed like the perfect meal.

"Five minutes." I caught another disgusting look at her left buttock peeking out from under that red and white striped uniform, taking my appetite with it bouncing down the aisle. These skirts would make great cheerleading outfits, but in the diner, I am surprised no one has complained. The sight of a man bending down to pick up his fork as she walked by answered most of my questions, and I made a silent vow to never enter that diner again under any circumstances.

"So, Jason..." My attention was snapped back to the situation at hand.

"Yes?" Wow, this was awkward. I was positive that he felt it too, but I just assumed that he might be used to it. Everyone he met must have gone through a similar ordeal. Why hadn't he told me over the phone that he would be entering that diner under the power of a motorized chair? I would have appreciated a little heads up on the matter.

"I bet you are wondering why I didn't give you any details on my physical status." Oh my God! He can read my mind! Maybe whatever left him in such a horrible state gifted him with extra powers like Dare Devil, and now he is a psychic. He's probably still doing it. Stop thinking!

"No." Now he thinks I'm a liar.

"I find that people aren't as accepting as I had once thought," he said calmly. "It may be a little unethical, but I tend to think that it is easier in my situation to sort of trap people rather than letting them dodge me on the phone." At this moment, the ability to dodge this situation was an option that I would have paid for.

"You don't have to be one hundred percent cool with my situation," he continued, "but I just like for people to talk to me before they rule me out as a human." It was becoming obvious that this guy must get burned a lot. It makes sense, as I wouldn't have agreed to our lunch time meeting had I been aware of his physical obstacles. There were more than one of such advertisements he had hanging on that Library bulletin board, and I could have called them all. I was sure that the others wouldn't have placed me at a diner in front of a man who needed my assistance to pick up a menu.

His theory was sound. I was here, and in a much more difficult position to simply write him off, while after touching his hands, I greatly wanted to. In a public place and face to face, it made it more human, and therefore, I was unable to bolt out the glass door leading me back out into my freedom.

"Ok." I wasn't cool with his situation, and I am sure he could tell. I was fumbling around like a complete asshole, nearly working up a sweat upon hearing his simple menu request. But this was completely new for me.

"So," he said. "I need a ride." It became obvious why. He couldn't drive himself. Like lifting the menu up into a suitable position for reading, I would have to do it for him.

"My accident was recent." I thought a story would follow that I didn't want to hear, but he simply continued explaining the ad that he must have had someone else pin to the wall in the bookstore. "In the confusion of the hospitals and visitors, my car was overlooked, so to speak, and now, I need to get it home." I guess that made sense to me, but I couldn't help but wonder why a family member or a friend didn't do it for him. It didn't make sense that he would randomly select an individual out of a hat to escort him all the way back to Kansas, and then pay for his bus fair back to Missouri.

I had a lot of questions, but I didn't want to ask them. Tony seemed like a to-the-point sort of guy, which was the one factor I sought out in a person. I hated it when girls said, "Yeah, OK," and then needed to wash their hair, or guys said, "sure thing bro. I'll stop by," leaving you to an empty apartment lighting the candles of your own birthday cake. And while I did feel a little deceived as he chose to omit the detail that he was in a chair, he was shooting me straight now.

"Look," he continued, "I'm gonna need a lot of help, but I will pay you. I left that off the ad because I don't want someone who is looking for a job. I want someone who just wants to drive home."

.

John Dooley
Broad Daylight
2004 (rev.)

//

Dooley is a long time poet and humorist with writing credits too numerous and obscure to mention. Born in 1960, this aging "Irish-Americanish" hooligan has crab-apple kidneys, a ham-size cranium and to date, has only suffered one slightly humorous heart attack. He enjoys drinking, smoking, and sexual intercourse.

I saw your girlfriend with another man
At the market, then again minutes later
She was kissing this guy in the parking lot
between a Jeep and an old Ford Falcon

She had her hands all over him
and they both seemed incredibly horny

From my car
I could see her pull out his schlong
He was pretty good looking
Big, muscular, bronze
legs like tree trunks

Pretty big root too
if you follow the metaphor

Anyway, your girlfriend
goes down on him right there
in broad daylight

Sucks it all in like a three dollar professional
I'm expecting the thing to pop
out the back of her skull

He seemed nervous, glancing around
He could have been worried
someone would take his shopping cart
full of protein supplements

I dunno
But I don't think they saw me

Just about the time I think he's going to shoot spunk
She stops
Lifts up her skirt-no panties by the way
and starts jacking him hard

You never told me she shaves, man
You know I eat that shit up!

Anyway, she lays down on the blacktop
Guides it in with both hands
sticks two fingers up his ass
And Dark Fabio starts laying pipe
in front of me, God, and everybody!

You never told me she was a Holy Roller, man!
Jesus Christ! Oh FUCK me, Jesus Christ!

But that wasn't my point
At the market
I got a really good deal on paper towels

I felt generous so I bought a case
Take as many rolls as you want
Something tells me
you're going to have a pretty big mess to clean up

And I've got plenty of my own!

Sleeping with Snakes

Notes from the Los Angeles Underbelly

Kathleen Maraschino
Moving Forward Fast
July 2004

Kathleen grew up in numerous small towns all over Central Texas before calling Los Angeles her home. As a child a lot of her time was spent on farms and in the middle of nowhere, therefore she would live in her imagination and alleviate her boredom by writing stories, continuing the narration as the years went by. Honest yet elusive, she likes to push buttons and strike chords in others. She also enjoys storytelling through song. Kathleen writes both fiction and non-fiction, with plans of more publications in the future.

There are devils hiding in every corner of the nocturnal wonderland they call the nightlife.
You want to dance? I do.
You want to fuck? I don't.
Thanks for the drink. Bartender, give me another shot of unknown sin, it's on him. We're only friends, you know. We both just sang songs of lovelorn tales and playing with fire, and it's time we celebrate. This is what we do, make people sweat and burn, provoke thought, and get feet moving on the dance floor.
Tonight is our night, right?
Sure, I'll have another.

Beauty in brilliance, he thinks he's a genius. I'm not attracted to him, but perhaps he is intriguing. Maybe I could derive some amusement in a little game of mindfucking, but the clock is ticking and I have somewhere to go. Okay, sure, why not. It is late and I am bored. My lips touch his and it is my first mistake.

Babe hold me.
(Don't touch me.)

Fast forward.
Oh fuck, I fucked up. Today is my dying day and I'm seeing stars. My head is swimming with guilt and sickness. I feel nothing, yet I have bite marks and lovesick bruises that serve as a reminder of a hazy night laden with alcohol clouding my judgment. Yes, this is my judgment day. I need an angel to pull me out of this mess. I can't take back time. I can't retrace my steps because, well, I don't remember. I gave into temptation and now I'm on my knees. I'm a good girl who walked the tightrope of trouble and I fell down fast.

Rewind.
An invitation for infiltration.
Tell me about your sexual history, he said.
It's impressive, I responded proudly.
Oh yeah?
Yep. Only two people.
You're lying.
Nope.

Who?

My ex.

How long were you with him?

About five years.

That's a long time.

Yeah, we were each other's first love, first relationship, first sex, first everything.

That is beautiful. What about the other?

Eh, a drunken rebound.

I see. That's all???

Yep. I only have sex if I'm in love.

Uh huh, he murmured as his tongue began tracing circles around my nipples.

(I just wanted to sleep, I wanted to be good.)

I'm so attracted to you, he said.

(Get in line, take a ticket.)

I'm asexual, I countered, and I don't have casual sex.

Okay. So do you want to cum? He asked as his tongue slid up my inner thigh.

Um, I don't do this type of thing.

Uh huh.

His tongue found its way up higher and higher, pressing inside me, wet and hot. My legs, they shook like an earthquake. My mistake.

Fast forward.

I'm tossing this secret in a jar with the others. Tying it tight with a pretty pink ribbon. My best friend shakes her head in disgust when I slip through the door at six a.m. I climb underneath the sheets and try to put an eraser to my memory. I'm trashed and tired from my own treason. I can't fall asleep. God and his minions are whispering their opinions in my deaf ears. I know, I know.

Rewind.

I love fucking but I don't fuck, I told him.

I hate to break it to you dear, but I just fucked you, he brazenly answered with a smirk.

Take me home.

(Take me home.)

Sleeping with Snakes

Dan Fante

Caveat Emptor

2003

//

Dan Fante was born and raised in Los Angeles. He hopes someday to meet a fat waitress and learn to play the harmonica.

For once the firing squad in my head was quiet. The result of three hours of solid sleep and no hangover. It was 5:30AM. Just dawn. The long bus ride from Mar Vista to my taxi garage near La Cienega Boulevard had been made easier by revisiting a thin volume of e.e. cummings' early poetry. It was mid December in L.A. and a hot spell of Santa Ana winds was coming in off the desert. Already seventy-five degrees at street level. By seven o'clock that night, I would lose another five to seven pounds of sweat. Twelve hours on the seat grinding out a living in my un air-conditioned cab.

I picked up my trip sheet and found #627 parked in the sea of yellow in the lot next to the taxi dispatch office. For once, the inside of the rear passenger area was fairly clean. Whoever had driven the cab on the last shift had had a slow night.

Rolling all the windows down, I started the car. So far, so good. No clunking in the engine or screeching fan belt noises. I checked the radiator and the oil dipstick. They were both okay.

Inside the cab behind the wheel, my next order of business was to copy the odometer mileage on the top of my trip sheet in the slot provided. I read the numbers off the dash and transposed them to the green box on the card: 94,261. #627 had been a new Dodge taxi thirteen months ago. These days it gasped and pinged and regularly needed work twice a week.

It was now fully daylight. The blazing orange fireball above the Boneventure Hotel was working its way up between the tenements in East Hollywood. My boom box was on the seat next to me beside my poetry notebook and my Cummings paperback. I clicked the "on" button then dialed to the 'all news' station to get the day's forecasts: 90-93 degrees. Smoggy. Forcing #627's gear shift down into "D", I punched the gas pedal.

In five minutes I was up La Cienega and crossing Wilshire on my way to Beverly Hills where the fast money is early in the day. My two daily steadies, both downtown financial guys, weren't due for their pick ups until after eight o'clock, so I was in the hunt for my first fare. With no one hailing me, I turned east on Santa Monica Boulevard. That's when I saw her.

Being an L.A. cabby requires a highly-tuned sense of danger. Vibes and street smarts are everything. After several years of hacking, off and on, after being held up and knifed, I was no exception. The woman on the curb looked okay. No problem. In her late twenties, Mexican or European, lipsticked, and dressed in a maroon warm-up outfit. Her died-blond hair was combed straight back and tied with a ribbon. But there was something else as she got in and recited her destination. It may have been her smile, or the way she said the words with the trace of a Latino accent. Something genuine and open. Special. For me, a guy always on his guard against people, a guy who spent his days and nights alone as much as possible, drinking and reading and typing, or just drinking, it felt like I had walked into a flower shop for the first time.

I make it an imperative to say as little as possible to passengers, but a conversation started anyway. The name tag on her jacket spelled out *Leslee*. I learned that she was a massage therapist at BLOW UP, a high-rent gym on Melrose Avenue, and a college dropout - Art major. Born and raised in Boyle Heights.

When we got to the address on Melrose and she paid her fare, her smile filled the back of my cab. "Thanks," she said, swinging the door open; "jou're a nice guy, Bruno. Hab a wonda-ful gooo day. I mean it toooo." "Ditto", my inarticulate idiot mouth replied. "You do the same." Then she was gone.

As it turned out, the next day was a repeat of the first, only ten minutes later in the morning. I had gotten a slow start because #627 needed a gallon of green radiator coolant. On my way up La Cienega, after no one hailed me, I again turned east on Santa Monica Boulevard. There was Leslee. This time she looked rushed. But the smile was there like the sweet blast of air conditioning. "Hi Brunesimo" she said, in her wispy south of the border accent, remembering my name. "Wha a nice surprise. Goo to zee jou?" I nodded and tried my best to return the smile.

"Koo jou hurry up? I'm late. I been burnin' my cannle ah bot ens."

This time my unsophisticated yap did better. A hip, literary answer, courtesy of Edna St. Vincent Mallay herself. "Oh", says I, quoting: "*Your candle burns at both ends…it will not last the night…But ah, your foes, and oh, your friends, it gives a lovely light.*"

Her smile back said it all.

Leslee's fist massage client of the day would be an intense Beverly Hills CEO who arrived at 6:15 sharp every morning. A hundred bucks plus tip. She wanted to know if I would be willing to pick her up on a daily basis so she wouldn't have to worry about being late for the guy and calling cab companies so early in the morning? "Okay. Sure. No problem", I said eagerly. "That's fine. I'd like that."

So that's the way we began. That first, deep puncture of the ice pick.

Slowly, I began to open up to her. It was tough for me, this sudden, clumsy candidness. But by week's end, after a coffee date in our free time, and a couple of long phone conversations about who and how rich her massage clients were, and her wanting to see my poetry and me viewing two books of her drawings, eventually, rebelling against my own prescribed isolation, weary of vodka and porno videos and my seething, genocidal thoughts, I convinced myself that I might somehow be starting to care about somebody else.

Then, on Friday, a clammy, drizzling Los Angeles morning, as I was dropping Leslee off, she leaned forward across the back of my seat to pay, as usual, and I got a surprise. A kiss. A firm, determined tongue forced itself between my lips then withdrew quickly. "I been wantin' to do tha all week", she breathed.

"Me too", my throat croaked.

Soon after that came the time, the only time as it turned out, that we made it. It was in my cab. That too was another ad-lib surprise. I had picked her up from work at five o'clock and we were heading west on 3rd Street in the heavy rush-hour traffic. "Hey", she whispered, "jou wanna see somethin'? I been keeping it kool for jou?"

At the next red light I turned and looked back over the seat. My passenger was naked from the waist down in the bumper to bumper traffic. Shaved pink crotch. Legs apart, wearing her beaming, million-peso, grin.

I should have known. The flashing orange caution light going off in my brain was delivering a steady message: THIS IS ALL TOO EASY... SOMETHING'S WRONG... But, in truth, in hindsight, I know I was lost. Nothing else but that wondrous thing resting itself lovingly on the vinyl of my back seat mattered. I had never gotten it on with anyone in a cab in open daylight before. Between parked cars.

It was the following Monday that I had my first symptoms. A redness between my legs. An itching. Then a blotch in my pubic hair that, by the end of the day, became a dime-sized sore.

When I mentioned my problem to Leslee on our ride the next day, her response was blasé. No big deal. Whatever it was would go away. Then the smile. The no prisoners - gimme all your cash and credit cards - I love you forever - smile.

Two days later my herpes sore was in full blossom, oozing and burning like mad. My cab company's fat HMO witchdoctor took one look and diagnosed the condition immediately. Along with his free medical opinion came a stern warning to ease up on the juice, a flash of brilliance I'd put together for myself years earlier.

Leslee denied everything then unaccountably disappeared.

By the end of the following week when none of my phone calls were returned, and she was a steady no-show on the corner of Santa Monica Boulevard in the morning, I took matters into my own hands, stopping by her gym after parking #627 at a meter on a side street a block away.

The desk guy at BLOW UP eyed me up and down as I walked in. He was muscular and smiling, an iron-pumping geek. Intentionally unhelpful and acting busy. He'd pegged me as a slob in blue jeans and a drip-dry shirt. A non-person in Hollywood.

Finally, after two requests, I got louder. It was then that he buzzed into the massage area from the switch board intercom. After he hung up the George Clooney charm was back. He eyed me up and down again and announced. "Leslee is presently *occupied* with a client."

I had all day, I said. I would wait.

So, for the next hour, I sat in one of the expensive gray leather chairs outside the spa area keeping my eyes on the little window in the massage room door. Finally, another guy in a towel from the male exercise area sat down next to me. "Who you waiting for?" he whispered. "Which girl?"

"Leslee", I said back.

"Hey, me too. Jesus! Shit! Maybe she double-booked herself!"

"I don't have an appointment", I said.

His eyes narrowed, then he snickered. "Well", he whispered, "you'd better sign up and get in line from now on. You won't be sorry. For an extra fifty she'll give you the whole deal, the total-body massage. And, for fifty more, what do you think you get?"

"I already know", I said.

THE END

Sleeping with Snakes

Notes from the Los Angeles Underbelly

Chris Iovenko

Reunion (an excerpt)

1997

//

Chris Iovenko is a writer and filmmaker who lives in Los Angeles.

Sleeping with Snakes

This morning at work it finally happened; I got over Susan. I don't have my own tools anymore, and I was sweating grease, wedged under this Jap shit-box trying to get the rusted 8mm bolts off the exhaust with a borrowed half-inch socket. I had both hands on the extension bar pulling like a bastard, and the socket winged off, kicking the metal arm into my mouth.

And you know what, a funny thing happened; I didn't fling the wrench across the floor, start cursing, and jump up screaming at everybody for making me use the wrong tools. I just lay there for a minute on the ground feeling this sharp bite crossing my mouth. I lay there and took it. One of my front teeth had a wiggle to it, and I could taste blood. I pushed the tooth with my tongue; felt the nerve pinch, then just picked up the wrench and refitted to start again.

I finally got the bolts off, and was pulling the exhaust down when I heard a woman call my name. I didn't so much as flinch. I just stayed cool. Then I realized that she was calling not for me, Walker, but for Walter, the owner. I realized then that I was over Susan. Like the tooth I could take the pain of it lying down, just let it go by. I knew I was done with her the way you realize you're done sleeping, or done eating, or done crying. Just finished, over; I would no longer need Susan or see her face in a car passing by, or eating a burger through the window at Johnnie's.

I'm walking home now and I feel cured, free, pumped for my new life. Even the hot August sun, spit brown in the smog, feels good and friendly. Walking by the Lighthouse I feel like celebrating so I get a fifth of peppermint schnapps, Whitley's, not the cheap shit. Back at the apartment I put the beat-up old air-conditioner on high and sit down in front of the tube. It's even worse reception than before, only two channels, but at least you and you alone decide which to watch. Not that they put anything on TV anymore that you can enjoy, anyway, just this weepy-ass Dr.Phil-Oprah shit.

I put it on Oprah thinking maybe I'll get a laugh out of it, but instead I just get irritated. Everybody on these talk shows just sits and whines about how their husband won't sleep with them because they're ugly or abused or can't find a dress that fits. It's like they are so busy feeling sorry for themselves that they can't get on with their lives, can't just fucking forget about it and move on.

I want to change the channel, but don't bother. I just sit very still, trying not to think. The air-conditioning isn't working. I'm sweating out of my eyeballs, just drinking the warm schnapps, listening to the bitching, and suddenly I'm not feeling like celebrating anymore. I'm drinking the way I used to drink, mad as hell shouting shut the fuck up at these stupid women who just don't get it, who want to suck you down, kill you with their problems. Then a girl comes on, a curly blond like Susan, in this flirty yellow dress, and I think finally somebody sane in this crappy world. Somebody who gets it; who doesn't buy the bullshit.

She's looking right at me talking, her tits sticking out like lemons, and I think Jesus Christ how long it's been since I got laid. Maybe I should call the TV station and get her phone number. Then I start listening to what she's saying, and she's bitching about her ex-husband who beat her up, and chases her around, won't let her see other men, won't let her lead her own life. Her own life. What about the things she probably did to him, the way she probably flirted with his friends, the way she maybe tore up his valentine because he was too broke to take her out to dinner? What about his life? Why isn't he allowed to sleep at night knowing where she is, knowing that she isn't fucking her way around town making an asshole out of him?

Everybody always takes the woman's side, they see her pretty and crying, and always say you're the monster, the Hitler out of control, but do they have to live with your eyes? Pretty soon I throw the empty schnapps bottle through the TV screen and the downstairs neighbor starts shouting up at me and banging on his ceiling with a broom.

Don't want the cops coming over, so I decide I'm going to chill out. I get my pen and my ledger out and I sit back down. I keep a list of favors owed me, favors I owe. Mostly it's people who have some evil shit coming their way if they cross me again. Everybody is in my ledger book, my father, my lawyer, Susan. Some of them are in many different places. But everybody is in there on one page or another because everybody I meet right off the bat either fucks with me or helps me. Owe me or I owe you, that's the way life works.

It usually calms me down everyday, making the entries. It makes me think how great it will be when I decide to call in all the favors owed me. Flipping through the pages I keep coming across Susan's name on every page, always in the "Owe Me" column. I try to start a new page, but I can't think, I can only write "Susan" over and over again. It's like she's here watching, spying on me, not letting me bury our sleeping dogs.

I decide to write her a letter and pull out an empty page and write on the back:

Fuck you, Susan, fuck you, you fucking cunt. Fuck you, you know what I mean. It's over between us, I mean it, I got married, young Walker Junior's on the way. No, but seriously, fuck you, I mean it. I've thought about it now, had plenty of time, it's over. Done. Fuck you, really. Seriously. Don't ever think of calling me to apologize, don't even think about it. Seriously, don't call, it won't work, I won't talk to you. Well, maybe I will, but see, just to be nice. And I'll pick up the phone real slow and won't have much to say. I'm over you- done, finished, end of story. You are no longer in my dreams, or on my TV, or in my coffee when I pour the cream in.

So, if you do call, do not for one moment think I will go grab a drink with you at Trickie's, because I might, just to be nice, but never as a date or a reunion or anything. Maybe we could sit in a booth there and drink a pitcher, but don't think or expect me to hold your hand and tell you how I can't hardly get up to go to work for dreams I don't want to leave, or how walking to work I put fifteen extra minutes on so I don't have to walk by the Wee-Wash where you wash your clothes, but if I don't walk down Victory then I have to go up Whitsett by your sister Annie's house and what if you were spending the night there?

If I saw your car I'd probably have to stop and think for a while, and wait to see if you came out by yourself, or see if maybe you were walking out with Annie or another friend. But what if it was Tony coming out with you? Then I'd have to think about that, just think about that, and maybe start walking over looking around for a broken bottle and...

I quit writing the letter, crumple it up, and throw it in the broken TV set. The smartest thing is to just go and find Susan because once I see her I'll know it's over for sure, and I can just tell her to her face that it's over. It's just when I start thinking that I get a little crazy.

Marna Bunger
Talking Dirty
2004

//

Marna began her writing career in the 1980s as a Pentagon intern. Her early exposure to $500 toilet seat press releases made her appreciate creative nonfiction writing. She continues to find humor in her own life and beyond as the creative force behind dontmincewords.com.

Bedroom dirty talk is the convergence of creativity and tolerance. I've been a dirty talk connoisseur for about twenty years. I have classic and timeless standards. At this point, I rarely need to add to my repertoire. The other night, I heard a new one.

I would be willing to bet that most people get into dirty talk via long-distance relationships. I know I did. During my first college break, I called a boyfriend to wish him happy holidays. Shortly thereafter, on his request, I began to describe what I was going to do to him when we got back to school.

Dirty talk sentence construction is a no-brainer and one- and two-syllable words prevail. "The next time I see you, I'll be wearing my black lace teddy and then... I'm going to pour honey all over your chest and lick it off slow and easy."

Once I converted from a phone sex dirty talker to in-person, I had to be more serious in my delivery - no more filing nails and multitasking on the phone. My sentence constructions needed to merge with all the senses. "Show me how happy you can make me with that hard cock," I would say with wild eyes.

I enjoyed watching reactions to my nasty soliloquies. Dirty talk became my favorite sex accessory. For my partners, my lovers lexicon was a value-add that packed the kind of excitement you have when you see large shrimp at the all-you-can-eat brunch buffet.

My latest prospect and I had a lot of good chemistry. There seemed to be some kinda-sorta-maybe relationship hope, not that I really know what that is (my only definition being I'll know it when I feel it). We had good conversations and good times... until the dirty talk. I'm creative and I can keep up with any smut-mouthed male. This time I was stumped.

"Suck my cock like mommy," he said.

My brain uttered a big Scooby "*Arrrgggggg?*" and I blocked out the statement and moved on before the mood was crushed by analysis. Later on, pillow talk turned into story time.

"So, do you want to hear the story about my mom?" this 40 year-old man asked.

I was anticipating share time - that time when lovers bond over dysfunctional pasts and grow closer. It appeared, as a 14-year old, he let his mother orally service him. This was not the story I wanted to hear. What ever happened to having an abusive father and an alcoholic mother? This was not my movie... this would never have a happy ending.

One day my life will not feel like a string of *Sex in the City* episodes; however, now I can say, I heard one I'd never heard before. Creativity and tolerance ceased merging that night and a contact was permanently deleted from my address book. Can a girl ever be better than mommy?

Trevor Nathaniel Rager

Holidays From Shenfield Travel

October 2003

//

Trevor Nathaniel Rager was born in Rochester, NY to an English mother and American father. He has spent the past 6 years traveling across the world, playing music, and laughing. And as the great Kurt Vonnegut once wrote, "Everything was Beautiful & Nothing Hurt." It is his mantra. He is 23 years old.

For five straight Saturdays I had sat on an old iron park bench on the corner of Raymond St. & Chalkstone Ave., in Providence, Rhode Island. I was the Marketing Rep for Montgomery & Kee, an upstart electronics company that had, in its first and only three years of business, gone from deficit in the thousands to a net profit upward of almost thirteen million. It was my job to gather the results of focus groups based on ethnicity and age and sex and determine whether or not a conceptual product had a place on the market. If it did, I was to find out just how much of the hide we would be able to skin. And how much profit we would make. And how much everything would cost before being placed on the market. And so on. And so on. And so on. And I was exceptionally good at all of that.

During my first week at Montgomery & Kee I had made the acquaintance of Lance McKinley, a very tall, heavy set, sandy haired, pimple faced good-for-nothing who wore flamboyant dress shirts everyday, God bless his soul. We met in an elevator on the way back from our lunch break. Lance had gotten on at the 4th floor, forcing his massive body to swim against the laws of physics, wedging himself into an already full space. He nudged and squeezed and sucked in, holding his breath for a good amount of time.

The second time I saw him was at the men's urinals on the ground floor of our building. Lance had walked into the Men's restroom wearing one of his usual fucking terrible shirts and hobbled over to the sink and filled it up, splashing his face every few seconds. I cocked my head sideways and to the right trying to figure out what he was doing. His eyes were bloodshot. His breathing was heavy. His knees started wobbling and then he collapsed onto the tile floor just as I finished my leak. A normal person would have gone to get help. A normal person would have checked to see if he was still breathing. I didn't do any of that. I ran out of the bathroom and down the hall and into the cafeteria and grabbed one of the stainless steel food carts used for carrying frozen goods from one refrigerator to the next.

Lance was trying to pick himself up off the tile when I returned with the cart. His hands braced himself against the wall and leaned his plump body against the corner as his legs wobbled, trying with all their might to lift the impossible. I bent down and put my head under his left arm, helped him rise to his feet, and then laid him down onto the makeshift stretcher. Using the front end of the cart as a battering ram, I shoved open the door and slid out into the empty hallway. No one had seen anything transpire. There wasn't a soul in sight. I was more than relieved. And with that, I gently pulled the cart towards my chest and then thrust it outward; casting Lance's floating body in one direction while I went in the other. From that day on we were the best of friends.

And so there I sat, on an old iron park bench in front of an antiques store almost two years later, wheezing and puffing and sucking in all the oxygen I could, my throat horsed. Lance was running from off in the distance towards me. He ran like an old pregnant woman on her way to the hospital just before giving birth. And he had been trying to catch up with me for the good part of 7 blocks.

"What in Gods name was all that about back there, Kurt? You nearly gave the old sonuvabitch a Goddamn heart attack with all that yelling and hollering."

"The old geezer had it coming!" I laughed. "Didja see the look on his face? Priceless! Fucking priceless I tell you!"

"You threw a Goddamn tantrum," He coughed, releasing Hiroshima into the air. "I've seen babies pushed around in strollers that act older than you sometimes. The man nearly had a Goddamn heart attack."

Lance knelt down beside me, bearing the bulk of his large frame onto his knuckles, which were turning white as the blood rushed out of the tight spots where his skin was pressing into the wet concrete sidewalk. In the process, the back of his shirt had come untucked, letting his enormous stomach claim its natural shape and exposing his rear side to a group of small children playing across the way in Davis Park. He slid his right foot back and under him, using his heel as a bench and easing the pressure off his hands. Wiping the sweat from his brow, he fingered out a cigarette from his shirt pocket, placed it on his lips, and lit it, taking in a long hard drag.

"You keep scaring the shit out of people, buddy, and sooner or later one of them will clock you one upside the head or maybe worse." Lance licked the palm of his right hand and brushed aside his thinning grey hair.

"Naw, they wouldn't clock me. They're all just pigeons. You know that. No better than pigeons, in fact- sitting there and bobbing their heads up and down and cooing and shitting on people."

"How do you figure that?"

"You see them?" I pointed at the children in the park. "What's the difference between the kids over there and those Goddamn pigeons? Do you know?"

Lance took another long, hard drag of his cigarette.

"Besides the obvious 34 year age difference? They don't go around hitting people with Wiffleball bats. I have no idea. What is it?"

"Fucking Christ, stop being sarcastic," I yelped.

"You want to go around hitting people?" Lance laughed and smiled. His laugh was the kind that could fill a room, stopping everyone mid-conversation in hope that they might find out what it was that he was talking about that was so great.

"That's not what I meant. What I meant was; just take a look. Take a long hard look and tell me what you see."

Lance paused for a moment. "I don't know." He said briskly, rubbing his elbow. "I see a bunch of children goofing about."

My eyes shifted, fixating on the travel agency located four blocks down.

"Those pigeons, they're just a Goddamn shell of who they use to be. They walk and talk and eat and shit and breed but that's about all they have. They've forgotten the important things in life, buddy."

Lance lifted his right hand, extended it outward and flicked the bottom of his cigarette, releasing the trapped ash into the air. "I don't think they're that bad off. I mean-"

"Not that bad! Look at them! Look at them!" I laughed with a slight cough. I lifted my head and pushed aside the hair from my brow and glanced over at Lance. "They only seem natural to us because the majority of people who lived before us have said so. All of us get caught up in the rut of our daily lives. And most of us forget about the simple things, the things that make life worth living."

I arched my back, leaned slightly forward and to the right, extended my left leg, and reached into the front left hip pocket of my trousers extracting a folded up brochure. I then carefully unfolded it, turning it from fourths to halves and then finally back to its original shape. Lance leaned over towards me, getting a good look at the piece of paper. He was always doing that thing- poking his nose around and looking over people's shoulders.

"What's this?" Lance flicked his cigarette into the gutter along the street side.

"Oh, just something I've been thinking about for a while."

"What do you mean?"

I stood up and rubbed my sore ass. "I've been stuck here for how long now… something around, oh, lets say about six years? Yeah, that sounds about right. I've been stuck here for six Goddamn years. I'm starting to feel like one of the old soaks back there."

"You are an old soak." Lance leaned forward and pushed himself up off of the wet concrete.

"Fuck off! I'm not even close, and you know it." I laughed.

Lance's face flushed red as we headed down Raymond St. He was trying to force his shirt back into the rear of his pants. "Wait up! Wait up!"

I stopped at the corner of Higgens Ave., turned around, and

leaned up against a tall, rough, wood telephone pole. Lance was fingering out another cigarette from his shirt pocket and slowly making his way towards me.

"Where are we going?"

"To a place where the sun never sets. No more pigeons; only brochures!"

"What? What the fuck are you blabbing about?"

"Relax. We're headed over to this store I've been meaning to go to. It's just up a few more blocks on the corner."

Lance stopped, lit his cigarette, and resumed walking his normal sloth speed.

"Have you ever thought what you would have been like if you weren't born who you were?", I said. "I mean, if you were born in Spain but were generally the same you are now - how you're life would have turned out? I think if I was born somewhere else and under different circumstances I'd like to have ended up owning a restaurant. I always wanted to be a chef."

"Yea and I've always wanted a best friend who wasn't Goddamn nuts."

"Seriously, Lance. Think about it."

We crossed over Higgins Ave. and stopped under the archway of the store.

"I'm not sure. Under different circumstances, you said?

"Yea I said-"

"Maybe a record producer or something like that." Lance angled his left elbow out and down letting a newspaper rack take a bit of his weight. He extended his right arm outward and held out the cigarette, examining it like an oddly shaped twig. He brought his arm back in, placed the cigarette on his lips, and took in another drag then releasing the exhaust through his nose.

"Isn't your uncle a record producer?" I said.

"Well, yea but-"

"Doesn't count then. You could be that now if you really wanted to. Think about it. Anywhere in the world! What would you hope for?"

"I don't know. Maybe work with dolphins or-"

"Dolphins? As in 'Sea World'? What the hell!!! Out of anything you could hope for, and mind you; you could grow up as Tarzan if you wanted to. But out of anything and everything you could hope for you'd want to swim with dolphins?"

"You're the one who wants to be a chef."

The clouds overhead started getting a bit thicker with each sentence that passed between us. We had been standing outside the store for what felt like 30 minutes when it started to rain.

"Come on, let's go inside." I said.

"But I just about to have another smoke!"

"Forget the smoke. You can have one later. Come on."

"But I just-"

"Take the rain as a sign to get the fuck inside. Come on." I said motioning to Lance and opening the door.

The shop was medium sized with one clerk behind an old wooden counter. The two walls to our left and right were covered with scenic photographs and posters of sorts trapped in by a thick red border that lined both the ceiling and floor. Behind the counter were a few boxes, a roll of masking tape, one loaf of bread, a jar of peanut butter, a buttering knife and, of course, the clerk. She was an older woman. Mid 60's, I'd say. And she was smacking her lips together in an obvious attempt to tongue a wad of peanut butter from the roof of her mouth. It wasn't working very well.

"Welcome to Shenfield Travel. May I help you?" she said pursing her lips.

Lance's whole demeanor shifted slightly. He let his shoulders hang down, stuffed his hands into his pockets, and his body slumped forward. He looked up and over at me as though he wanted to say something but for some reason couldn't. I just looked back at him and smiled. I turned towards the clerk.

"I've been thinking about taking a trip for a while." I said "But I'm not really sure about all the packages and details. I just want to get away."

"Well sir, where would you like to go" the old cow mooed.

"The Arctic Circle." The Arctic Circle. Circle. Circle. Circle. Circle. It was playing over and over like a loop in my head. Circle. Circle. Circle. The Arctic Circle. The Arctic. The. Circle.

It sounds like water- rain maybe. I'm not wet though. Not wet. I'm...

"Take it off. Easy now. Ju-"

"Careful! Watch it."

"He's awake."

"Kurt, can you see me? Open your eyes. Can you... Kurt? Can you hear me, Kurt?"

My head hurts. Pounding. Throbbing. What's going on...

"Kurt, can you hear me? You're at Fairbanks Memorial Hospital. It's going to be all right. You were in a plane wreck."

David Villanueva

Them People

2004

//

David Villanueva is a struggling freelance writer who graduated from an
over-priced, small private school, where he earned a useless B.S. degree
in Fashion Marketing. He currently resides in sunny Redondo Beach,
where he is working on a novel.

They are everywhere. And when I mean everywhere, I mean everywhere. They lurk behind closed doors, sit amongst the common people (though they are uncommon themselves), and mingle like a spring time breeze passing through a town on a quiet afternoon to create some disturbance to the mind. But I ain't one to gossip, so you didn't hear it from me. All I can do is give an honest to goodness account. Who am I to pass judgment? Little old me just needs to be expressive and tell this tale about when my life was changed, for the good that is.

I live on Eucalyptus Court, in a town called Meadow Lake, a small town in California that could never be pinpointed on a map, not because it doesn't exist, but because it's so small that it could easily be missed in a blink of an eye. Get the picture? And I am in the sixth grade, though that really isn't important in this story. My mother and father all reside under one roof. My bedroom is on the far right of the house next to my baby brother Jimmy Jones. Next door to my house lived a family, the Otis clan. An unusual bunch I might add, "them people" my mother referred to them as because they were never sociable with their neighbors.

One springtime day I was sitting underneath a tree in my backyard, sitting amongst the sparrows chirping melodies, taking in the scent of roses blooming, and enjoying a glass of homemade lemonade (which I made myself), and coloring in my jumbo sized coloring book that my mother bought me at Loretta's Pharmacy (Loretta has no significance in this story. She just owns the pharmacy, and is a busy body anyway, and smells like Ben Gay, but that isn't important). Things were as peaceful as can be, until I heard the voices of my neighbors and saw them for the first time, Tallulah and Ojani, who were around my age of eleven. I think they were twins, but I could be wrong.

The windows to their house were always open, even if it was cold outside. Each window was propped open by a stick, a book, an old hammer, I guess whatever was convenient for them. I'm not one to make a fuss over nothing, but I happened to put down my red crayon, and listen to these voices registering in baritone and soprano tones, in a coordinated manner that you could tell that there was a conversation going on amongst two people.

A hedge separated my house from their house, but the hedge was only waist high, so their backyard was visible, just as mine was too. I could see their back sun porch, where white pillars (you know the kind that are from the south, Confederate pillars my mother calls them) held the roof with strength. I saw this nappy headed girl with blond hair, my age I might repeat, running across the back porch in a pair of stiletto white high heels, with her blond hair in curlers, wearing a summer dress that had a sailboat on the right hand corner. A lady should never be seen in public prepping for the day's appearance my mother once said to me. I guess Tallulah's mother never gave her that advice because she paid me no attention, and acted like she had no cares in the world, despite being in her condition in my presence.

I pretended that I didn't see her when we made eye contact accidentally, but for some reason I was fascinated by this heathen and her unusual antics.

She walked up to the hedge, and then spoke in a high pitched, nasally voice.

"Wanna smoke?"

"Pardon?" I asked.

"A smoke? A cig?"

She reached her hand over the hedge, holding in between her pointer and middle fingers a white cigarette with smoke emitting from its tip.

"Oh goodness, those are just awful," I announced.

"They ain't so bad when you get the hang of it sis. My momma always says, 'two tears in a bucket, this bitch says fuckit'," and when those nasty words released from her mouth like a locomotive, she took a puff from her cigarette and then blew three tiny smoke rings in the air.

"I don't think you should be smoking," I scolded as I walked closer to the hedge.

"Yeah, that's what my pap says. Says I should drink bourbon instead, good for the spirit he says, and a better hobby than toting on a puffer. But I'm hooked on these." She took several puffs from the cigarette, and then when she was finished, she squished it in the ground with her pair of white stiletto high heals.

"I think that is inappropriate behavior Miss...Miss?"

"The name is Tallulah Otis...Tallulah, Queen of Sass and a Little Class," she announced with authority, and then she winked at me, which I then noticed she had sparkling blue eyes with a little mixture of green. Her curlers bounced around the top of her head, some even seemed to loosen by her vibrant movement.

"Tallulah? Queen of Sass..." I was confused. Not only by her self appointed title, but also by her vulgar use of words.

"Yes, and a Little Class. A little never hurt anyone, too much class is hypocritical. You gotta name sister?"

"I am not your sister; you are not part of my congregation at church. I'm sure I'd know if you were a sister at the Providence Baptist Church."

"Oh geez, a Baptist...Lawdy Miss Clawdy, you're a real winner." Tallulah stepped back and then bowed. "It's a pleasure Miss Baptist."

"My name is Ellabelle mind you."

"Ok toots, it was nice meeting you," she quickly interrupted. "And next time you spy on someone, make sure they don't make any eye contact with you," she said as she curtsied. "Eye contact is a welcoming committee whether you like it or not," she answered as she walked away and back up her porch. "Sometimes people are afraid of what they welcome," she shouted over her shoulder as she entered her house.

I was dumbfounded. I didn't quite know what to say, so I stood mute like an invalid, standing at the hedge, unable to move.

For a split second I became deaf. And then I felt someone tapping my shoulder as my eyes focused on the white columns at the Otis house.

"Ellabelle," my mother said. "It is getting a little cool out, come inside and put on your cardigan and drink some tea before you catch a cold."

I turned around and stared into my mother's brown eyes. She then reached her hand to stroke my golden brown hair, and then led me back into our house of perfection.

The house was rather dim; my eyes didn't quite adjust to the darkness so easily. I could hear my little brother crying in his crib, which my mother immediately vanished to care for him. The sound of my father crinkling his newspaper every time he turned a page was loud and clear, yet his eyes never left the black print on each page as I stood in the dining room to have my cup of tea.

My life felt like a dream. I took a sip of the warm tea, and it penetrated through my veins, allowing me to feel like myself once again. Several more sips greeted my lips by my command, and as I peered across the wall where my mother had hung a long mirror over the side table, I noticed the reflection of an odd fellow hanging his feet out of the window on the second story of the Otis house.

At first I thought I was seeing things, but when I turned around, a white trash boy gazed out of the window, his dirty feet were dangling from the ledge, his brownish blond hair was combed forward into his eyes, he was wearing a pair of jeans cut into shorts, and he was shouting something that I could not understand.

"I'll jump pap, I swear this time!" the boy repeated loudly.

"Ojani, get the hell out of the window and stop playing games," I heard an adult male's voice blast through the walls.

I walked to the window and peered through the lace curtains that my mother had made, and as I opened the window out of curiosity, I noticed that the boy named Ojani jumped right down to the carpet of green grass.

"No jumping out of windows if you don't have shoes on your feet," the boy's father scolded. "A man should always protect his feet, don't want your feet all beat up and have your toes looking like monkey fingers!" The man shouted out the window. He was peculiar. Not handsome, but not foul. He had a thin mustache, graying hair, a pot belly that stuck through his white night shirt, and a pair of boxers that had yellow ducks on them.

"Pap, I am fine...get a life and let me be," the boy scolded as he laughed and ran through the side gate while digging into his left nostril with his middle finger.

I quickly closed my curtains before anyone could see me, and then retreated to my bedroom to relax on my bed. The pillows were nice and fluffy, soothing to the soul and a relief from my day's encounter of weirdness.

As I closed my eyes, I heard music blaring from the second story at the Otis house. It was coming from the bedroom that was directly across from mine. Though the window was propped open with an old broomstick, I could not see into the room. But the music that was foreign to my ears greeted me with curiosity.

My feet tiptoed to the window, where I found myself sitting on my window bench. I poked my ear out of the window, only to find myself alarmed.

"Spying again sister?" Tallulah said sternly as she had her arms crossed against her chest. She was standing in front of her window looking into mine, this time without her curlers on.

I tried not to let her see me, but my feet got clumsily tangled together, causing me to fall to the floor and pull the curtains off of the silver rod.

My head hurt. Cautiously I arose, almost embarrassed that Tallulah caught me again. She remained looking out of the window in her bedroom, eyeing me with her eyebrows arched in the air like mountain peaks.

"Sorry," I said, "I didn't mean any harm."

"Don't apologize. Why don't you come over sister?"

"I don't think I should."

"Why not?"

"Um..."

"Exactly. Now get those panties out of a bunch, and climb on over."

Tallulah disappeared into the darkness of her bedroom, and then came back into the light with a yellow rope in her hand. She looked at me with a devilish grin, and then smiled, revealing her pearly white teeth that had a gap on the top row.

"What are you going to do with that rope?" I questioned.

"You're going to tight rope walk on over," she shouted as she threw the rope to me.

I fumbled with the rope, almost dropping it to the ground. And as I held it in my hands, my forehead began to sweat and I could taste salt on my upper lip.

"What do you mean?"

"Are you a re re?"

"Re re?"

"Special? Retarded?"

"I am insulted by your comments."

"Geez sister, get a grip. You're either missing some marbles, or you are totally clueless and somewhat useless."

There was awkward silence for a second. Tallulah then reached down on her ledge and picked up a cigarette. It was already lit, so she took two big puffs of it, and then smashed it in a crystal ashtray that kept reflecting a rainbow of colors from the sunlight.

"Go tie that rope to your bed. Make sure you double knot it, 'cause Lord knows you don't want to expire having a little fun. But then again my mama says that having fun is dangerous, and there would be no point in having fun if it weren't dangerous. Do you understand what I am saying toots?"

"No."

"Didn't think so. Now go tie the rope to your bed. And when

you get in two good knots, let a sister know."

I did as told. I pulled the rope and tied it around my bed post, using two knots like Tallulah ordered. I felt her pulling on the rope, and when I did she hollered for me to come to the window.

"It's sturdy," she said with confidence.

"Shouldn't I just use the front door?"

"No, my dad is trying to sleep in the living room. He hates when we make noise after he has six cocktails. We'll scare the bejesus out of him with an ounce of noise."

"But..."

"Don't worry. Just do as I do."

To my surprise, Tallulah climbed out the window, and stood looking down to the ground. She kicked off her white stiletto high heals inside her bedroom, revealing her toes, which were big and round, and pink like sausages. She tested the strength of the rope with her feet a couple of times. She loosened her arms and stood on the rope, almost looking in a crucified manner because her arms were straight. And then she started walking along the rope heading for my bedroom.

"Goodness Tallulah, is all of this necessary? If my mother sees you in this condition she will faint."

"Sister please, I used to do this all of the time. When I was six I walked across two buildings in New York City. This is all kiddy fun, very harmless. And you'll find it easy when you try too."

My heart began to beat. I could feel it thumping through my blouse. The second that Tallulah reached my window ledge, she jumped right into the room and became a quick observant.

"Nice," she answered, referring to my bedroom. "It looks like a princess room. A little too perfect and sweet, but nice."

"Thank you," I said cordially, not sure whether I should take her opinion as a compliment.

"Now, you have to be careful when you walk across. Don't go too fast, and don't look down. If you experience vertigo, well then good luck sister, 'cause you'll be dead as a doornail with your head splattered like a smashed watermelon. Brains and blood will be everywhere."

"I don't want to do this," I protested.

"I'm kidding. Damn, you are so easy to scare. You'll be fine. And if you get scared you can hold my hand like a queer," she laughed.

She climbed back onto the window ledge. She stood on the rope once again, and then looked back to make sure that I was coming along. Even though I was scared, for some reason I couldn't resist not walking the rope.

"Hurry up, this won't take all day," Tallulah said sternly. And with those last words, she was quickly jetting across the tight rope with relative ease. I staggered slowly, stepping with caution. I could feel butterflies churning in my stomach, making me slightly nauseous. Suddenly sweat dripped down the side of my temples; I accidentally looked down to the ground.

"Oh no," I screamed.

"Shit," she said. "Did you look down? God damn it, that was a rule not to do."

"I'm sorry."

"Stop apologizing sister or you'll be one of those people apologizing for their lifetime."

Tallulah turned around because she was already near her window, and then she walked back to me as I became frozen in time. I could feel that my knees were starting to buckle, and I could feel tears starting to develop in my eyes.

I didn't feel Tallulah grab my hand because I was so nervous, well, and because I closed my eyes. But I could definitely hear her chanting a rhyme, a rhyme not like the ones my mother read to me as a little girl, but one concocted by her lively mind I assume.

"Hey hot lips lets go on a date, my mama's not home so don't be late, kiss me sugar a thousand times, bring me flowers bring me wine, shake your tail and I'll shake mine, hey there sugar lets have a good time," Tallulah repeated several times as we walked into her bedroom.

When I opened my eyes I saw that the room was a mess. A mattress was on the floor, a red quilt was torn in two places, the walls were a faded pink color, fashion magazines were thrown in every direction, feather boas were hung around a twisted looking lamp, and several records were scattered around the floor. I remained by the window with my heart thumping. Though the sun was shining outside, inside was rather dim, so I had to squint my eyes.

"Don't be such an ass, relax Ellabelle. Come here and shake your shimmy," she said in a lively tone of voice.

I didn't know what she was talking about, but when she

grabbed my arms I had no choice. Tallulah started shaking her chest and jiggling her small bosoms. I almost blushed at her behavior, and as I tried to cover my mouth from emitting an embarrassed laugh, Tallulah shook me by my arms so that I could shimmy with her.

"That's it toots. My mama says that a girl who can shimmy is a queen, and is talented in more ways than one."

The sound of the record player scratching in the background didn't bother Tallulah one bit. She picked up a pack of cigarettes from the floor, swiped a match against the wooden floor, and then lit a cigarette that she placed in her mouth. Tallulah looked like a grand dragon as smoke filled the room.

She walked towards her record player, which I thought was unusual because people my age have CDs and CD players, and then she grabbed a huge black record with a purple label off of the spinning wheel. She fumbled through her collection of records scattered around like gypsies, and then yanked one out of its paper sleeve. I observed her every move, and when she placed her record on the spinning wheel, a woman's voice blasted out of the speakers while a crackling noise surfaced throughout the background music.

"I've got the blues," Tallulah announced as she began to sing along to the record.

"What kind of music is this?" I asked because the music sounded dated, unlike the pop tart music my friends and I were accustomed to.

"Are you for real? Tough titty, I'll be doggone, you've never been schooled in taste?"

"What?"

"Is that your favorite word sister, what? Let me tell you something, blues is a feeling; it's in your soul. Mama and pap say it's the best form of music ever."

"Who is singing?"

"Jesus Christmas Ellabelle...where have you been all of your life? This is the Queen of the Blues, the Queen of Rock and Roll...Etta James!" she shouted at me as she flopped down to the floor to hold a record with a woman with blond hair on its cover. "See, this is the queen. She was famous long before we were a twinkle in our parents' eyes."

I looked at the record cover and read: Etta James, At Last!

"Sit down with me Ellabelle, its time you got schooled."

I sat lady like on the dirty floor, almost disgusted by its filth, but interested in knowing Tallulah. She handed me records every second it seemed because the weight of them piled around me in clusters.

She flipped the records, posing them in front of my face and then reading off the names of each singer. "This is Big Maybelle, this is Sippie Wallace, and this here is Esther Phillips, oh and this one here is Billie Holiday, and my God, this one here is Sister Rosetta Tharpe...did I miss this one? This here is Bessie Smith...I got me a Lucille Bogan hard to find record...and the lovely Dinah Washington is here...another Etta James...Myra Taylor...Memphis Minnie is a good one too."

I didn't know what to say. I've never heard of any of the singers she had mentioned. But looking at the record covers of each singer, I was able to tell that they were black, in furs, with diamonds, and were from the past.

Suddenly the door burst open, scaring me easily, which caused me to become on guard. Ojani busted through the door with a cowboy hat on his head and red cowboy boots on his feet, and then smacked his sister on the back of her head.

"Ouch you bastard."

"Good to see you too," he said as he sat next to Tallulah.

"This moran is Ojani, my brother," Tallulah introduced. "He won't be staying long," she said as she gave him a dirty look.

He paid her no attention, and then took out something from his pocket. He kept it hidden in his hand, which didn't allow me to see what it was. I tried to sneak a peek, but Ojani held his treasure secretly.

"Got any matches?" he asked his sister.

"What for imbecile?"

"None of your never mind."

"It will be in a few seconds when I kick your ass."

"Calm down," he said sarcastically as he opened the palm of his hand to reveal something white.

I didn't know what it was. It looked like rolled tissue paper, a very small piece of tissue paper rolled up like a thick cigarette. Tallulah cared what it was that instant because her eyes bulged like a gold fish, and then she handed her brother a box of matches that were lying around near her records.

Ojani took a match and then struck it against the box. He

placed the match slowly towards his rolled up piece of tissue paper, and then I heard the crinkling sound of paper burning. A smell that I had never smelled before run up my nostrils. It was foreign and strong.

"I'm first," Tallulah ordered as she grabbed the rolled up piece of tissue paper from Ojani's hand. "Let the pro show you," she laughed as she held the thick tissue closely to her lips.

Tallulah took a big puff from the tissue paper, and then held her breath for what seemed like five minutes. And then like a raging bull, smoke released from both of her nostrils that were flared wide and round. She handed Ojani the rolled tissue paper, and then he took a puff from the tissue paper. I was looking back and forth between the two of them, and each time I did that they both laughed at me as if I were a clown.

"Here try this," Tallulah suggested. "It's a little somethin' for the mind," she laughed like a hyena.

"No thank you," I said as I turned my head.

Both siblings began laughing at me again, which annoyed me. I wanted to leave, but I forgot that I had come in the house through the window.

"It's hot box time," Ojani declared as he quickly ran to the window to shut it.

And before I could register what was happening, both siblings were passing the rolled tissue paper back and forth and blowing smoke in my face.

"Stop that!" I ordered. "That smells," I declared.

They paid me no attention. Every second a cloud of smoke was plastered against my face. And soon I was coughing very deep and hoarse, which made the smoke circulate through my chest and into my lungs. My head began to feel light, my eyes started to squint, and I found myself wanting to laugh for no reason. Tallulah and Ojani found my behavior amusing.

"She's soaring like a kite," Ojani laughed.

"More like on cloud nine," Tallulah giggled.

"What is happening to me?" I questioned as I soon started laughing.

"Sister, you are educated," Tallulah informed as she lay on her back and started laughing.

I began to laugh loudly when I saw Tallulah's skinny legs kicking in the air. I even blushed when I saw her purple panties when her dress flew up her thighs. She didn't care; she was laughing her head off every time she stared at me.

"I'm soooo hungry," I giggled.

"She's got the munchies," Ojani shouted as he fell on his back and started laughing some more. The room seemed to be spinning. I couldn't make out anything. The walls looked warped, the blues music blasting on the speakers of the record player continued, and every time I moved I felt dizzy.

Tallulah stood up from the floor, and then she yanked my hand so that I could stand up with her. She opened the door to the bedroom, and then down the dark hallway our footsteps pounded against the wooden floor. Tallulah kept giggling, while I tried to concentrate on regaining my composure. But everything Tallulah said or did tickled my funny bone until my stomach hurt.

She motioned for me to be quiet, and as we passed a bedroom with its door cracked open, I saw a semi nude woman staring into an oval mirror. I've never seen a naked woman before, but I stood looking into the bedroom watching the curvaceous woman shaking her hips, wearing a pair of black platform shoes, watching her long platinum hair sway with her movement, dancing very provocatively, in a pair of lace panties, but without a blouse on.

"That's my mama," Tallulah informed. "She's the best titty tasseler in the world. They don't call her Titty Tassel Tyra for nothing."

"What's a titty tasseler?" I questioned.

"You are so juvenile Ellabelle I swear. Haven't you ever lived a little?" she giggled. "My mama is an entertainer at the Sugar Shack on 4th Street and Avenue B. She's a dancer, singer, the whole kit and caboodle. Men come from every corner to see her perform."

And then this woman, Titty Tassel Tyra, turned around revealing her pearl white breasts covered with tiny things pasted on her danger zones. I gasped, but she paid me no mine.

"Hey there sweety, brought a friend over?" Titty Tassel Tyra questioned her daughter. She waved hello, and smiled wide her crimson painted lips.

"Whatcha doing mama?"

"Practicing my bumps and grinds," she said as she turned around to stare at herself in the mirror.

"You still got it mama," her daughter encouraged. "But swing a little more harder on your right swivel shake mama," she suggested.

"That's your mom?" I questioned.

"Yes, isn't she fabulous?"

We walked further down the hall and then proceeded to the staircase. It spiraled down into a dimly lit room. I could still feel my head spinning, but I still managed to laugh. All I could think about was food. I was as hungry as a horse, and before I could mention my hunger again to Tallulah, she was sliding down the spiral staircase.

"Meet you at the bottom sister," she yelled as she continued laughing. "Come on, don't be a puss, grab a hold and slide down," she ordered as she reached the bottom.

I climbed aboard the hand rail, wrapping my feet tightly. There was an ounce of fear inhabiting my body, so as I let the grip of my feet loose against the rail, I began sliding slowly until I had no control over the movement. I shot down the staircase like a bullet, tickling my stomach in the process.

As we reached the first story of the house, we heard a man snoring on the couch. His legs were wrapped over the sides, but I could not see him. It was her father, because I could see his boxer shorts with ducks printed on them. Tallulah paid him no mind, she took my hand and we headed to the kitchen.

The kitchen was a mess, worse than Tallulah's bedroom. Dishes were piled high in the sink on the yellow tiled counter. Cupboard doors were off their hinges, the refrigerator had an assortment of magnets on it, the dining room table was missing two chairs, there were cracks in the walls, and there were several empty wine bottles scattered on the floor and on the table.

"Don't mind the mess. Mama says that a mess just shows that someone is busy, and busy is what we are. Remember this Ellabelle, perfection is something that is never attainable," she giggled.

I stood in the middle of the kitchen watching Tallulah. She climbed up on the counter, jumping onto it like a jack rabbit frolicking in the fields. I could see why she wore stiletto high heels; she was as short as could be, which I only noticed at that moment.

She opened a cupboard that had its door still intact, and then brought out two small glasses.

"Cocktails anyone?" she laughed as she jumped back to the ground. I laughed along with her, but not as loud as her.

Tallulah opened the refrigerator, which contained a gallon of water, some containers with something inside of them, a jar of green olives, and a huge bottle of Vodka. She poured the Vodka in the glasses, and then with her skinny fingers she opened the olive jar and plucked four olives with her fingers to place two in each glass. "Cheers," she said as she handed me a glass. I did as she did. We tapped the glasses together, and then took a big swig at the same time.

I thought I was going to be sick. The vodka dripped down my throat like wild rapids floating downstream. And as I squinted my eyes, I could feel my throat burning and my nostrils flaring.

"What is this I questioned?" The words emitted from mouth with disgust.

"Punch for a lady. Mama says cocktails are a ritual for a lady, gotta have one at least once a day," she smiled revealing her gap on her top row teeth. She took another sip of her cocktail, and then grabbed an olive from her glass to eat.

I took a small sip from my glass, but it burned worse than my first sip. I started laughing, why I don't know. Tallulah found my behavior rather tickling as she finished the last drop of liquid from her glass.

"Okay toots, this party is done over. I gotta get back to my business," Tallulah said as she grabbed the glass from my hand. "Let's do lunch cocktails tomorrow," she said in a British accent.

"Tomorrow? I got school," I answered through my cloud of confusion. "Don't you go to school?"

"Hell no," she quipped with authority. "Mama and Pap says as long as you can say your ABCs and add and subtract, then that's all a person needs in life."

She took me by surprise. And though I wanted to question her some more, the hunger pains I was experiencing wanted to make me vomit.

"Come on, I will walk you to the door," Tallulah said as she grabbed my hand.

"But I'm hungry," I announced.

"Here," she said as she handed me a box of crackers. "Eat these Ellabelle, these are light. A woman must always keep her figure."

We walked through the kitchen to the entry of the house. The front door wasn't closed, so Tallulah kicked it open with her feet, causing it to hit against the wall with a loud thump. I held the box of crackers in my hand not quite sure what to make of the situation.

"It was my pleasure sister. You are all right when you loosen up a little," Tallulah said as she blew air kisses on both of my cheeks. "Don't be a stranger toots, and don't spy on people either, eye contact is a welcoming committee for the least expected," she reminded me.

I didn't pay attention to anything because everything that happened seemed so surreal. And as Tallulah walked me to the front gate, I noticed that clouds were appearing in the sky. Ojani ran outside holding a kite in his dirty hands. He skipped around his sister chanting something that didn't make any sense. I paused for a moment to stare at him, and I saw that his eyes were bloodshot and he still had the giggles.

Tallulah grabbed the kite string because it was long, and together Ojani and her were running across the yard trying to make it fly. They seemed to forget about me as I stood dumbfounded on the sidewalk holding the box of crackers.

All of a sudden with no chance for reaction, a lightening bolt swooped across the cloudy sky striking the delinquent Tallulah and Ojani. My eyes widened as the bolt made a sound like a cracking whip. It struck both siblings across their heads at the same time. There was no sound coming from either Tallulah or Ojani. They were dead. Dead as a door nail.

The smell of burnt hair was atrocious; it lingered in the air as the clouds passed through Meadow Lake. I stood in front of the gate staring at the charcoal colored bodies of my afternoon hosts. They laid flat on their backs with their legs high in the air, while their kite flew across the sky on a swift breeze.

I shrugged my shoulders because there was nothing that I could do, opened the box of crackers to eat one, giggled a little, and then walked home with no concern. I guess the lesson learned was that when you can say that you are not offended by anything, then that is being normal. "Them people" taught me that.

Todd Eliassen

Schadenfreude

2001

//

Raised by a lesbian on a Sioux Indian reservation in the Badlands of North Dakota, Eliassen and his dog moved to Los Angeles in 1993. A horribly unsuccessful television writer, he now enjoys bowling, drinking, and collecting scars. Todd enjoys life immensely. The dog, however, is dead.

"Me-Ville?" Kermit was mortified. "Did you just say, 'take a trip to Me-Ville?'" he asked in his odd, throaty voice.

The psychiatrist used a pen to scratch at the back of her neck. "Well, I..." she stuttered, "it's metaphor." Though many of the doctor's patients were seriously disturbed, she'd never had one become violent. This fellow, however, seemed to have such potential. "Do you... understand metaphor?"

"Lady. I'm a fucking *muppet*. I *know* metaphor." Months of therapy had come to this, this cheap psychobabble. "Tell you what," said Kermit, a thin metal rod twisting his green fingers in tiny circles at the psychiatrist, "you want a cute little saying that will make me feel better? Try this: 'Kermit, here's a one-way bus ticket to Get-That-Pig-Bitch-On-My-Johnson-Town.' How's that, doc? Hmm?"

"Why don't we end here? For today, I mean..." said the psychiatrist in a tone that belonged more with 'I'm quite scared of you, frog.'

Mustering as much panache as one can with a hippy's hand up one's ass, he marched in sideways awkwardness to *[BACKSPACE BACKSPACE BACKSPACE]*

...to the door, to a life without love...
Drivel.

Elmer sat back in his desk chair, pondering the crisp new sheet of innocent, thirty weight bond he'd just slaughtered. He'd been homicidal like this all week. 'The Last Lilly Pad' wasn't a book - it was a bloodbath in ink; first degree verbicide.

"Tank god for comf-wa-table chairs," muttered Elmer as he lit a joint, "dey awow a man to contempwate more eef-wect-uvee."

Though Elmer's current novel was going badly, one could never call this celluloid hunter a failure. From the wasteland to which Hollywood condemns it's no-longer-popular stars, he managed to cultivate a fresh career in the world of scriveners. Sure, he was finding his fingers less nimble these days, reluctant to tap out his bidding, but his house in the Hollywood Hills was paid for in full and he had the grudging respect of his peers. Phillip Roth once called him 'an ordained legend, a Dostoyevskian bastard.'

His had, indeed, been a productive life and retirement would not come with shame.

His ego growled back, "No no no. One musn't give up. Musn't caw it quits just yet."

He fondled the keyboard, pushing the spacebar, the backspace key, the spacebar again... Where was Kermit going? Would the frog recover, find a new reason to hop through the muck of life? Or would he sink deeper, hiding in the pig's shrubbery; a vespertine stalker waiting to murder 'la belle dame sans merci?'

Elmer considered those oft-told tales of novelists running the well dry and dying from word-thirst like dogs in a Grub Street desert. He sucked at the joint in three staccato puffs, then gently pushed the roach into a ceramic snuffer next to his Corona typewriter. His large, round eyes grew red veins as he recalled the days when observers would've thought he was taking dictation when he wrote. But now, nothing.

Michael wondered if there might be something in the other room of more interest than writing about a cartoon character in the throes of writer's block. In recent weeks, the man had taken procrastination to theistic heights. His favorite activities were masturbation, hosing down the sidewalk, and wandering around the living room, admiring how he'd left untouched each item his wife threw at him in their final brawl.

The writer pushed his laptop away and stood. It was almost noon. Noon's a good time to jack off, he decided. Then he would make a final push and finish this story that no eyes would ever read.

"A Literary Triumph" wrote one critic of his third novel, "To Cry for the Sun". "An Epic Masterpiece of Unfettered Brilliance" wrote another of Mr. Fudd's trilogy, "The Hare and the Hunter".

But what will they say about him now? Will they say his smooth, bald skull no longer holds the burning embers of creativity? Will they retroactively condemn his past works, suddenly portending that pounds of binding glue have been wasted on his entire oeuvre?

Elmer cringed in his chair as he watched a smudge appear on his imaginary Nobel; a non-existent medal which he carefully polished every day

"with a lust-colored chamois!!"

The problem, Michael realized, with pretending one is typing on a 1912 Corona Model 3 is absent-mindedly slamming at the carriage return and knocking your laptop off the desk. The problem with drinking scotch in the afternoon is more serious; it's one of focus. He decided adding a joint to the mix would be appropriate. To take the edge off.

Kermit the Frog, onetime star of stage and screen, now a lovesickened muppet, wandered the streets of Manhattan, ambitionless, mentally impoverished, abulic. There are no statues of frog saints to val *[backspace backspace backspace]* warrant existence, there are no reptile messiahs *[backspace backspace backspace backspace]*

"Shit. It's aw shit."

Elmer knew his options had run out; the time had come to either box up the typewriter or do the obvious: take on a writing partner. The idea horrified him.

The corn on Michael's left big toe burned as he climbed the spiral staircase and crossed the hall to the master bedroom. In the master bath, he began rummaging through the remnants of his estranged wife's medicine cabinet. He touched the bottles lovingly; Caprisopodol, Percaset, Prozac, OxyContin (often called 'Hillybilly Heroin,' a term the writer quite liked). He felt very mature at how deftly he opened the childproof caps. And plinking one pill from each bottle into his throat, he felt that if he couldn't hold her again, at least he could make love to his wife's addiction.

The chemical goulash kicked in quite nicely and, as so many unsuccessful writers do, Michael took the buzz as his cue to pound at his typer.

But where does one find a writing partner? wondered Elmer. Not in Hollywood, of course. The hackneyed scripts he was forced to perform lo those many years ago were proof enough of that.

"Wuckiwee I have a magic door..." grinned the cartoon hunter-

"Magic door? Christ, I'm really high." Sighing, leaning back in his chair, Michael scratched his chin and pondered the computer screen. This had become the most familiar of trends; that initial excitement of a story idea tapped into a beginning, a middle, and never an end. "I'm sorry, Elmer. I don't know what to do with you."

"How about making me king of the action romance novel?"

said the voice from behind.

"I don't see where that'd get me," Michael uttered through a well-cottoned mouth.

"I couldn't be more indifferent to where it gets you, friend. But it might get me laid and in this I have a vested interest," said the voice. Michael nodded that special, earnest nod which males frequently offer when the Great Hope of Willing Vagina is mentioned.

The writer reached for the keyboard again, stopping short at the realization he was talking *to* another person, not as another person. Partly from fear, partly to avoid nausea, he turned his chair in a slow, horror movie spin.

"Elmer... Fudd?"

"All my life, unfortunately. And I've been dying to tell you, Michael, I don't speak with that silly affectation. That was called 'acting' you half-wit."

"Okay." The problem with drugs, thought the writer, is they prevent one from being properly stunned.

"So, Michael, are you going to offer me a drink and some smoke or will you be vulgar and force me to get them myself?"

Months had passed since Kermit cared about things. Now, living on the streets of Chinatown in a melting shitake mushroom crate, his only concerns were of keeping his gear clean and finding the next scrap of tar. Money, of course, was always an issue. Begging for change had at first been swell; his being a muppet, he often garnered more alms than the next guy. But soon the pocket scraps of passersby fell short of supporting his ever-deepening drug habit. After succumbing to the lure of old-man-cock-sucking money, Kermit made the unusual switch from crack cocaine to heroine.

His lighter worked the spoonful to a boiling frenzy. The needle sucked up the thick brown liquid, the point ripping easily through his cloth skin.

As the sweet hotness moved like a snake through his veins and wrapped its tail lovingly around his eyes, there the image of She appeared. Her long blonde hair. Her pink evening gown and gloves. Her large, round, upturned nose. Her monstrous breasts.

"Oh, sweet Missus," uttered the frog as his body gelled and fell smoothly onto a newspaper pillow, "Daddy's here. Daddy's here..."

"Perhaps this should be his last hit, don't you agree? Kermit lies there in a heroine induced paradise and dies bearing the first smile he's had in months."

Elmer rolled his eyes in disgust. "Thank you for chiming in, Walter Mitty, but our hero is on a Sisyphean quest."

Michael secretly chuckled at the ease with which Fudd referenced both Thurber and Homer in a single sentence.

"Laugh now, but do so knowing that I'm right. I'm always right. It's one of the benefits of living in fiction. I can choose the least plausible of any number of possible answers, and it will still be fact." With that, Elmer lit a thin black cigarette, toked twice before inhaling, then let out a long stream of smoke which hung in the air and formed the word "FACT" before disappearing in a puff.

Over the last few days, Michael had grown to simply accept that Elmer Fudd, this most likable of hand-drawn protagonists, was indeed a reality and was here in his house. In truth, he quite enjoyed the hunter's company. Unlike the usual male bonding experiences of his past, Michael found himself sharing with Elmer the dreams, fears, and secret needs that are normally acknowledged only by the self and only then in the shower where sound and steam provide adequate cover.

"You see," Elmer continued, as much to himself as to Michael, "in the world of fiction, facts are *chosen* by the individual rather than born of some universal veracity. True, in the real world, too, what're called 'facts' are often little more than preferred ideals or molested half-truths adhered to for self-benefit, but in the literal sense, facts must be those statements which can be empirically proven; those which possess objective reality."

Michael adored sciolistic babbling. "Hmm. Yes, I see."

"Now, in Fiction Town, a fact is congenital to both objective reality and molested gospel."

"Ah. Politics."

"Epistemological flexibility.'"

Michael grinned -- If there was one thing the failed writer enjoyed more than any other, it was a drug induced logomachy.

"By your, should I say, 'ill-informed' presupposition," started Michael, making the bullshit up as he went, "I must infer that in all the books and movies and songs and plays throughout history, each character is more a microcosmic demigod than simply the meanderings of some creative, sentient being."

"Sentient! Hah! Honestly, Michael, you're one banjo string shy of being a Smothers Brother."

"Harsh."

"Well, you obviously refer to this 'creative sentient being' with yourself in mind, do you not? You honestly believe this is what you are."

"Of course I do," Michael answered, surprised at the tentativeness in his own voice.

"Then you've proven my point. After all, *I am here*, am I not?"

Michael's heart skipped just a beat before he recomposed. He knew who he was and *that* he was. He didn't have to believe in Elmer's absurd theories. After all, a little red hat with flaps tied up in the center does not make one Jean-Paul Sartre. Still, a little time to gather his thoughts wouldn't hurt. Michael needed to stall.

"Hungry? Hasenpfeffer, perhaps?"

Elmer gave only the smallest of courtesy chuckles before his demeanor turned. He stared at the ground for a moment, as if a memory had become lost somewhere in the white shag carpet.

"Elmer?"

The corner of Fudd's top lip curled upward to the side of a nostril as his gun blue eyes found Michael's. "You know, few people saw my last film in which I caught and ate that rascally rabbit and his entire fucking family. Then I bagged that duck friend of his and raped it. What do you think of that?"

"Potato salad. I have potato salad in the fridge. Be right back."

It was in this place, this Heroin Valhalla that Kermit dared remember the days of his lilly-padded youth. Fly catching, stump hopping, babysitting tadpoles for a measly two flies an hour...

Mrs. The Frog did not approve of his leaving the pond to become a muppet in Hollywood. She knew that the dangers he would face had razor teeth just like the scaly asps she called 'neighbor.' But these other creatures, these Studio Executives, hissed even louder than their reptilian counterparts. Indeed, it was one of these snakes that first offered a star-shaped apple to the young, gullible frog. He soon found himself in Sodom; a West Coast Gomorra of fast cars, cocaine, all-night parties, and a seemingly endless supply of soft puppet pussy.

His mother's letters had come weekly, sometimes biweekly. The frog sent a single telegram home, imploring her to cease her entreaties for him to return to the pond; he'd gone fully prodigal and he was no longer interested in her or her simple ways.

Then, from some sick corner of this black paradise came She who would most assuredly be his downfall; She who was two hundred and fifty pounds of the most beautiful swine in all the world; She who would make his cotton heart suffer like the slave who'd picked it.

Michael's laughter turned to a sick, marijuana-burned lung hacking.

"'Soft puppet pussy?' 'Slaves picking cotton hearts'?" Michael pointed a finger, "You, old man, are a twisted bastard."

Elmer wiped the laughing tears from his eyes, giggled a little more, then collected himself.

"See?"

"See, what?" Michael asked, his side hurting from the first laughter he'd experienced in months.

"That's just it, friend. You called *me* the twisted one. But I *didn't* write that."

"Well, neither did I," said Michael, a final, nervous giggle slipping out of his throat. "You must've written it; it is writ, after all."

Elmer let out a long breath, lit a cigarette and crossed his legs. "Michael. You're forcing me to say it. You know that."

The writer cleared his throat. "The story. It's done, isn't it? We're finished?"

"Finished."

Michael narrowed his eyes, opened them wide, and narrowed them again; his wife was gone, his career had followed her, he was a junky, and now his only friendship was a fact chosen rather than offered.

"Then say it, Elmer. Just say it."

In a soggy cardboard box somewhere in Los Angeles, the star of a long-running children's TV show loaded his gear to a chilling capacity. As the lethal dose of brown made a final lap through his vessels, his left eye closed softly, the right unable to follow as it had been torn off earlier that morning by a feral dog.

An impossibly beautiful bar of light broke through the smoggy, summer night air and illuminated his makeshift home, cooling the frog's weathered body. Kermit's face worked hard to smile because his smiling muscles hadn't been used in many months. "Well, I'll be damned," he said in a weakened voice. "You'd think I, a muppet, would've known..."

Post Script: *(North Hollywood, California)* **A writer today finished yet another lame short story, lit a cigarette, and blew a puff of smoke into the air. He was oddly disappointed when the cloud of carcinogens formed no word above his head.**

Notes from the Los Angeles Underbelly

GN Harris

The Business Trip

2002

//

GN Harris (aka Gregory Harris) is an ex-poet hitchhiker now WGA screenwriter whose creative talents have been tapped by Universal TV and 20TH Century Fox. He thumbed to California from Florida long ago, published essays in the *LA Times*, magazine stories and fitness books, and three novels, *Connecting the Dots*, *Beat the Machine* and *Highlights From a Lowlife*, all available at BarnesandNoble.com. He is still on a roll.

I've always attracted psycho chicks. One wanted to show me the razor cuts on her calves. Another called and hung up repeatedly the first month I knew her. That same one sprayed perfume all over me in an argument. A different one had me fuck her in dirt once, and then really hard on a seawall. The ex put a tail on me when we were together. Most of these chicks were in therapy. Two were therapists. I've never been able to shake this karma. Even when I landed a spot at a reputable firm and they sent me on a business trip.

It wasn't so long ago I swiped an *LA Times* off a doorstep, drank coffee at Burger King, lived with my mother. But I wear suits these days, and ties. I charge drinks and meals to the company. The hotels offer turndown service, with candy. A valet I never see collects my dry cleaning. I sign my name everywhere I go, that's all, just sign and go. It gives me a kind of immunity. I'm bolstered by perks, insulated by corporate connections, excused for long lunches, saved by do-it-all secretaries. But my status change hasn't freed me from this peculiarity I have. I just attract more expensive lunatics now.

She came up to me in a DC pub and asked for a cigarette, but said she doesn't smoke. My mother smoked for fifty years. This one had almond eyes and carried a suitcase. She pulled legal papers from her purse-parts of a lawsuit, crumpled, wrinkled, lipstick and food smeared. A judge would have laughed them out of court. She was suing her husband. He had tried to have her committed. She had fled her apartment and was staying with an Arab record producer. She said her father was a legendary songwriter who had willed his lyrics to her. My mother's will was a small scribbled note that said, "take everything."

There was ice on the sidewalks outside. We took several taxis to clubs that would not let her in. My mother took me to bars as a kid, put me in a booth with a soda. A man with tattoos on his arm and beer on his breath used to come around on Saturday nights. The psycho chick wanted to run away to Sierra Leone. I mentioned they were beheading people there. She stopped the cab to call an animal shelter and plead for custody of a cocker spaniel. Most of the drivers seemed to know her. I gave one a hundred dollar bill for a ten seventy-five fare. She carried a painting with her into a restaurant, one of hers that she felt close to. She spoon-fed me tortellini at a cheap bar. At the next stop she ordered a sixty-dollar bottle of champagne. We toasted my company.

She asked a maid who was better looking, me or a photo of her husband. She unloaded her suitcase on my hotel bed. In it were a Muslim rug and a belly dancer's belt. We had sex once on the toilet and twice on the sink. I closed my eyes rather than look at myself in the mirror. She stayed up until three a.m. singing. Her audience was a snow flurry and lights from buildings twenty stories high. My mother had entertained the troops during the war. I saw her once in the bathroom, wearing garter belts and applying makeup.

The walls shook and the TV came on by itself while I slept, the psycho chick said. I had a hard time shutting her up. I was scheduled for an early morning meeting, the kickoff to the entire project. I have an internal clock and never need a wake up call. The men at work wear the watch and the ring; it's a tribal thing, I've decided. She heard pounding on the ceiling from the room above, she said. I have never missed a deadline. My mother held my hand and said she wanted me there the rest of her life. I have tried every drug except crack. Someone is trying to reach you, the psycho chick cried.

I used to be unable to imagine twenty years at the same place. Lately I eat lunch at my desk. There is no longer a number to reach my mother. I am surrounded by coworkers with capped teeth. They know where they will be tomorrow, and the next day, and the following months, and for years, until the end.

The psycho chick had demos, killer songs, she swore, guaranteed hits, locked in the apartment. Coffee has become the most important ingredient of a day. It bothers me that the little thin strip won't stay put behind the wider section of my tie. She demanded cash for breakfast and settled for eight dollars. My mother's voice was only a whisper at the end. I'd tried to calculate how much time she had left from its sound. I was wrong by two days.

I used to hate flying, but now I believe the middle of the sky is where I belong. I had always shirked the nine-to-five routine, ridiculed that way of life. I'd resisted conformity in my clothes and attitude, was not interested in clocking in or climbing the ladder. Now I have accepted my metamorphosis into a good, middle-class citizen. There is nothing dangerous or unpredictable about me anymore. I have gained a few pounds and don't have that lean, hungry look. I've become comfortable, dulled my edge, cleaned up my act and gotten in line, merged into the masses, moved on to the kind of life that others understand.

Alexis Lockman
Disgust
2004

//

Despite parking tickets, shitty jobs, over-draft charges and boundless anxiety, Alexis hopes to one day not regret leaving the house. Among her favorite things are family guilt and/or gatherings, going to friend's weddings alone, standing in long lines, disappointing birthdays, avoiding phone calls, working retail while her friends have "careers", public laundry mats and taking online traffic school. Alexis's reason for living continues to be her three whip-smart sisters and one clever brother.

Clearly the disgust of waking up next to someone whose name you forgot is something one tries to avoid. That is if someone cared about names. I got up and stretched my arms over my head and looked around the room. We were at my place which meant I couldn't do the lady-like thing and "have to go because I have a million things to do, give my friend a ride to the airport etc, oh it was nice meeting you....sweetie" and gracefully slip out. I looked at the large mirror by my bed hoping my reflection had some good advice; or at least a foggy account of last night's escapades. My bare chest looked good in the mirror, plump round breasts with small pink nipples hardened by the shock of getting out of those hot sheets. I pushed the body next to me. He moaned and buried his face in my pillow. Gross. As a germ-a-phobe this sent chill-bumps down my arms. I pushed him again. I had to get rid of this one. I could tell he was no good. He was in my bed and I couldn't remember his name; a clear indication he was no good. I had a knack for picking bad men when good alcohol was around. I piled my hair up, pinned it and slipped into my robe.

"Look, I've got a million things to do; I've got to get going." This was a clear and polite way of excusing, well, someone rather than yourself.

He pulled his arm from under the covers and pulled me back in bed next to him with one erratic swoop. Now usually this was something cute and sweet I would sigh over, but thus far he was nameless, I was nauseous and I needed him out of my site.

"No, I really have to get going." Cue the fake smile.

He squeezed me this time with both arms and climbed on top of me and placed a threatening face above mine. His dirty mouth came at me and those wild eyes stared out of a tattooed skull. *Must think good thoughts, must think good thoughts.* His kiss landed all over my face rather than my lips. I felt dirty instantly. What was this stranger doing in my bed? How much did I drink? I thought this phase was over, but apparently not. I wiggled out from underneath him and stood up. I needed to shower; I needed to boil my skin till it was pink; until I was sure every trace of him was completely off my body. But I knew if I jumped in the shower now he would still be there when I got out. He wasn't the savvy kind of one night stand that all women deserve. The kind that gently slips out when one is sleeping and leaves no trace. That's the kind of lay I deserved, that's the lay I had failed to find. But I was a determined young thing.

"Ok, get up." And out.

I pulled the covers and exposed him. That strangers body lay there in my clean sheets, beautiful and sanitized sheets. I felt sick. My stomach turned over and over, but was it the gin or the company? It didn't matter now, I needed to be alone and assess. I began to get anxious, as though the more time he spent in my bed the more permanent he'd be. No I didn't need this. Electricity ran through my skin and vomit was lounging in the back of my throat. Suddenly he stood up on his knees and looked at me with an intense glare. I thought he was going to attack me, but I waited for him to make the first move. He jumped up and stood on the bed completely naked and began to yell.

"I don't want to leave, I want to stay here. I want to spend the day with you. You're mine now!"

Sweet Jesus No! Now things were serious.

"No, no you have to go right now because I have to do things. There are things I need to do. I have to go. Do things. So you have to get your clothes on and go." I smiled and said the words but I wasn't sure now that he would leave. How was I going to get him out? I began to dress as quickly as possible; if I was going to fight him I was at least going to be descent. I may be a slut, but I was still a lady! He jumped off the bed and grabbed me. His octopus arms squeezed and his face smashed against mine. Our lips may have touched, I wasn't sure. Then to my surprise he turned around and began to dress. He made quick, jumpy movements like a skipping record. It was irritating like a little boy that can't sit still on a coast to coast flight; everything in my mind said slap him, but I didn't.

He put on his hat and kissed me with his stale alcohol mouth and stared right into my eyes.

"I'll call you later" he said and walked out the door.

I sighed deep and stretched my lungs to capacity. I picked up my cell phone, turned it off, accidentally catching a glimpse of my reflection in the mirror. She looked at me and rolled her eyes. I smiled apologetically and slipped back into bed, stretched my limbs to the edges of the mattress and fell into the sweetest sleep.

Mark Webster

Workday #32

2004

//

Mark Webster suggests that the next time you hire a day laborer through a labor hall you should tip him or her directly. Tip the worker no matter what the labor hall charges you. If you do not tip the worker then you are a cheap fucking asshole and you can take the ten dollars you saved and shove it up your ass.

Lazy Eye said, "Could be worse. Shit, that Home Depot job down south was worse 'n this. They worked us like fuck. Was you on that ticket?"

I ignored his question. The refrigerator we were carrying was cutting into my palms so I bounced it higher to get some of the weight on my arms, anywhere but on my palms. Lazy Eye was on the bottom end backing down the stairs while I held my end up as high as I could. People say that the bottom end is the heavy end, but at least you can carry it with your body or put a shoulder into the weight. The man at the top can only use his back and his hands and his fingers to hold his end up. That ain't even half of what you need to do the job.

"Could be worse?" I asked. "Could be fucking worse? Dude, fuck that."

"Fuck what?"

"Fuckin' *no* job could be worse. They already payin' the state minimum. What they gonna do, tie a fucking bookshelf to my back while I hump a stove down four mother-fucking flights of stairs? I only got two balls to bust at once. I don't grow new balls at night you know."

"Easy fella," said Lazy Eye as he stumbled over a step. "One fuckin' step at a time. Ain't no bonus for goin' fast. We gotta look out for each other."

"No bonus? Ya think? Shit. We on our own, Fucker. Mama's in the cold cold ground."

My sunglasses were on my cap since I couldn't keep the sweat from messing the lenses up. Sweat had already boiled my leather belt. The cut on my knuckle had stopped bleeding, but each time I gripped the refrigerator frame I heard my future doctor ask me how I had managed to fuck my hand up so badly.

"A man's gotta earn a dollar," would be my resigned reply. "Gotta eat. A man has to eat real food. Ain't no fuckin' tooth fairy gonna cook me steak in my dreams and feed it to me with the gold forks."

"Helluva way to earn a buck, I said. "Enough to kill a healthy man."

"Shit. That Home Depot job makes this look like a Saturday morning blowjob. Hey! Workers was dropping like rat shit. Man, they didn't show no mercy. You don't remember?"

I couldn't see my feet so I was watching the refrigerator like a dance partner. If it moved, I moved. If it paused, I paused. Every step could end in a splintered shin bone followed by six weeks of stuffing envelopes as my "Workers Comp. assignment". I wouldn't last ten minutes in front of a pile of junk mail, let alone six weeks.

"I wasn't on *that* fucked up ticket," I mumbled, "and I wish to fuck I hadn't taken *this* fucked up ticket. I'm a human man workin' for crumbs. I got two hands and eyes like every other man. So why they treat me like an asshole?"

"Cuz that's all you is," was the reply.

"That's coming from the king of all assholes," I shot back over the dusty refrigerator.

"Shit," said Lazy." I take this ticket any day over that Home Depot ticket. They didn't know what they was doin', just fucked everyone up. Men wasn't the same after the Depot ticket."

"How much that gig pay?"

"Huh?"

"The Depot ticket. That pay good? You eat good at it?

"Shit. They wanted ten-an-hour work out of seven-an-hour men."

"That's more than this fucked ticket," I pointed out. "Plenty more."

"Won't argue with that. Better hope we get eight hours out of this ticket. Short day at the minimum wage is takin' food out of my mouth. I got to eat, motherfucker!"

I examined a magnet that a student had left on the top of the refrigerator.

"UCLA?" I said bitterly. "Bunch of bullshit. UCLA? Sure I *see* L.A. It's right over there and it looks like a big fucking pile of dog shit.

"It ain't right," agreed Lazy Eye. "It ain't right in my world."
"They don't know we gotta eat like every other man. We eat and shit like men."

"They don't care one bit, Dog, but this is a fuckin' Fourth of July pussy parade compared to the Depot ticket. I couldn't walk right for a week after that. Hey, buddy!"

He addressed a man in a damp gray T-shirt who had backed into a corner to allow us to pass with the refrigerator. The other man's name was "Barcode" or "Code Blue". Lazy Eye's real name was Hakeem. No one called him Hakeem or even Lazy Eye to his face. He was just the guy with the screwy left eye.

"Hey, Dog, was you on that Home Depot ticket?"

"I just got a quarter raise an hour, man," said Code Blue.

"You fuck the boss in the ass?" laughed Hakeem. "He give you a whole quarter to fuck his ass? Or is that an advance on tomorrow?"

This sounds funny now, but at the time I didn't laugh.

"Shit," drawled Code Blue. "Found a quarter in that last couch. Ain't no lie. A quarter and a pack of gum. I likes gum."

"If you find a dime bag of some Chronic then come talk to me. We'll go smoke in the shitter."

"Could you move your bitch ass down the stairs?" I asked.

"Hey, was you on that Home Depot job over in Inglewood?"

"God damn," said Code Blue. "Don't even remind me, fool. I go near a scaffold now and start pissing my panties. Heard Coach got hurt on that job. Twisted his ankle all up. Coach was a good worker too. Bullshit ticket."

Code Blue unwrapped his gum as he shuffled up the stairs to get another bookshelf from one of the dorm rooms.

Coach was an old timer who tried to keep the spirits up in the Work-A-Day Labor Hall by saying things like, "Count your blessings, boys." and "Every day the lord gives me is another day to spread his word ." I hadn't worked with Coach, but I assumed he was just another guy who came into this world with a strong back, a good work ethic, and an ambition deficiency. His getting injured, if in fact he had been injured, meant only that I'd gotten through one day more than him.

That's all it meant.

"See," said Hakeem to me, "Movin' furniture's easy money. Them motherfucking scaffolds were janky at the Depot. Couldn't hardly walk upright. OSHA man come out and shut 'er down right after I threw my back out. It was fucked. You couldn't pay me enough to walk them fuckin' planks. No, sir."

"Shit. You got standards all of a sudden?" I asked. "You Mr. Executive now? Watch out! Fuck!"

My back, the lower part of my back where the damp back brace was resting, ached terribly. Just when I thought my hands would give out I managed to bounce the refrigerator off of my thighs and regain a grip.

"You alright, buddy," asked Hakeem. "Your pussy sore? Your face look like you takin' a shit."

"I'm fucking perfect. I could eat my own shit for lunch. Close my eyes and think of *Chicken a la Fuck.*"

"Damn."

"Enough to kill a healthy man."

"It's better than that Home Depot ticket. This is easy money, believe that shit."

We were on the third floor now.

"A man has to eat," I said again. "They throw me crumbs like I'm some fucked up circus dog. Like I'm some kind of Chinese Hercules. You see a tattoo on my ass that says I don't need to eat like the other men?"

"Those Home Depot scaffolds weren't put together right from the get go," continued Hakeem. "Weren't nothing on that job right. I tol' the big boss man someone was gonna get hurt and you know what he told me?"

"Go fuck yourself?" I offered.

"Shit. Now Coach is down. It ain't right in my world. Ain't one thing right in this fucked up town. Not one."

"See? I've got a belly too. I can't eat sand and those fucking paper water cups at the labor hall like you do. They think I'm not a man? Send me out on this fucked job, movin' stoves and fridges for a couple bones? One of them beggars in Westwood makes more than me a day.

"Fuck that. Beggin' ain't no life."

"They think I'm some kind of special freak who doesn't need to eat? Mother fucking refrigerators? Fucking UCLA bookshelves? What they gonna do, work a man like an animal? Toss me in a dumpster with them janky mattresses when I can't carry no more? It ain't right."

"No sir."

"My mommy didn't raise me right for me to be here now. Ain't no other fuckin' explanation."

"This ain't even begun to get bad, buddy," said Hakeem. "This is a fuckin' walk down Pretty Panty Lane compared to Home Depot. This summer..."

A cramp started to build in my forearm. My fingers quickly grew numb and I could see the refrigerator slipping as my grip loosened.

"Shit, dude. Put this down. I gotta take a break. My fucking hands."

"You gotta put it down? Pussy sore?"

"No. It's my hands. I'm a man. Put it down."

"Take a break? Wait." Hakeem adjusted his grip. "Alright. I know how the lazy man works."

"Watch your fuckin' cunt," I said as I kneeled down.

"I'm just fuckin' with you. You a hard workin' Joe when you ain't jackin' off."

We lay the refrigerator down on the platform between the third and the second floor. I rubbed my hands and gently pushed the flesh on my knuckle over the hole where it belonged. Of course there were no band aids when I needed them. I'd probably have to shoplift some from the .99 cent store in Santa Monica.

The cramp slowly eased off. I needed a drink of water. Some dormant health trivia from High School reminded me that cramps were a sign of dehydration. The only thing between me and my water bottle was an empty refrigerator.

"You get cut? Want me to call 911?" mocked Hakeem.

"You know, I ate a fuckin' waffle for breakfast. That's it! A waffle and some cereal. That ain't a man's meal. Men need meat. Maybe an egg."

"Eggs is good," said Hakeem.

"I had a breakfast once up north. It was called the Lumberjack Breakfast. Big ol' sausage and eggs. Hot cakes with real butter and syrup."

"Good sausages? Big ones?"

"Not the big Italian ones. Little ones. But I ate ten of 'em. Real flavorful. Orange Juice. They just kept bringin' it out and I ate it all."

"You like them sausages?"

"I don't know. I just ate 'em up. Now look at me. I weigh one-sixty soaking wet. Lifting a fucking fridge with a waffle in my belly. Helluva way to earn a dollar. Treat me like an animal. Shit. Ain't no switch on my dick that turns me into Hercules, you know."

"A buck is a buck."

"I'm like one of them cats who carry shit in the mountains over in Tibet. What are they called?"

"Assholes?"

"No, they got names. The dudes who carry shit for the rich folks who climb the mountains. They don't get paid shit. What's the name they're called?"

"*Poor* assholes?"

"That ain't it. Fuck. This is gonna bug me all day."

"You ready, sissy?"

"Anyway, we're like them dudes who hump luggage up the mountain."

"We ain't humping shit with you sitting on your ass."

"I should just go home," I said without moving. "Fuck this. Thirty bucks ain't worth this shit. *Sixty* bucks ain't worth this. I might do this for a hundred. I mean, it's one thing if you pay a man for his labor, but The Hall gets paid more for sending me here than I take home myself. All they did was give me the fucking address on a yellow piece of paper. That sound fair to you? That sound like a way to live?"

"You done flapping your cunt lips?"

"You take a healthy man and send him out on this ticket and you know what you get?"

"I can call 9-1-1."

"You get a fucked up man. Shit, I'm weak. I need a sausage and some water. Look at that shit," I said as I showed Hakeem the cut on my hand.

"You sure is weak. You been beating off too much?" He asked.

"Shit. That's all I do."

"See? A body needs fuel, boy. All your fuel is in your balls."

"You a doctor now? You an M.D.? 'Cause my pussy's been itching lately."

"Listen, son. You know how it is when you fuckin' your bitch all day, when you hittin' that ass five or six times a day? You gotta sleep, right? Now, there ain't no finish line in this kind of work. It ain't like fuckin' your woman. You beat off in the bathroom and you get weak. That's your problem right there."

I started shaking my head as soon as he opened his mouth.

"Naw, it was from working in that office building for a week. You know last week when I was gone?"

"You went downtown, bitch?"

"Dead center downtown," I said before listing the high points of the week. "Ground Zero. Fucking KPMG tower. Twentieth floor. Business district crap. Thirty dollar parking. Gucci suits. Water fountains. Office bullshit."

"Damn."

"Made me soft. Those men aren't men down there. Pushing

pencils. Pissing in toilets. Talking on the phone. Fat fucks sitting on their fat cunts and shredding paper. That's not work. Just being around them made me soft."

"Ya got weak, huh? Bet ya wish you was downtown now. Easy ticket. Easy money. Not like the Home Depot job."

"You wanna talk about a shit job? Go change fucking florescent light bulbs for a week. Go transfer accounting files from the twentieth floor to the twenty-first floor all fucking day long. You go move boxes of 1997 quarterly reports into storage for two straight days and then we'll talk. Alright?"

"What the fuck?" said Hakeem in amazement, like a world he never knew existed had just been described.

"That's right. Shit. I fell asleep in the fucking elevator. Every floor looks identical. You have to read the number on the wall or else you get lost. Nearly broke my neck on a ladder. Fucking artificial oxygen piped in like sleeping gas. The boss was sitting on his fat ass. I'd like to see those executive fucks try to do this job. Just one day. I'd laugh my fucking ass off. I'd just point and laugh."

"What the fuck is artificial oxygen?"

"It's bullshit is what it is. Dizzy spells. Quarterly reports. File cabinets. All bullshit."

"Bet you saw some fine pussy downtown," said Hakeem dreamily. "All them pretty girls in them 'spensive skirts. Bet they loved your scrawny ass."

"Fuck 'em. I told the hall to give that ticket to someone else. Let *them* change light bulbs for seven an hour. It took two hours to get there on the Metro."

"Asian chicks is cute," said Hakeem. "Latin Mamas. Vanilla and Chocolate Pudding. That's some *fine* pussy right there. Itchy pussies, educated, rich too! Beats looking at my sweaty ass all day."

"That's no lie, buddy. I'm a man like the other men. But this," I kicked the refrigerator, "...this is fucked. Get an animal to do this. A fucking gorilla from the jungle should be moving furniture. Whip his hairy ass into carrying refrigerators. Listen: give me a monkey and a whip and I'll show you some furniture moving."

A young laborer named Tino walked by wiping his face with his shirt. He had a knife scar on his brown belly. He smiled and said,

"The shit," which wasn't bad English for a guy just out of the river.

"The shit is right," agreed Hakeem. "Downtown was an easy

ticket. You done fucked up by not going back there. That's a gravy train ticket right there, easy money, pretty pussy, and you got off to come move refrigerators."

"Three fucking hours by bus."

"You threw away a golden ticket, bitch. Ain't got no one to blame but your own damn self."

"I need to work, man. I'm not in this fucked town to change light bulbs for some cunt accountants. They sit on their cunts and answer phones and multiply decimals all day long. Type a memo, move some folders. They can't do nothing I couldn't do. Eat their sushi. Fuck those fucks. One of my work days is worth *ten* of theirs."

"That ain't no lie."

"If they all died I'd just laugh."

"Still, that's still a good ticket and you threw it away. You could eat good on that ticket. Get laid all you want."

"Fuck it."

"Bet them women were all hot and dripping for your Work-A-Day ass."

"When the fuck is one of them prevailing wage jobs coming 'round? That's what I need."

"You gotta walk before you run. Ain't no PW gigs for sissies like you."

"Shit. I can work circles around these other grunts. Give me thirty bones an hour and watch my ass smoke. Let the monkeys move bookshelves and shit."

"Ain't no golden tickets for the weak men. You said yourself that you was weak."

"Because I need a steak and egg sandwich. Put some cheese on there. Eat it with some chips and one of them cookies with the chocolate morsels. That's a meal for a working man."

"Ain't but one working man here."

Break was over. Lazy Eye picked up his end of the refrigerator and with great effort I picked up mine. I banged my shin on the freezer door.

"Fuck! Cunt!"

"You know that sign holding gig I told you about?" asked Hakeem as he slowly backed down the stairs. "Remember?"

"You didn't take that fucked up job. Tell me you passed it up." He smiled. "Four days a week. Guaranteed easy money."

"Jesus, dude. A mother fucking *sign*? They got wooden posts for that, you know? Bang a post in the ground, nail a sign to it, and you got your job. A fucking retard in a wheelchair wouldn't even do that. You got a whore's pride."

"Four hours a day, four days a week," sang Hakeem. "That's one hundred Washingtons in my wallet every week. Easy money."

"A whore's pride," I said again.

"I'm gonna get it up to five hours in the summer. The owner gives me a sandwich for lunch. That's a good ticket."

"A sandwich? What kind?"

"Fat old turkey," he said proudly. "Sometimes ham as thick as my thumb. Lettuce. A little mustard. Real good. His daughter brings it out to me. Sweet little cunt. Big titties. I'd suck the dog shit out of them titties."

"Good sandwich?"

"Easy money."

"You get a drink too? You get something to drink?"

"Anything I want as long as it can fit in a bag. No beer though. Get me a soda or a box of milk, bag of them salsa chips. Maybe one of them new lemon drinks they got now. Them are good. You try them yet?"

"Shit. This guy gives us fucking bottled water," I said referring to our current boss. "A real working man's hero. I get a frozen waffle for breakfast and a fuck in the ass for lunch. Enough to kill a healthy man."

"You work on that Home Depot job and you'll piss a different tune. A man don't come out of that in one whole chunk."

"Look at me now! Think I'm flying high now? Think I'm living large here? Think my shit don't stink now? Fuck. I ain't no winner with a fat belly like you. I ain't no executive like you with your cushy job holding up a sign. I ain't got no easy ticket to fill my belly and no cunt bringing me ham sandwiches."

"It's mostly turkey. I likes the turkey."

"I just got a fucking fridge and a cut hand. That sound like a winning lotto ticket to you? Shit. Who's the shoeshine boy now?"

"You want me to call 911? Get the paramedics out here to help you out. Maybe get you an IV? Get a hooker to give you a blow job?"

"Shit. A man ain't a man without food. Make a man too weak to work."

"You gotta get you one of them part-time jobs they got now over at Taco Bell. Three or four days a week. That's the way to go for a sissy like you. Give you time to jack off."

"So I'm a fucking asshole if I don't have a part-time job? I'm an asshole if I want more money?"

"You an asshole no matter what," laughed Hakeem.

"I move furniture for bottled water. What an asshole I am."

"Yep."

"My daddy didn't raise no asshole. Fuck a part-time job. I piss on a part-time job. How about that?"

"Get you one of them part-time jobs with some shade and a pretty boss. Get your dick sucked. Buy a slice of that pizza you always talking about. Shit on a clean toilet 'stead of these port-o-pots. Ain't nothing wrong with it. At Home Depot you ain't got shit. It's all over."

"It's all bullshit. Full-time, part-time, no time. Just different colored bullets."

"I'm just sayin'."

"Forget it. You and me ain't the same. You can hold a fucking sign for four hours on the sidewalk. I can't. You got ambition. I'm no good for this town. Los Angeles just wiped me out. Everyone said it would happen. I'm just another loser. Think I'm too stupid to see that?"

"See what?"

"Ought to move back home. Have mom cook me toast and bacon. Wipe my ass with the white paper. Get a girl to suck me off."

"Yep. I hold that sign right over my face so nobody knows it's me. Hold that sign, eat my sandwich, collect my check. That's a good ticket right there. I'll ride that for the summer. Buy me some good weed. Go to Hollywood Park for them Friday races. Take my kids to the beach on Saturday. That's a good ticket."

"Shit. Get yourself one of them fucking sun hats and you'll be Minnie Mae cunt herself."

"I know you ain't talkin' to me, buddy."

"Get a nice rainbow umbrella to keep the sun off of your ass," I laughed. "I'll throw my shit at you when I drive past."

"But I'll be fuckin' the boss's daughter and you'll be humping shit up and down stairs. That ain't no hero's parade. You ain't no pimp with a golden hairdo."

"Shit!"

Then I dropped the refrigerator.

My hands went from searing pain to a cramp and then to total failure in two seconds. I just had time to shout, "Shit!" and try to bend over to let the fridge down easy before I let it go. The fridge hit the cement steps and all 200 pounds took off with Hakeem at the bottom trying to hold it back. At first Hakeem tried to stop the fridge, then he just tried to get out of the way. An hour earlier we'd broken a stove when a handle snapped. Hakeem's advice then was, "Don't be a hero for no janky-ass, twenty-dollar stove." He was trying to follow his own advice as he backed toward this open portal that overlooked a lawn two stories below. The fridge hit the midfloor platform and Hakeem jumped out of the way just in time. The fridge then crashed into the wall and the door swung open.

It was still empty inside.

Hakeem's one good eye looked at me and the other one, the left one, looked at the ceiling over my right shoulder.

"Motherfucker! That's *twice* you fucked up, bitch. Once with that bookshelf when you got cut and just now. You fucking high? Huh, cunt? Two times you fucked up. Ain't no three strikes in this game. You get hurt and that means you can't jack off for a week. I get hurt and that means my ex-wife's lawyer be callin' me at two in the mornin' wantin' my pork money. See that, fucker?"

My right middle finger was still cramped closed and I struggled to pull it open. Code Blue came around the corner followed by another refrigerator he was dragging across the concrete walkway.

"Dude, a little help?" Asked Code Blue through his chewing gum.

I looked at the refrigerator and said, "Do I look like Superman to you? Huh? Am I wearing the Superman cape? We in Hollywood so call Batman if you want some help."

I pushed past the refrigerator as Lazy Eye stood with his hands on his hips. I wanted to get a drink of water.

"You think this shit's gonna move itself, dude?" asked Hakeem as I banged my knee on the railing.

"I can't carry no more shit, man. My fingers don't work."

"Bullshit! You carry the bottom then. Bitch! We ain't *never* gonna go home!"

I stopped and threw my arms up.

"Fine. What does it matter to you if I'm crippled.? I'm just a punk. L.A. ain't gonna notice me when I'm gone. No half-mast flags for my corpse."

"You got to remember one thing."

I made a point not to look at Hakeem. I could never look at him in the face without trying to get the attention of his wandering left eye. I looked out the window to the south where the hot smog clung wetly to the palm trees.

"Listen, the Labor Hall is your pimp. Plain and simple. They pimpin' you out. Right?"

Code Blue nodded his head silently and chewed his gum. I slapped my palm on the fridge.

"That's what I was *sayin'*."

"Well you got to remember to keep your pussy tight. See?" Hakeem closed both of his hands together in front of his waist. "You givin' your ass up too easy."

"Fine. Everybody's an expert on my life. Everybody's got an opinion. I must be a fucking idiot."

"Now grab this fuckin' fridge so we can go home. My bitches be waitin' on me!"

I helped move the refrigerator into position over the edge of the stairs and then lifted the bottom. Then I backed down two steps. It was much easier because I was able to put my arms around the frame rather than just hold onto the bottom lip with my fingers.

"Wait, Buddy," said Hakeem as he struggled to crouch low enough. "Wait. I can't get a good grip."

"Take the tampon out of your cunt and grab the thing," I taunted. "You afraid to grab it? How you gonna hold up that sign if you can't carry a little refrigerator?"

"Just wait."

Hakeem attempted a dead squat of his end and barely budged it. His cheeks blossomed red. I stood easily with my end in the air and a big grin on my face.

"How 'bout that Home Depot job? Which is worse? Who's the hero now?"

Lazy Eye squatted again and with great effort lifted the fridge to his knees, then to his thighs, and then to his waist. His face looked like he was taking a mean shit.

"You ready yet, bitch?" I asked. "I can stand here all day and wait for you to eat your Wheaties."

"Just go, buddy. Don't drop your end again."

"My end? This end don't weigh shit. How you doin' up there,

Mr. Home Depot? Your pussy feelin' good?"

"This ain't shit," said Hakeem. "Any man can do this."

Slowly, we turned the corner of the mid-floor platform and descended the final flight of stairs. I looked up from the refrigerator and into Hakeem's face, hoping for a sign of forgiveness. One of his eyes stared critically at me while the other eye, the lazy one, was drawn like a dream compass through a portal, over the green lawn, and toward the haze of West Los Angeles.

Ray Sikorski
Something Worse If I'm Lucky
1997

Ray Sikorski escaped the New York suburbs and moved Out West, where he worked in National Parks and ski areas for thirteen years. While there he wrote many short stories and a short novel, which he compiled into a book called *Driftwood Dan and Other Adventures*.

Sikorski enjoyed his time in the mountains immensely. After that he moved to California, for a girl. He enjoys the girl immensely, but he hopes it will snow soon.

You might say Mary-Jo's chunky, and you might say she's fat, but I wouldn't say either cause I know her to be a mesomorph. By mesomorph I mean to say that she's big-boned - she's got broad shoulders and broad hips and a big butt, but she ain't fat. She's got big arms and big legs, too. Marilyn Monroe was a mesomorph, but nobody ever called her fat. Course, Mary-Jo's got a big head, in addition to all her other big parts - a big head with big eyes and a big, juicy-lipped mouth. I don't know if her big head is part of her being a mesomorph. I think her big head's just part of her having a big head.

That's the first thing I noticed about Mary-Jo when I started working in the Old Faithful snack shop - the next thing I noticed was her negligence with the mushrooms. She was putting thirty-five, maybe forty mushrooms on those pizzas, like mushrooms are growing right out of the floor. So I tell her, "Twenty-nine mushrooms per pizza," and she gives me a look like "Who gives a damn?"

But, now that I'm thinking about it, the look wasn't "Who gives a damn." It was more like, "I know the mushroom rule, but I'm having a hard time with it, and I don't need you telling me about it." Which, I know, is a lot in a look, but she's got that big head, so I suppose she can fit a lot in a look. That's when I started liking her - the big body parts and the look.

So I like her, but she's a bear to work with - not just the mushrooms, either. College girl, about fifteen years younger than me - I don't know what she did back in Boise, but it probably wasn't anything resembling work. Work doesn't interest her, she tells me, and I can't say she's got a firm grasp on what exactly her role is, there in the snack shop. She likes giving stuff away for free - free ice cream, free pizza, free hot dogs, free hamburgers, free brownies, free lemonade.

Now, I'm not her boss so I'm not supposed to care, and I don't say anything. And not that I'm Mr. Honest or anything, but we've got this tip jar, and she starts ringing up the customers for less and putting what's left-over in the tip jar. Which we split up evenly at the end of the shift, so when before I was making like, seven bucks in cash a shift, now I'm making twenty, twenty-five dollars cause she's not stopping at anything. It's like she's begging to be fired, but whenever Ricardo comes down and checks the till and sees how goddamn slow she works and her problem with the portion control

- I of course am keeping my mouth shut cause I, you know, kind of like her - she just gives Ricardo a *look* with that humongous head of hers and he's just like, "Forget it."

So Mary-Jo and me, we're working together for about ten days, and we're talking. She's telling me how she needed some garlic, cause she was coming down with some sort of glandular illness on account of the elevation which she's not used to, and there's no garlic in Old Faithful, except for garlic powder that the cooks use. So she's telling me she got one of those sous-chefs or whatever you call them in the dining room to order her fresh garlic from Sysco. Well, she didn't *get* him to order it, she just told him her garlic sob story and he just went ahead and ordered it, and now she's downing two, three cloves every morning, and she stinks! She tells me she stinks, but she doesn't have to tell me cause I smelled her about ten minutes before she got to work, that's how much she stinks.

Anyway, I'm thinking she must have given this sous-chef one of her big head looks, cause why else would he just up and put garlic on the list? Ordering stuff Trans World Recreational Services doesn't need is a fireable offense, far as I can tell. Course, maybe this sous-chef likes her big body parts as much as I do.

So I'm thinking about her body parts and she's still talking about garlic or glands or whatever. I can't say I know what all she's muttering on about, I'm just kind of staring at her, looking at her name tag, which says "Mary-Jo Idaho," cause she's Mary-Jo from Idaho. I'm thinking about this, thinking it's kind of funny, and then she says, "And I really miss alfalfa sprouts."

This brings me back. "Alfalfa sprouts?" I say.

"Yeah," she says, "we don't get them out here."

"Good thing, too, cause they taste like dirt."

Now I'm expecting this mentioning of dirt will somehow turn her off, maybe get her irritated, maybe she'll even give me one of her big head looks. But no. Instead, she says, "Yeah, I love dirt. A big, fresh field of it, I could go for some right now. I used to live next-door to a farm, and that smell! I'd go over and just dive in and stick my whole face in it."

I don't know quite what to make of this, so I tell her, "Look. I ain't gonna put alfalfa on no list for you, but if you want dirt there's no shortage of it right outside. You want me to bring you a cup?"

Then she gives me a look, and it's a good one. Says, "I'm trying to express myself, maybe get a little alfalfa out of you, and you're being a jerk. But that's okay." After that we were friends. Being friends with Mary-Jo means one thing: Stealing. Not just in the snack bar - stealing applies to the gift shop, the camp store, and any other store we might be in. Now I never shoplifted anything more than candy my whole life, but with Mary-Jo, anything goes - she'd steal Old Faithful if she could get her arms around it. She gets me pocketing key chains and snow paperweights, thermometers, fridge magnets and bullshit like that, but meanwhile she's going for the gemstone jewelry, the hand-crafted rock and arts-and-crafts stuff - things with a price tag. She'd slide five sets of earrings in her pocket, then ask the sales-lady for help, hand in her pocket the whole time, feeling the stuff, just loving the thrill.

She'd have contests with me, like who could steal the most or the most expensive, but of course she'd always win. Until one day in West Yellowstone we're in the supermarket, actually buying groceries for real, and she doesn't get anything. Nothing - she forgot, she says, she was just buying groceries like any other private citizen. But she doesn't hesitate to praise me for the twenty-three-ounce jar of strawberry preserves I nabbed for myself. "So big!" she tells me.

That night was the night we kissed. Yeah, I smooched with those big lips on that big head, right there in her room in her dorm. Her room's got bunk beds, and we were up in her top bunk, and she was a pretty good smoocher too - aside from the garlic, that is.

Course, then her roommate what's-her-butt, the waitress, has to come parading in - turning on the lights, rattling shit, tossing things around, making all sorts of goddamn racket. Mary-Jo wants to keep on smooching, just ignoring her. "C'mon, Driftwood," she whispers to me, "what's the problem?"

"No problem," I say, but then what's-her-butt starts ignoring us, and by that I mean she starts sliding out of her waitress uniform. Now, it's one thing when she's taking off her apron and those ugly cheap-ass K-Mart waitress shoes, but when she unhooks that bow-tie and starts unbuttoning her shirt, that's when I start getting uncomfortable. Not that I don't want to look - shit, she's practically busting out of that skimpy bra of hers - but with Mary-Jo and me cuddling up like we are, it just doesn't seem appropriate to watch. So I turn my head away, and Mary-Jo thinks it's kind of funny.

"What's the matter, Driftwood Dan?" she whispers at me, poking me in the side. "You afraid of seeing something you can't identify?"

"C'mon," I say, "a woman's got a right to some privacy, don't she?"

"You think she'd be doing that if she *didn't* want us to watch?" Mary-Jo says. "You don't know her like I do - she's figuring she'll give us a show, then she won't feel guilty listening to us getting it on."

"What?" I say, cause I ain't used to this sort of behavior in roommates.

"Isn't that right, Amy?" Mary-Jo leans over and asks.

Amy, meanwhile, is standing bare-assed naked in the middle of the floor with all the lights on. "Ain't what right?" she says.

"Are you looking forward to hearing us?"

"Well, shit," she says, "it's about time *somebody* got some action around here."

"See?" Mary-Jo says to me. "Do you want to ask her to leave, so she won't hear anything?"

"No, no," I say. Woman's got a right to her own room, doesn't she?

"Don't worry," Amy says to us, "a team of mules ain't moving me from this room tonight."

Needless to say, I'm not much in the mood for loving knowing Little Miss Naked's just waiting around listening for it. So Mary-Jo and me, we just go to bed then and there, on the top bunk, with all our clothes on and everything. Course Mary-Jo tries a few of her shoplifting moves on me during the night, but when those bed springs start singing, shit, I'm afraid that bed we're in is just gonna give out and fall on top of what's-her-naked-butt, snoring away down below, and squash her like a hamster.

* * *

Next morning I wake up in a knot. I'm pressed up against the wall, and I got one shoe on and one shoe sitting next to my head. Feels like one eyelid's been crazy-glued shut, the other one can't stop winking. Mary-Jo's gone, what's-her-butt's still snoring away naked down below, I don't know what time it is and I can't barely move. I look at the clock, says noon, which means I'm two hours late, which ain't good - I don't like being late.

Mary-Jo was scheduled to open, I recall, so she's been at work since eight, making coffee for all the goddamn early-rising bird watchers, and probably laughing her ass off at me by now - she doesn't care how late I am.

I roll off that damn top bunk, tuck my shirt in, hop into my shoes, give my regards to what's-her-butt, and rush on out to the snack bar. Halfway there, I see Mary-Jo wandering towards me. "Aren't you supposed to be at work?" I tell her.

"I got fired," she smiles. "Ricardo caught me giving away a brownie. Figured I'd see Old Fartful go off one last time before I split - it's blowing in five minutes. You keeping me company?"

"What?" I say. "Am I fired too?"

"Nah," she says. "Ricardo says I'm a bad influence on you, and once I'm gone you'll be back to normal. So you might as well come watch with me - you're golden, as far as he's concerned."

So we walk on over to the viewing area, and find ourselves a good bench to sit on, right up close. Most of the tourists aren't watching yet - they never seem to figure out when Old Faithful's gonna blow until it actually starts blowing, and then they come rushing out from everywhere all crazy-eyed with their cameras and video equipment and shit, shoving everyone out of the way like the world's ending and they gotta get at least one good picture of it.

"That's the best part, the tourists," Mary-Jo says. "Someday I'd like to get me a movie camera, and just film the tourists watching Old Faithful go off. Seems like some of them don't even care to see it, as long as they got the video running - I suppose they can just watch it when they get home. But there's some who forget they're supposed to be taking pictures, and they just watch the geyser - because, you know, even if you've seen it go off a thousand times, it's still kinda cool."

"Yeah," I say. "I hate to admit it, but yeah."

So just when the thing is gurgling and steaming and getting ready to blow, Mary-Jo gets up off the bench and walks forward ten feet and turns around and sits down in the dirt, watching the tourists. "Come on, Dan," she says.

So I go out and sit down next to her in the dirt, and I watch everyone come running cause it's about to blow. Old Faithful can be kind of sneaky - it does a few pre-blows, just to see if you're paying attention, just to get everybody in the geyser mood before the real performance. So it's doing these pre-blows, and everyone who does-n't know any better thinks it's going off for real. "Don't look at it," says Mary-Jo. "Just look at the people."

It's kind of hard not to look, what with all the oohing and ahhing going on - I know it's not the real thing yet, but I just want to turn around and look to see where it's at, how much longer it's gonna be. Meanwhile people are taking pictures, and I know they're staring at us because here we are, looking like two idiots, sitting in the dirt, facing the wrong way. So they're probably taking pictures of *us*, so they can show the folks back home what a bunch of nuts hang around Old Faithful.

But then it's going off for real. I know it's going off for real because people are really screaming now, and they're taking pictures, and some of them, just like Mary-Jo said, are forgetting to take pictures cause they're too busy screaming their heads off, and Mary-Jo and me, we're getting wet from that hot steam that's coming down on us. It's not so hot that it's burning us, but it's warm and wet and it stinks like sulfur.

First comes the steam, then we get little sprinklings of warm water, and after that we start getting splashes, like Old Faithful's dumping buckets on us. Mary-Jo and me, we can't keep our eyes off the tourists, cause we're too busy laughing and screaming from Old Faithful blowing all over us.

Course, it doesn't last forever, and slowly the tourists start filtering away. Mary-Jo and I sit a little longer, waiting for everyone to leave. After a while she says, "I better get going," serious all of a sudden.

"What's the rush?" She's wet and muddy when she stands up, and that red-and-white uniform shirt of hers is clinging to her big body. Everyone can see her nipples right through, but it's not like her to care.

"I grabbed eighty dollars from the till on my way out. Ricardo's gonna figure it out soon."

"What?" I ask. I'm still staring at her nipples.

"Yeah, Ricardo would have to be brain-dead not to notice. I better get the hell out of here."

"You stole eighty bucks? You're damn right you better get out! What are you still doing here?"

"I wanted to say good-bye to Old Faithful. And..."

"And what?"

"And I thought, maybe..."

"Maybe...?"

"Maybe you'd like to come along?"

And she looks at me with that big-head look, although that see-through wet shirt doesn't hurt any, either.

* * *

"It's my roommate's," she says, stepping out of that 1975 Ford Country Squire station wagon - a true vacation vehicle.

"What's-her-butt?"

"Yeah, Little Miss Naked."

"She's letting you borrow her car?"

"Well, no, she's not in, but I left her a note. I figure I'll get it back to her someday, and if not I'll just kind of let her know where it is."

"Great, so now we're in for Grand Theft Auto, too."

"Are you gonna get in, Driftwood, or are you just gonna keep flapping your gums?"

So I get in, reluctantly. Hell, I'm always up for adventure, but this time I'm just not sure what I'm getting into.

"You better drive," she says, soon as I get comfy in the passenger side. "I get easily distracted driving. I have a tendency of running into things."

Now I've never seen the girl drive, but do I think Mary-Jo'd be a bad driver? Hell, I'm surprised the girl can handle walking, let alone driving. So I get out and walk around that tugboat to the driver's side, without saying a word. I fire that monster up and we start rolling, all the time tallying up in my head the crimes I'm committing just by hanging around this big-head mesomorph.

Mary-Jo isn't talking much in the car, but that's not unusual - when she's in a talking mood you can't shut her up with a can of glue, and when she's not in a talking mood, well, I sure ain't gonna bother. If she's got something to say she'll say it, and if not her face will give her away, sooner or later. The only thing she says the whole way to West Yellowstone is, "I need a shower," and I sure ain't gonna argue with her on that.

So, instead of talking with her I just do a lot of thinking with myself. Mary-Jo had given me one of her big head looks, saying, "It's time to go," and I figured, "Hell, what's the difference?" I'm no stranger to "It's time to go," cause every job and every situation has its rightful end, and this seemed as good an end as any for that two-bit soda-jerk shit snackshop. Though I'm not foreseeing anything as good or better coming my way any time soon. Something worse, maybe, if I'm lucky.

*   *   *

Lucky for us we make it to the park entrance in West Yellowstone without any rangers stopping us, and I want to keep on going, just in case. But Mary-Jo, she starts whining about stopping to get dried papayas, how she needs the nourishment. So we stop at the store that has dried papayas, and I sit in the car waiting and grumbling and getting madder cause she's taking forever.

Then she comes skipping out, all smiles and happy and, "Okay, honey, let's go!"

"Honey, let's go?" I say. "Where the hell are we going?"

"I don't know," she says. "Wherever. Wherever this thing feels like going!"

I don't say anything, so she says, "What's the problem?"

"What the hell do you mean, 'What's the problem'? Am I your summer tour leader? Is that why I'm giving up my job, room and board, everything I had going on back there?"

"Oh, come on, Driftwood, don't give me this bullshit - you'll get another job. Besides, you need an adventure. You're so repressed! C'mon, it's like we're Bonnie and Clyde!"

"Yeah, right," I tell her. Here I am, driving this big-boned moody-assed thief around the Wild West, so she can get some kicks. I don't need this kind of shit.

"Can you tell me why I shouldn't just kick you out of this car, turn around, and go back to work?"

She just sits there, surprised-looking. She's not saying nothing, just moping cause apparently I'm not having the same fun she's having. "Well?" I say. "Or you want me to live a life of crime with you?"

"You always have to be the dad," she says. "Why do you always have to be the dad? I already got a dad and he's plenty!"

"Somebody's got to be the goddamn dad!"

She's silent for a minute. Then she says, "I hate you," just like that. After that she gives me one of her big?head looks, which just ain't necessary cause all it says is "I hate you."

It hurt me. She just sits there in the passenger seat, getting

Sleeping with Snakes

teary-eyed and looking mean, and I don't know what to do. All I can think to do is fire up the Country Squire and start driving. I'm thinking maybe I'll drop her off at a bus station or something, or maybe take her to her dad's? But hell, Boise's a day away. Maybe she'll just disappear.

*   *   *

So I drive. I drive for hours, and now it's dark and we're going through Idaho's atomic Neverland. This area always gives me the creeps - someone's always spotting UFO's or their cows end up getting turned inside-out or something. Mary-Jo's still just sitting there whimpering. "Are you gonna drop me off somewhere?" she asks.

"I'm thinking about it," I say.

"Well," she sniffs, "there's a car wash up ahead. Let me at least wash the car before you throw me out."

"C'mon, now, I ain't throwing you out."

"Just let me wash the car. Then we'll be even, okay? Then you can go back to Yellowstone and get your job back and give the car back to my roommate all nice and clean so she'll forgive you. And you'll never have to see me or talk to me or anything again because we'll be even."

Well, it's tempting, getting my job back, getting off the hook. Plus, the Country Squire really does need a wash.

We crest a hill, and there it is. It's one of those coin-op do-it-yourself deals, and what in hell's name a car wash is doing out here I can't say. The car?wash mist reflects in the Country Squire's headlights, making the place look like it's sitting in a cloud. No other car is around.

I pull in. Mary-Jo tells me to stay put, she's gonna take care of everything. She gets out with her plastic bag full of change, heads to the coin slot, and then decides she's gonna take off her shoes.

She unties the laces, then slips off her shoes and her socks and rolls up her pant legs, and for the first time I notice her ankles. I'm told a lot of men are into ankles, but I never noticed a pair myself. What's appealing about an ankle?

But the thing with Mary-Jo is, she's big. She's got that big head and those broad shoulders and hips and that big butt, but her ankles, they're not big. They're skinny. Dainty, even. So I'm looking at her dainty ankles like she ain't Mary-Jo, but she's definitely Mary-Jo, cause now she's spraying that car-wash soap from the high-powered soap gun like she's never soaped a car in her life. She's getting wet, too, which isn't surprising. Wet and covered in soap, which she seems to be enjoying.

After she's done soaping the car, she starts soaping her feet, cause I guess they need it. I don't think she's taken a shower in a week, judging from her smell, but you never can tell with that garlic of hers. So after soaping her feet she decides to unzip her pants and unbutton her shirt and slide out of every piece of clothing she's got, and she exposes to me and the Country Squire every big part of that mesomorph body that can be exposed.

Now I've never been a peeping tom and I wasn't planning on starting at this point in time, so I avert my eyes. Course, that didn't last for long. I'd spent a lot of time in the last couple of weeks wondering just what that mesomorphic body looks like unclothed, and now here it is, right in front of me. I won't say that body was begging me to look, but it was at least asking me nicely.

So I look. And there she is, big as day, trying hard as she can to spray her naked self with that soap gun. Those car wash soap guns are about three feet long, so they're not exactly designed for personal showering. Mary-Jo's having a hard time with it.

For a while it's fun, looking at her struggling with the thing - stretching those large arms out far as they'll go, but not quite far enough - but I can't just sit there watching for long. After a few minutes I get out of the car, go over to her, and take the soap gun out of her hands. "Mary-Jo," I say, "this isn't working."

She gives me a look, one of her big head looks, which says, "If you're not gonna help then mind your own business, but if you're gonna help then help."

So I help. I do the soap gun for her, and the foam brush, and the high-powered jet rinse, and I buff her dry with a towel.

Then we do the same with the car. Mary-Jo puts her clothes on, and we get in the Country Squire. And finally, we're back on the road.

Gavin Hignight
A Letter From Clyde Wilcox
May 2003

//

Gavin Hignight is a writer and filmmaker living and working in Los Angeles, California. He has put-in seven years in the "city of snakes" and *A Letter From Clyde Wilcox* is just one of the many stories inspired by his time here. To read the continuation of the story or others visit www.gavinhignight.com.

Sleeping with Snakes

They're watching you. They're watching everything you do. They're watching me, they're watching us, they're watching everybody.

My name is Clyde Wilcox. I should start this off very simple so it's easy to understand. My entire life I've done everything right. I've always followed the rules, that's what got me into this mess. Breaking the rules is what's going to get me out.

All of this started almost a year ago. I had just come home from work. At the time I worked at the SureSystems copy and messenger service. I wasn't a messenger. I was one of the poor saps that would be in the office for 8 to 9 hours a day smothering under the choke of the florescent lights. For 8 or 9 hours everyday I would organize, copy, bind, staple, rebind, and recopy documents. But that doesn't matter. What matters is that one night after another day at that job I came home.

I had been at home for a while. I was eating dinner. Nothing glamorous. To tell you the truth it was cup of noodles. Not the actual brand Cup of Noodles. It was some cheap Korean version I got at the bargain store. They were really cheap and I was on a budget. I had to be on a tight budget all of the time because of my job at the copy place. But that doesn't matter. What matters is that one night while I was sitting there eating yet another package of the generic ramen noodles someone knocked on my door. I answered the door and no one was there.

No one was in the hall. No one seemed to be anywhere around who could have knocked on the door. That's when I found it. On the ground, on the floor in front of my apartment door was a package. It looked blank except for a tag on the front, which had my name on it. It was printed and addressed neatly to Clyde Wilcox. That's me. And that's when everything changed. The night I found that package at my front door.

I suspiciously got the package into my apartment and didn't open it for a while. I sat it on my table and in my head went through all of the scenarios of what could be inside. Could it be a bomb? Who would send me a bomb? I don't even know anyone who ever remembered me enough to hate me and send me a bomb. You really have to love or hate someone to send them a bomb. Could it be an old fruitcake or some relic from a Christmas a long time ago, something from a relative I didn't know I had who mysteriously came fourth to send me something. I spent some time wondering if it could be small pox or maybe anthrax. Everybody is always worrying that someone is going to send them some disease they don't want. Well, why not me? Someone could have sent me a disease. I ruled that possibility out. So I opened the box.

Inside were two compact discs. The kind you put in a CD player or a computer. They had the same neat labels on them. White label, black simple print. On one of the discs were the words play me. I looked at it for a second, and then I put it into my compact disc player. Nothing happened. Who would send me a CD that doesn't play in a cd player? So I decided to place it into my computer.

Once the disc was spinning in my computer a window opened up on the desktop. On it was a man I had never seen before. His name was Mr. Williams. I never found out his first name. I never found out if Mr. Williams was even a real name. The strangest thing is that the message he recorded on the disc was to me. He was speaking to me.

-Hello Mr. Wilcox, you may find this unimaginable at first. I suspect you will find it very hard to believe. But please, bear with me. We have your best interest at heart. Right now you are probably asking yourself, "Who is "we"? How does this man on my computer know who I am? Why did they send this to me?" Well, it's simple Mr. Wilcox. We want to offer you a job. You have lived a model life. You have been the utmost moral. You have been the best possible citizen you could possibly be. And that's why we are contacting you. That's why we have chosen you to be rewarded. And now your probably asking yourself, "How does he know all of this about me?" It's simple Mr. Wilcox. We've been watching you. That's what we do. That's what we've always done. We watch over everyone. And now that's what we would like you to do for us.

So that was the beginning of the end of me. At the time I was very confused. What did he mean they were watching me? How did they know who I was? How did they get into my building? How? What? Why? When? Where? And did I mention Why? Why?

-Mr. Wilcox, my name is Mr. Williams. I am responsible for an agency called the Network. You probably have never heard of the Network. There's a reason for that. No one is ever supposed to know of the Network. That's how it works. That's how our system works. We represent a vast network of the highest technology developed by this glorious government. The reason the Network exists is simple. To watch for and prevent anti-government activity. We at the Network, are the eyes and ears of the nation. We are the silent shepherds always keeping a watchful eye on our beloved herd. It's an honor for you to even be made aware of the Network. It is even more of an honor to be asked to join the Network. To be made one of our agents whose sole purpose is to be that watchful eye. We are extending that offer to you Mr. Wilcox. Without even knowing it you have passed the ultimate screening. A test you weren't even aware of taking. If you choose to be one of us, if you choose to be an agent in our network you will never have to report to a normal job again. Housing, food, income, vacations, transportation. It will all be awarded to you. In return we ask for two things. The first being your watchful eye for 5 to 6 hours a day. You can work from home, at your convenience, whatever hours you choose. In this job you make your own hours. The second thing we ask is your silence. You may never discuss what you see, what you do, or what the Network is to anyone. As, I've said, we've watched you, we know you and we trust you'll make the right decision. That's why we have contacted you. If you choose to join us, if you choose to work for the solidarity of your country then place the second disc into your home computer. It will install the proper software to connect your computer to the Network. After that you and your computer will work with us to make a better America. Thank you for your time Mr. Wilcox.

And with the last of his words the image blanked off. I sat there staring at the computer screen for hours. Surely it had to be someone's idea of a cruel joke. Maybe it was one of the guys from the office. They were always messing with me. Maybe they made all of this up. But, what if they weren't making this up? What if it wasn't a joke? I deserve something like this. At least that's what I thought at the time. So I stuck the second disc into my computer. It began to spin. It dialed up something through the modem and then the computer screen went black. It was black for two days. Until another package showed up at my doorstep.

A knock on my door. I got up from what I was doing at the time and answered the door. No one was there but this time in front of the door was a box. I looked down the hall each way. No one there. I then brought the box inside. Inside the box was more equipment to attach to my computer. Beside that was another disc. I plugged in the disc.

-Hello again Mr. Wilcox. I can't tell you how pleased we are that you have decided to join us in our ongoing campaign to keep this country and it's people safe. It will take you a short while to get the hang of navigating the software running the Network. If you have any questions you can e-mail us at the link provided. As promised you're living expenses will be fully compensated. Check with your bank tomorrow to find that over the evening we have made an electronic fund transfer to your account. Keep up the good work and every two months the Network will make a substantial deposit into your account. And don't worry. We give raises yearly and bonuses for jobs well done.

Was that it? Was it that simple? The next day I did find a large deposit of money into my account. It wasn't even a deposit. It was just there. There was no record of it being entered, or deposited. From that point on every two months there was just more money in my account. After the first deposit without haste I went into my horrible job and quit. It was a great feeling. I was being taken care of now. I did the right thing all my life and was finally being rewarded for it.

My job was simple. I would get up every morning and work in two shifts. When I started I tried doing one long shift but found that my eyes would hurt from staring at the screen to long. Staring and watching. With a voice command the microphone they sent me (That worked with my computer) I could give the command for different camera locations anywhere in the country. ANYWHERE. I don't just mean busy traffic intersections or bank lobbies. The Network was larger than I could have imagined. They had cameras everywhere. EVERYWHERE.

Streets, houses, hotels, libraries, police stations, apartments, bathrooms, bedrooms, shopping malls, bars, farms, parking garages, airports, backyards, front yards, grade schools, kindergartens, high schools, colleges, day camps, summer camps, night-clubs, government facilities, governors mansions, consulates, embassies, you name it and the Network had a grid of camera locations inside and out.

As you can imagine that's a lot to take in. There were no rules for me to follow except for the two. Watch for anti-government activity and never communicate with anyone about the existence of the Network. I could bounce around looking at whatever, whoever, or wherever I wanted. If I found something suspicious I would mark it by hitting a certain key and it would be flagged. I guess at that point it would be passed through the Network to some kind of superior or upper management and they would assess if it was potentially dangerous to the security of the country.

It was very hard to adjust to the idea that I was watching people. Watching them live. Watching them eat, sleep, shit, screw, walk, talk, work, you name it. It was now my job to watch them at their jobs. (Offices, factories, shopping malls, hospitals, etc...) It was now my job to watch them on the streets. (Dark late night street corners, subways, highways at rush hour, Etc...) It was now my job to watch them in their homes (apartments, houses, kitchens, living rooms, bedrooms, bathrooms, etc...)

As you can imagine this incredible freedom at times could be very distracting. For me it was very distracting. I've narrowed some phases I went through into 4 categories.

1. Pervert Phase: This of course is the most obvious phase. You would think it's great. All of the sudden I had access to any act of lust, lovemaking, or debauchery, the Networks camera system could catch. The montage of images I saw was unforgettable to say the least. It was like having a free subscription to a porno channel. It's a big country and there always seemed to be someone somewhere who was getting it on. But, here's the thing. I saw everything. Everything. Every shape, every size, number of participants, sexual preference, tricks, toys, boys, girls, goats, even an attempt at a feline. What I'm saying is that the pervert phase didn't last very long. Very quickly the subjects you are watching become just that. They are like meat. Or like animals. You lose the human connection with them very quickly. I'm sure there were others like me. I'm sure some of them never got through their pervert phase. As for me, after you see all those different people hump each other in all of those different ways, you kind of loose your taste for watching it.

2. Fine Art Phase: After the dehumanizing aftertaste I had from my pervert phase I decided I should become more cultured. I spent most of my time during that phase looking at art in museums. Or graffiti in alleyways. I would connect to cameras that were in movie theatres. I would boost my sound output and watch movies. I watched all kinds of movies. I tried to limit it and focus on work but sometimes needed the release. The most notable part of this phase is Jazz music. On camera 17-A in the NYC set up I found an old man. He was special. He had a saxophone and would play in the Subways. It sounded incredible. Even through the crappy sound of the surveillance microphones. This old Jazz Man, like me was a creature of habit. I could always find him on the same trains on the same nights playing music for tips. I envied him. He lived in a much more simple world than the one I was now a part of.

3. Stalker Phase: The longer I worked for the Network the less I was going out into the real world. My view of the world was very much through the little porthole of the surveillance system on my computer. I was becoming much more accustomed to seeing the world through the Networks black and white monitors than on my own, on foot, in the real life color world. I went out maybe twice a week, usually for groceries. I began to realize that I was very lonely. It was like I was in a cage at the zoo. I could see all the others walking around and living around me but I was stuck in the cage and couldn't communicate with them. This is a feeling I had much of my life. Even before I started working for the Network. I realized that with the help of the Network I could finally start meeting people. I needed a good woman in my life. My entire life I never had anything in common with the girls and never knew what to say to them. Well, with the Network I could find girls, follow them via the camera, find what they were all about, find out their patterns, where they would be and then accidentally bump into them and "hit it off". This plan didn't last too long for obvious reasons.

GIRL A: She lived near my building. I ran into her at a coffee shop. After instantly knowing about and demonstrating my knowledge of everything she liked she was freaked out, to say the least.

GIRL B: After working out the kinks of my last attempt I planned to run into Girl B while waiting in line for a movie near her college campus. I had learned from my last attempt and would make it a point not to be overzealous. Although better I was still too much. It's safe to say I freaked her out as well.

GIRL C: Was an absolute success. I had all of the knowledge about her; her needs, wants and desires. I had worked out a system to play it cool and let on a little at a time as not to freak her out as was the case with Girls A and B. The only problem is that it worked so well that it freaked me out. Without any real effort this young lady was eating out of my hand. It didn't feel right. I had to get the hell out of there.

Now, I didn't move into my next phase for a while. I'll get to that in a moment. For a couple of months I was a model employee (or agent) for the Network. It took an adjustment period but I really got the hang of the equipment, the camera placement, and the strategies for surveillance.

Here's the thing. Much of the time you're looking at nothing, a whole lot of nothing. Empty streets, people watching television, people sleeping, people eating, shitting, walking and talking about the most mundane things. A whole lot of nothing.

If you weren't watching people do nothing, then you were watching them be bad. I was constantly watching acts of disrespect. Vile acts, disgusting acts, embarrassing acts. People violating rules, each other, and themselves. I began to see just how disgusting we can be as a species. This is where I first started to loose it a little.

I saw:
Beatings
Theft
Sexual Assault
Vandalism
Animal Abuse
Wastefulness
Littering
Spousal Abuse
Child Abuse
Murder

Now, here's the thing. I witnessed all of that, and none of it has anything to do with "Anti-Government" activity. So that means the only thing I could do is watch. Sit there and watch. One can imagine how that would make me think less of the human race. After watching all of this thoughtless crime it really made me realize how we are not that different from animals. In some ways we are worse because we should know better.

I hadn't heard from anyone at the Network. I had to assume they were happy with my performance because the money kept reappearing in my checking account. I would watch and flag down "Suspicious Activity". Not being able to do anything about all of the crime I was seeing is what led me into my fourth phase. But, I'll get to that in a minute. First I should discuss my first successful "bust".

The time of my bust is also when I heard from Mr. Williams for the first time since he offered me the position with the Network. It is ironic because I was watching two cases very closely at the same time. Two groups of men. I had already flagged one of the men and was sent an email from an unknown contact within the Network to keep following his activity. With the software I had the ability to flag certain camera locations like a normal person would place a bookmark on his or her internet browser.

I would get up in the morning, fix a cup of coffee for myself, boot up the computer and open the link to this man's apartment. I had other camera locations noted, like a dry cleaners he frequented and a diner he would eat at with other men. I can't recall what about him seemed suspicious, if anything really, but I was told to continue following his progress so I did.

I had come across the other group of men I was watching at the time on accident. Sometimes when I would get bored I would just type random camera locations into my surveillance system. I would just pull up any location and camera number that popped into my head. One night at about 11:30 I found this group of men. The camera location was the backhouse of some apartment building and they were using it to make methamphetamines. They were drug dealers and drug makers. This isn't considered anti-government activity.

I emailed my faceless contact at the Network and was instructed that this was indeed a crime but not a concern of the Network or it's representatives. I was also noted to cease surveillance on these subjects and focus on the other man that I had been observing. I got this job for following the rules and that's what I was going to do. So I focused on group one, the group of men who hung out at the dry cleaners. It bothered me that here was a group of people, obviously breaking the law and endangering people, but it didn't matter to the Network.

I kept following the "dry cleaner man". That was now my nickname for him. With the Network, I had mapped him out; his friends, his hangouts, and some appealingly suspicious behavior.

On one particular night, very late in the evening, the dry cleaner man awoke by alarm. He got dressed in dark clothing and picked up a duffle bag. I watched all of this through the Network. As he left his residence I had the instinct to flag him again and send a warning to my superiors. I followed him until he got to a warehouse with some of his other regular contacts.

Almost immediately, right before my eyes, the building was stormed by some type of SWAT team. There was a lot of confusion, a lot of smoke and gunfire. I very clumsily navigated through different camera locations and angles on my computer to see what was going on inside the warehouse. When I got to a certain camera I saw one of the SWAT members gun down the dry cleaner man. Watching all of this unfold on the monitor was surreal. It was almost interactive. I was removed from it, yet I was a part of it. It was like a video game where I was killing bad guys. Only it wasn't a video game. It was real. These people were dying and it was my fault.

I never found out what exactly they were up to. I never found out who the dry cleaner man was or what was in his duffle bag that night. I never found out why they had to be killed or why it was important that I pointed them out. I never found out who exactly those guys in the SWAT uniforms were. Nothing. I was never told a thing.

There was a knock on my door the next day. I found a letter addressed to me. Blank envelope. Plain white label, with my name printed in black letters. Inside was a letter from Mr. Williams.

Mr. Williams
Sector Five
Third Division
Lead Officer

Dear Mr. Wilcox,
Congratulations! You have proved yourself a valuable addition to our team. You made your first bust in record time for a new agent. You have excelled not only in your training to the Network protocols, but also above my personal expectations. Keep up the good work! If there is anything you need or anyway I can help you, please feel free to e-mail your contact and he will forward the message to my desk.

Sincerely,
Director Williams

So that was that. I did my job well, congratulations they said. I was responsible for people dying. That isn't easy to just forget or let go of. If I hadn't said anything that guy would still be alive. Of course, if I hadn't said anything he might of done something horrible. Other people could have been killed. I may have prevented it. But it didn't matter either way because I didn't know. I needed to know. But they would never tell me.

Notes from the Los Angeles Underbelly

Carla Garcia
The Strongest Poison
2004

//

Heartache makes you stronger. Heartache makes her a better surfer.
Tears taste like the ocean, where you are most likely to find Carla in the
morning. In the late afternoon she returns to her life as an indentured ser-
vant to the Editors of *The Real World*.

"What would you like to drink?" I asked as I led him up the stairs to my apartment.

I had not had a drink in a couple of days or so I remembered. But sure enough, the bottle of bourbon was empty.

"I don't drink anymore," he said rapidly.

"Good thing. It seems that I've finished my last bottle."

"Well, you shouldn't drink so much." He leaned against the counter next to me and replaced a stray auburn lock behind my ear. He glanced around the spacious, newly renovated kitchen. "This place is wonderful."

"Heaven knows I looked long enough for it. Would you like the official tour?"

We walked back into the living room and dining room. Then, I led him down a long hall to my room and let him have only a glance.

"I like what you've done with your room."

"Thanks. Let's go sit in the backyard."

"You even have a backyard?" I sensed a strange momentum building, as one feels a much-anticipated event drawing near.

"How does it feel to be out in the world, now?" I asked thinking of my own answer to the question - overwhelming and lonely.

He chuckled and spoke in his rapid East Coast way, "You make it sound as though I'm a debutante who has come out."

"Well, aren't you? And I'm the suitor? The unsuitable suitor of course, I'm poor, you see. I have to work for a living. It's sad to not lead a life of leisure but so long as I can keep myself stocked in cheap liquors, used vintage noir paperbacks, and a modicum of food, I feel as though I'm the greatest success."

His face held a pained expression of pity. His long lashes fell over his dark brown eyes as he bent forward and rested his arms on his knees. "I wish you would give up drinking." His tone was autocratic. He was the prince of a large law firm that his great-great-great-grandfather had established.

"I don't *really* drink. Only on occasion. In fact, I believe the last occasion was Valentine's Day. I was quite alone, no, not quite alone. I was Cinderella playing with the mice, waiting for my prince. Only the magic couldn't turn my pumpkins or slippers into much of anything, let alone a prince, and the fact that I didn't have any pumpkins or slippers put me out of the mood as well."

"You're quite talkative today. But, you're talking like a 1930s tough guy in an old film."

There must be something wrong with the universe at the moment. I usually sat across from him listening to the garrulous young man spouting many names of famous criminal lawyers and law cases while I nodded my head and brooded over whether or not I was good looking enough for him. Well, that wasn't all I thought about, occasionally I did pay attention to him. At this moment though, I was wondering how I was supposed to go about trying to be a professor, assistant professor, I mean. Perhaps I should have taken the bar?

"Please, by all means, don't stop. I like listening to you for a change."

He looked down at his hands, and then, with a furtive lifting of his head, his eyes landed on my belly. I placed both my arms over my abdomen to shield myself. He sat back and ran a large hand through his black kempt hair. He was brooding. There was something big on his mind

"I'm thinking about going back to New York."

"No!" I shrieked and tore out my hair and lay prostrate, spitting and hissing in a fit. Or so I imagined as my gut reaction. I clutched at my sides to keep my trembling hands from showing. How could he stay so calm after practically destroying me with one sentence?

"When?"

"That's it. Can't wait for me to go? When?" There's his anguish, buried under his bravado.

"No. I mean. Carlos, no." I couldn't get the words out. I shook my head.

We had spent the entirety of our graduate school years in a state of insufferable celibate companionship. His ambitions were far greater than mine and, if I couldn't find the time to be with him, I knew it was hopeless on his side. Not until I saw the struggle in his eyes at this moment did I realize that what we could never express was mutual and not merely a fantasy. I did not have his brilliant mind. My memory for cases was terrible and I had to chant myself to sleep with these simply to avoid failing the next day's exams.

His brown eyes gained courage and hope as he looked into my slate green eyes. Kiss him! I jumped out of my seat. Instead I walked over to the grass to pick up a fallen walnut in its furry casing. I hit it against the edge of the chair and cracked it open. I ran my thumb over the shell of the walnut and threw it back over my shoulder, feeling stupid for my uncontrollable impulse. I felt my legs tremble.

"What are you thinking?" he asked.

"Would you really like to know?" I looked with an embarrassed hope, trying to steady the shaking in my breath.

He glanced away when I looked up at him.

"Yes, Philippa."

There it was, the truth in the way he said my name. My heart decided to stop and then, in an attempt to make up for loss of pressure, beat overtime.

"I can only think about kissing you before I never have the chance again."

He cleared his throat as he glanced at my mouth and then held one of his beautifully formed hands up to his lips in subtle defense.

"That's it?"

"No," I straightened my back and smiled at him, "I don't want you to go."

"Have you considered giving up drinking?"

I suppose." The lie was evident to him as I looked away to the ground where the last syllable seemed to drop.

"Let me rephrase that. Would you be willing to give it up?"

He finally looked up at me. The real question was clearer in those brown eyes that would only see the other side of the country.

"If the circumstances were right," I replied. I was nervously fidgeting, my left foot tapped on the ground quietly.

He subtly wiped his hands on his pants and got up. Placing two fists on his hips, he walked over to the tree and seemed to confer with it before returning to where I sat. I could smell his warm virile scent as he leaned over me and spoke.

"I want you to come with me."

"I've never been to New York." My defenses had risen. I wanted to strangle myself for not allowing my true enthusiasm to come through.

He backed away from my chair as though I had sucker punched him in the gut. Well, perhaps not so melodramatically. He sighed in calculated disappointment as though he had expected rejection. But I knew he was deeply wounded.

"Just say no if that is your answer." He snapped at me and paced with his hands gripping tightly in fists. He was a frightening figure. I had never realized how much I enjoyed watching him agonize over something. It was a rare treat. He was usually so phlegmatic.

"What would I do about my apartment?"

I watched him take the turn at the end of the patio and walk just a few feet in front of me before turning again.

"Who thought you would just move like that? I couldn't believe you hadn't mentioned it to me, especially when I had mentioned that I was thinking of going to the East Coast to work and."

He stopped in front of me.

I had done my best to be stoic, but there, one tear slipped and then the other. He looked with intolerance at my wet eyes.

"I'll go," he turned and walked across the lawn to the back door, which I knew he couldn't get out of because it was locked.

"Oh don't. Can't you give me some time?"

"How much more time do you want? You've had three years, now."

I was astonished at the accusation. Was it *me* who had neglected to initiate the relationship? Could I have been blind to his subtle hints? Am I really as idiotic as I was feeling? It would have been much simpler if I had kissed him. All those years I should have just kissed him.

"Do you plan on marrying me?"

"What?" He was caught off guard. This had never figured into his life goals. "I'm not ready to get married. You know that." I knew the question would infuriate him because he had recently made it clear that it was a goal of his to avoid marriage.

"I know."

I'm not sure if I was imagining it but I detected a scent of peach blossoms in the air. I had a strong desire for just a taste of prussic acid. It would be a much faster way of dying than this. I touched the back of my hand to my forehead and wiped off the perspiration caused by mortal panic.

He stood before me and slipped his hand under my fingers and searched my eyes for my honest response. I leaned forward and settled my lips on his soft mouth.

"So your answer is no."

"No." I had to make my point, even though I was not certain why. "Not now."

Notes from the Los Angeles Underbelly

Mike Golden
LALALALA
Mid-90s

//

The Editor-Publisher of *Smoke Signals**, Mike Golden has written for, among others, *Rolling Stone, The Paris Review, Between C&D, Film Comment, Vibe, Spy,* The *LA Weekly*, and his short story *The Unbearable Beatniks of Light Get Real*** gave birth to the infamous downtown NYC guerilla writers & artists collective known as The Unbearables. Over the last several years of the 20th century, he worked on assignment covering the King family's attempt to reopen the MLK assassination investigation, and did the last face-to-face interview with James Earl Ray, as well as serving as a commentator on Court TV's coverage of the King vs. Jowers "unlawful death" conspiracy trial. After working on it for close to 30 years, he finally finished *Memphis*, a novel set during, and 30 years after, the MLK assassination, that, after reading part of it in early draft, Bukowski called it"That Big 60s Novel We've All Been Dreading!". His book *The Buddhist Third Class Junkmail Oracle****, on the art-poetry and mysterious unsolved death of the last poet put on trial in America for his language, Cleveland poet-publisher d. a. levy, is presently being developed as a feature film from his NEA award winning script.

* www.carminestreet.com/smoke_signals.html
** www.thinicepress.com/mikegolden1.html
*** www.sevenstories.com/Book/index.cfm?GCOI=58322100707970

Usually the light at the end of the tunnel in Hollywood is nothing more than somebody else burning out. But in the early 00s, *Big Brother* cut through the shit he had missed in the 80s and 90s, though not exactly with what you'd call a sharp blade. Pabulum was still the formula, but something was happening Mr. Jones, and nobody really knew what the infomercial was selling, other than more of that same-old, same-old Survival Training.

Orwellian studio politics and the usual politically correct angst of the usual *Newspeak* aside, when the umpteenth "Year of the Woman" cleared it wasn't so much that the game had changed, because ultimately the game never changes, just the players. It doesn't matter who they are either, because they're all heroes and they're all cowards at different points in time. You can't be one without the other out here. Depending on the deal, everybody you meet will at some critical point rise to their hype, but at other critical points in the action completely sell out. You can never tell which, even about yourself, unfortunately. I mean, I'd like to tell you I'm a hero, but after eating shit for so many years, the best I can guarantee is that I'll do it again, as long as I can order the wine.

These are bizarre times. The culture we live in has become such an insatiable virus it even devours itself. And this is no metaphor for the condition our condition is in; the woods are full of *infomaniacs* spouting meaningless statistics to prove one pointless point of view or another. Information, which was once thought to be our salvation, has turned into the enemy, unnecessarily trashing even the most nubile minds at the most critical moments in *the history of the growth of history*. In short, we're lost in the program, trying to find the key to unlock the door to a knowledge that will provide us with the *crazy wisdom* to get out of the shit storm we've rained down on ourselves, and make the transformation to the next level of growth. Where or what that will be no one who isn't totally full of shit can say right now, though I figure it's safe to say *technology*, for all practical intents and purposes, has completely trashed *ideology*. And until we see where the former is leading us, it's safe to assume the latter has turned belly up, just satisfied it's got a ticket in line to suck hind tit.

Not that it matters to me one way or the other what happens in the future. Or for that matter, what happened in the past. I was never one of those guys that lived for tomorrow or pissed and moaned about *the good old days*. When you get right down to it, unless you're on top of the game there's not much difference between *the good old days* and *the bad old days*, except for recapturing the sunshine or shitstorm of your precious youth. In my case I could barely remember which was which.

It was all like looking at the dream through a glass eye, to me. There had been a war to fight again somewhere back there in the beginning, so there was alienation from the powers-that-be, which led into a lifetime ride through the alternative hills and valleys of fringe weirdness; a trip that demanded a concentrated meditation in order to understand the addiction to a process of trying to make some sort of sense of a generation's spent youth. Which ultimately was like an emotional cripple trying to pay off a psychiatric loan he thought was a scholarship. What came out of this folly was a cryptic little book of schizoid but didactic tales, which were mistaken for genuine gospel by the *blinder than thou* set.

To paraphrase Clint, *it made my career*. It didn't make much of one, mind you, but it was enough for me to say, *hey mom, hey dad*, I was wrong, not only did I live long enough to reach 30, but now that I finally can't be trusted like the rest of the so-called *adolts*, they're actually paying me to jerk-off. Writing additional dialogue for the mavens of Development Hell is like working for the Pentagon building wings for bombers that no longer exist, but still have budget dollars left over that have to be spent. I'm not proud of what I do, but if they have to give discretionary money away to somebody, why not to the immortal wise guy who first asked, "Who do I have to blow around here to find out who I have to blow around here?"

To negate that negation (as the screenwriting gu-gus like to put things in perspective out here), before I pried myself free from my little New York rat hole I heard the novelist Gerald Green tell a story at a Writers Guild symposium about the major monster of his day, Harry Cohn. At the time Green, who could've been the model for *Barton Fink*, had just sold a novel, and been flown out to Hollywood to meet the mogul. He was picked up at the airport, rushed to the studio, and ushered into the mogul's office and immediately embraced by *Dirty Harry* himself, who stepped back, smiled, and said to him, "My boy, my boy, I actually cried real tears, real tears when my secretary read me the synopsis of your novel."

To make a long *Horatio Alger* a short one, the infamous *Glitz brothers* sent me a round trip ticket, and for awhile I was the new young hot one that's always being thrown up against the wall to see if he sticks around. My agent Howard (the duck) Lipshitz had had the manuscript of my book sitting on his desk for close to a year. It had been given to him by my editor, whose brother was Howard's lawyer, and had recommended that he take me on as a client even before the buzz started on the book. Howard, who's motto was "I read everything I sell," unfortunately, hadn't been able to read the book, even though he knew three months in advance that I'd be in town on this preordained day. Of course he could've given it to his reader, but he couldn't give it to his reader, he explained, as he looked around at the wall to wall piles of manuscripts stacked from the floor, 12 feet up to the ceiling, surrounding my chair on three sides. I noticed the only place there were no manuscripts was in back of his desk, where there was a window that dropped six floors down to the Beverly Center's parking lot. I suddenly imagined Howard hyperventilating, which wasn't difficult to do, because as he explained to me that he had found out his reader was filing false reports, he started gasping for breath. He stood up, turned and faced the window -- for a moment I imagined he was going to jump. Later, he confessed he did too. But it was merely *transcendental hyperventialtion*, a malady I've learned is much like momentary rapture of the deep, and has recently become the new *Epstein-Barr Syndrome* of the *infotainment* industry.

When Howard turned around he was crying. His reader, he confessed to me, was telling him that scripts submitted to him were no good, then taking them to a studio on his own, and claiming he was the agent. From what he said, it was happening all over town. Ambitious young sharks were cutting the legs out from under their mentors, and there wasn't a damn thing anybody could do about it other than take six months off, and hope the *dyslogia* cleared up and they had enough to hold them over until they could begin focusing on the page again. Either that or hope there was enough flour left over in the barrel to open a *Burger Chump* franchise. Because once you're out of *the biz*, you're out of *the biz*.

Ask anyone trying to beat the cost of postage down that long winding hall to Development Hell, and what you see is not a pretty picture. And like the news of the day, it never ends either. As they say, *deals go down where even chumps fear to tread.* . . then the phone rings, and the overnight sensation who used to be you wakes up 10 years later and for the second time realizes you not only didn't die before you were 30, but didn't die before you were 40 either, like all those *live fast, die young* heroes you always thought you were one of.

The shock of finding out there's no tragic out comes the morning you wake up 10, or in my case 12 years later (two years after I figured out I was living in Dylan's *The Ballad of a Thin Man*), and realized I wasn't even doing what I always thought I was doing. Which in my case was writing some sort of real life experience down after it happened and figuring out what it was. The reality was I didn't have a *real life*. And if I did, it didn't matter what it was. *They* didn't care what it was. Or what I thought it was. *They* cared about caricatures of so-called good guys and bad guys, cool assed cops and bad assed wops and trendsuckers and pig fuckers and psychotic monsters with chain saws and teenagers getting laid by harmless but derivative looking aliens or just plain killers from outer space on a bloody Saturday night binge.

Which was a lucky think for me. I could always come up with weird shit like that, especially if I didn't have to live through it myself. *Sure, we'll send the kid into the jaws of the elusive snapping pussy of yonder yore. Why not? Let's see him get out of this one alive.*

So for 10 years, I not only made my nut by putting heat and meat and juice in somebody else's flat, lame, empty imitation formula script, but somehow managed to be invited to play in every game on the circuit, from tennis to flag ball to round ball to soft ball to celebrity wiffle ball to bridge to backgammon to craps to gin to ping pong to wild card poker, featuring all those old favorites like, Mr. & Mrs. Acey-Ducey, Night Baseball, Indian poker, and the killer of killers, *Two Card Rosen* itself, which was how I won the most valuable possession in my life: a pair of prime Magic *Laker* season tickets from two shit blind speed freak soft core porno producers, whose major goal in life was to make an erotic remake of *The Sound of Music*, with Madonna in the Julie Andrews role.

This little *Rosen* got me the seat of seats next to the swine of swines, *Mr. Deal* himself, Avery *(Fast Guns)* Cosata, who gave me that once in a lifetime opportunity to crash through the closed doors of *The Club* itself, merely on the strength of writing the highest grossing gross out of all time for him, the one and only immortal *Pig Meat*.

Showtime at The Forum, of course, brought us together. The rest as they say was history, Hollywood history, folks. From an unknown Script Doctor to the A-List in less than a year, which is something that probably couldn't have happened in MoTown, Big D, Houston or the Meadowlands. Probably not even The Apple, where people are too suspicious of worms to invite you inside their domiciles, sometimes even if you live there with them.

Cosata, though originally from Brooklyn, was way past that kind of Woody Allen neurosis. And though he carried his share of New York guilt around with him, at least he wasn't guilty about being guilty. Money can buy an awful lot of things, and this town is probably the home of every new kind of radical therapy that's been invented since Freud missed the train for catharsis, after arriving at the depot six hours before his so-called trip to that elusive vacation from his own brain. Something that would never happen to *Mr. Deal*. He may have had to act out being a major scumbag all day long to get to the top of the heap he was climbing, but he was smart enough not to bring the role home with him. I met his built-in consciousness insurance policy the day after I signed the Contract to write *Pig Meat* for him. She was a gorgeous six foot two inch two hundred plus pound Afro-German body builder who answered to the name Ms. Ingrid Lock, if you had the guts to address her.

I didn't, since the minute we walked in the house she lifted "The Boss" up by the back of the neck like he was a sick kitten, threw him over her lap, pulled down his pants and then proceeded to spank his bare bottom until he cried and begged for mercy. That done, he pulled his pants back up, and led me into the Rec Room, where now completely relaxed from the day's tensions, he racked up the balls for a game of snooker. This, he assured me, was his daily routine; how he beat the pressure, how he avoided ulcers, how he achieved *satori* without the benefit of checking into a monastery, and how he was able to get up refreshed, clean and invigorated every morning, and go back out into the jungle as the most ruthless, vicious, backstabbing lowlife in Beverly Hills. He smiled at me expectantly, like he had just given me the secret of life.

"Thank you for sharing that with me," I strained a smile back, praying his check wouldn't bounce. So if we're talking testimonials and I'm ever called up in front of *The Academy* to receive an award for the slickest shlock or something, I probably won't make it, so I'd like to take the opportunity now to thank my benefactors. And as long I'm at it, I'd also like to thank my allergy.

If I wasn't allergic to toot, folks, if I didn't blow it all over the table everytime I tried to suck it up my nose, they'd still be offering it to me through a sawbuck instead of threatening to shove my brain, like thigh cheese, through the hole in a genuine New York bagel. And I would not be standing here before you today urging you to just say NO!

Say NO! Yes, NO! Right, NO! Yo, NO! Just NO!

Of course that NO was before the word got out that I was not only writing, but would be directing *The Revenge of Pig Meat's Revenge*. I was no longer *the asshole*, I was *the asshole in charge of the money, baby*. But by then it was too late to do them or me any good either. I'd already met Maggie Rector and was no longer a free agent.

If we do choose our own futures, as the New Age bimmies proselytize, what I always used to ask for was: *Please bring me back as Magic Johnson*. Though it seems more than a little dubious knowing what we know now, it was exactly what I was thinking the moment I first laid eyes on Maggie. It was *Showtime* at The Forum, folks, and though that act seems a millions miles away from everything but the highlights in my brain now, it seems like it was only yesterday that Magic and Sir James were in high gear swooping down the court like the *Blue Angels* on a two on *Bird* fastbreak when she comes sliding down the row and just at the strategic moment Magic makes his sleight of hand pass moves in front of my line of vision.

"Fuck!" I exploded, leaping out of my seat like Worthy elevating to the hoop.

She whirled on me, her baby blues blazing incredulously. "What?"

"Shit!" I snapped, as Bird hit the floor and went sliding into the photographers under the basket.

Right in my face she glowered, "What did you say?"

"You're in my fucking way!" I was looking directly into those eyes, getting sucked deep into a pool that wasn't the normal shallow vat of Valley *nada* they put in the backyards out here, but still couldn't stop myself from exploding again. "Get out of the fucking way!" As I said it I had the overwhelming desire to pull the words back into my mouth and stuff them down my throat and send them on a one way ticket down the shoot and out the back door. But it was too late.

The whistle blew. Larry *the fucking Legend* had drawn the charge on Worthy!

"I beg your pardon!"

"You're blocking my vision," I said with all the control I could muster.

She smiled politely, looked me straight in the eyes, then lilted the words, "Hollywood scum," and gracefully floated down the row to the aisle, went down to the first row, and sat down next to of all people, *Jack fucking Movie Star* himself!

"Good move," *Mr. Deal* lisped. "You just insulted Maggie Rector.

"Who?"

"Maggie Rector," Cosata laughed. "The hottest new director in town. Ever hear of *The Rivington School?*"

"That was great! She did that?"

"And *Little Lambs Eat Ivy.*"

"That too? Oh fuck!"

"Don't worry about it, Nickie, she be nothing but an over priced appetizer. One of those little birds that James Beard used to eat, beak and all, on the coast of France."

"What's she doing out here?"

"Selling her ass, Nickie, just like everyone else."

"That doesn't seem to be her style."

"You don't think so?"

"She doesn't look the type."

"That's what I like about you, Nickie, you're the last Romantic in Bimbowood."

"All you gotta do is look and you'll see she's serious, she's for real!"

"You're such a titsucker. What if I tell you she interviewed for your job?"

"My job?"

"To direct *The Revenge of Pig Meat's Revenge.*"

"Bullshit!"

"No, not bullshit. Real shit!"

"You're either a liar or a fool, Cosata! If you had the chance to hire a real director to direct this piece of shit, why'd you hire me? Because I was a cheap trick?"

"Nickie, Nickie, you have such low self esteem. You have to be more positive about yourself. This is your big break."

"Yeah, well I hope it's not in my neck."

"Funny boy."

"It *was* the money, wasn't it, Cosata?"

"Naw," he shakes his head. "Believe it or not, no matter how bad an agent you think Howard the Duck is, he's a real killer from outer space. I could'a actually had her cheaper than you. A lot cheaper than you! But she wouldn't blow me."

"*Touché*"

"Yeah, *touché. . .*"

The next time I saw her, only a week later, was at *The Racquet Club*, in Venice. She had the court before me, and was in a match point, sudden death that refused to die, cutting 15 minutes into my hour. When she finally came off the court she nodded coldly at me, and said insincerely, "Sorry. Again."

"It's ok," I said. "I love women who sweat." She gave me that look, that look that would become the famous Maggie *eat shit and die* look, and brushed past me. I had to admit, I liked the way she moved, though she wasn't my usual type. No starlet bazookas or round swishing mound of rebound on her backboard. Broad shoulders, solid designated hitter frame. And her face, though it must have been beautiful when she was younger, was chiseled now, you know, more handsome than beautiful, the kind of face you wouldn't mind being in a foxhole with, or up on the Matterhorn, out on the trail, a strong face, a face you could count on in deep shit because you knew it wouldn't take any shit, but like I say, she wasn't in my program as dream girl. She had the angles of a free safety, not soft curves you could lean into going around the track, definitely no MM job by anybody's long shot, though she ran some subtle streaks though her thick dirty blonde hair. And we were basically the same height, give or take an inch, depending on who was curved over the keyboard longer on a given day. The little bearded ones who run the numbers down out here, would go for her because they have a thing for the tall ones, the zons, the mommy figures who at any given point can tell them what to do, but in the meantime know how to keep their traps shut until it's time to hit the sheets, but that wasn't my trip.

Though I'm certainly no Redford, I don't exactly pass for kosher at first glance either. I mean, I've been an outsider all my life, even when I've hung with the outsiders. I don't know why. As Joseph Campbell might have put it if he had lived out here, it was some kind of personal myth imprinted from birth that I had to live down to. It's sort of like, you're given certain things, certain gifts when you come into this world, and in my case, those gifts embarrassed me. So I turned against them. I didn't want to be cute, which is what I was; I was cute. Even now, for a wild old dog, which is what my puppy wanted to be when it grew up, I was still too cute for my own good, which basically, if you can grasp the contradiction, was all that was keeping me alive. Though I didn't know that at the time. My hubris was sure it was my talent.

So it wasn't until the next time, that lucky, charmed third time, that Maggie saw through those dichotomies, and decided I was not only cute, but maybe worth saving from myself because I was. I was waiting for the court again, and she of course was sweating again, the veins on the back of her hands and arms standing out almost like Navratilova's, when her opponent, a young shark from CAA, went down with a twisted fin. As they say, I picked my spot, baby. Volunteered to fill up her hour. Bopped out on the court, even introduced myself.

"I know who you are," she said.

"You do?"

She looked right through me then. Laughed. "You think you're in the game, but I don't think you've ever played before."

"Oh yeah!"

"I'm not even sure you understand what the deal is."

We went at each other then. Long and hard, with no time for me to admire the scenery. This was definitely a woman who had come to grips with hating her father. She spun the racquet on the palm of her hand. It was no big thing. There are givens and there are givens. That was one she had already worked out. She played the game like a man, but never forgot how to use her givens.

"Game point," she glared, giving me a *FREEZE FRAME of the best of Maggie's legs*, and damn if I suddenly wasn't running it up the old flagpole.

She noticed of course. "Is that for me or do you just want to play with the dog?" Triumphantly her lips involuntarily spread across her ego, then she whirled and served.

In slow motion now: *I spin and then spin again and again following the flight of the ball from the side wall to the back wall to the side wall, and then throw my body into the rhythm and hit what I think is a perfect kill in the corner as I bounce off the wall to the floor, and watch belly down as she waits in perfect position to get just enough racquet on the ball to squib it home on the range.*

"It's like this," she explained later, over ice coffee outside the *Rose Cafe*, "I knew what it was going to be like when I left New York and came out here, and I said, Maggie Jean, you are either the horse or you are the rider. It's your choice whether you let the Beast's energy ride you or you ride the energy. I choose to be the rider."

After making it that first time high in the hills overlooking the great illusion I'd turned into my own love-hate dichotomy, I asked, "Am I supposed to be the horse?"

She didn't laugh. "This isn't a joke! Feel flattered. I didn't choose to fuck anyone to get what I want, I chose to fuck someone because I wanted to fuck them. Fucking a writer has absolutely no utilitarian value to me. You're totally useless. This is pure lust."

"Hey!"

"Hey!" she repeated, then swung back up in the saddle, and we did it again; Then even though it was overtime for Old Glory, one more time. Then forgot about foreplay and got into postplay, and I figured, *hey, maybe this is different. Maybe this is the real deal?*

It seemed like we could actually talk *to* instead of *at* each other, both before, after, and sometimes even in the middle without forgetting who we had come to the prom with. And though I can't remember the conversation -- just the grunts and groans, the *oohs & ahhs*, and guttural cries out of the night keeping chorus with the coyotes, wild cats and other creatures of the hills -- as we rubbed, stroked, squeezed, scratched, kissed, licked, bit and buried ourselves so far inside each other I couldn't tell whether I was me or I was her or this was a script I was writing inside my head that was just too personal to ever reach the big screen. Hard to explain, but it felt like a dream without an ending, just a sea, floating on a sea of new born innocence lost somewhere in time until basically a lifetime of cynicism was bathed in a glowing ethereal womb of *false* security. I knew the security was *false*, so obviously the cynicism went too deep to be dissolved in one fell swoop, but there were holes too, dreamless pockets of innocence I fell into where I neither had to be or choose not to be. Truly an *incredible* sleep. The best sleep I'd had in 20 years. It was almost like being back down in Memphis again. Almost like being 15 and innocent again, looking west, out across the muddy Mississippi and realizing for the first time the fucking ship you wait for your whole life would come in when you quit waiting.

Easier said than done of course. Every time that perfect zen balance ever occurred in my life it was always an affirmation of a practice I wasn't practicing, but knew if I wanted that balance as a constant I had to consciously surrender to it and let go of plotting the parlay.

That's what it was like meeting Maggie, though not for a minute did I think she was going to be the answer to a question I hadn't even formed yet. Just maybe another addiction, another sweet addiction in a long line of addictions.

Finally, 12 hours later, I broke. "Say something profound," I said, as I buried my face in her hair.

"If you can make decent Marinara sauce I think I'll keep you."

"Yeah?"

"Yeah." She pulled my head around to face her, and chewed on my lower lip. "As long as we're at it, I might as well ask for Salsa Verde too."

"You're eclectic."

"I know what I like."

"Do I have a choice in this?"

"Not if you can't cover the sauces. If you can, you've got free will."

"I don't even have the illusion of free will anymore, I'm a mercenary."

"That's generic out here for whore. I had hoped the man who wrote *I Love You But I Hate Your Life* could do better than that."

"You read that? You actually read that? Nobody but my mother read that, and she hated it!"

"You don't think I'd be wasting my time with the hack who wrote *Pig Meat* do you?"

"Well. . ."

"I actually liked *False Beginnings* better than *I Love You But I Hate Your Life*. It wasn't so precious, so, pardon the expression, *Salingeresque*."

"What would Holden Caufield do now if he realized his voice was being copped by every under-35 male and female lit light who wants to get in *The New Yorker*?"

"If he was too old to get it up again?"

I looked down at my wilted manhood, and for the first time in my life, felt like I was happy. "Yeah."

"He'd eat me, darling, then pray for rain."

After we finished making love again, Maggie rolled over, pulled an old script out of the bookcase over the bed, and two hours later woke me, because, my dears, I had created "a masterpiece" that had to be made!

I, of course, didn't have to make it. I didn't have to make anything except my nut, which had grown to the size of Brazil. When I wrote the script 10 years earlier it had been an honorable undisguised blatant rip-off of Kurosawa's *The Seven Samurai*, a film that had already been ripped off so many times that my major concern was getting sued for plagiarism by the original rippers. Originally set in a Space Colony in the year 007 of the New Calendar, in the next draft it got moved to Australia at the turn of the last century in order to capitalize on the Aussie tax break. But the Producer's wife left him, and there was something about the director going to Switzerland for the sleep cure. I forgot it for four years, and then a Yugoslavian who had just come back from Tibet said he was looking for a Tibetan script to pitch Richard Gere, so I went back into the computer and changed the names and locations, nothing else, but it was around the time the gerbil hoax was being faxed all over the world, so the Yugoslavian either went to work for *Disney* or ran away with the Australian producer's wife to Borneo, and it went back on the shelf until BINGO, three years later Maggie plucks it out of obscurity and spoils my latest illusion of true love by trying to beat me out of a free option.

The negotiations had begun.

Notes from the Los Angeles Underbelly

Thomas Fuchs

Cash Out

2002

//

Having spent much of his adult life writing and producing documentary
television, Fuchs has learned that there's nothing inhuman about evil, an
idea he's been trying to explore in fiction.

Satan, with that uncanny ability of his to be magisterial even as he is plunged into a frenzy of activity, had found yet another opportunity to tempt one of that herd of God's favorites - humanity - into error and sin.

"Don't take what isn't yours" is such a simple and useful piece of advice, and yet...

On this particular occasion, the Devil began his mischief by creating a bank error, a "mistaken deposit" of $50,000 in the account of a man named Roy Olson, whose actual wealth was more on the order of fifty dollars.

Roy didn't give a moment's thought to the morality of it. Who would? Particularly when money means the difference between life and death (or at least, a bad beating) as it did to Roy at that moment in his life. He owed money to his bookie; one of the bookie's hulking employees had only recently knocked Roy down and promised to return and do permanent damage unless payment was forthcoming.

An electric thrill went through Roy when he discovered the astonishing condition of his bank account as reported by the ATM. At last, a break in his luck, and what a break! He'd heard of things like this happening. His heart was pounding and his hand actually shook a little as he dipped into his newly acquired $50,000. How much do these machines hold anyway? He decided to ask for a mere thousand and was deeply frustrated to learn the machine would dispense no more than three hundred a day from any one account. Some sort of fraud protection. Hmmm... Roy wasn't a particularly clever fellow -- he knew that much about himself -- but he knew someone who was very smart, and for some time now he'd been looking for an excuse to see her. Now he had it. He went to see Lydia.

Lydia ran the office for her Uncle Buddy at his body shop, a place where in fact all kinds of work was done. Buddy was genuinely concerned about Lydia's well being and believed it was one of her smarter moves when she broke things off with Roy, clearly the kind of guy who, when he did go down for the third time, as he certainly would, would drag anyone attached to him into that final, fatal spiral. So, when Roy appeared, Buddy blocked his way with his body and various smart remarks such as, "Let me guess, you've got a sure fire way to double your money, only someone has to lend you some money to double" and "I know, the winning numbers for the Lottery came to you in a dream". This was an exaggeration of Roy's past appeals, but only an exaggeration. Roy had squandered money on a variety of disastrous schemes which had succeeded in swindling almost no one and cost him and Lydia more than one stake, such as the on-line time share, but that's another story.

Nevertheless, Lydia had had fun with Roy before things had crashed; he had all kinds of ways of pleasing her. If she hadn't been committed to eating on a regular basis and enjoying some of the other God-given rights, she might have stayed with him. So she was willing to hear him out. And he did have that transaction slip from the ATM that showed - sure enough, there it was! - a credit balance of $50,062.32. Lydia actually shook her head to clear her eyes. It had been so long since she'd seen any commas in a bank balance. She was cautious about allowing herself to believe something good had come their way at last, but there it was.

Now, not to screw it up. Not to let Roy screw it up.

"How," she finally asked, "how are you planning to get the money since the ATM won't let you take more than three hundred a day?"

"Tomorrow morning, the bank opens, I'm there with my checkbook," said Roy.

"Do you really think they're going to just hand over that much money to someone like you without checking very carefully? I don't think so."

Lydia's earlier experiences with Roy and other like-minded dreamers of easy money had taught her to be ruthless in her assessments and brutal in expressing them.

At one time, Roy, desperate to maintain his relationship with Lydia, had shoplifted and then actually read a book on relationships, so he was able to say, "You have a low esteem for me, Lydia. That's always been our problem."

Lydia hadn't read the book. "I used to have hopes for you," was all she said for a few moments. But the wheels were turning. Then she said, "You know what we could try? Cash a check for, say, five hundred. That might not set off any bells."

"Five hundred?" Roy was disappointed. Five hundred, when there was over fifty thousand just sitting there?

This was only the first step in Lydia's plan, the plan that was slowly forming in her mind, a plan that still had many possible outcomes, most of which she could not foresee. Along with that first check to Cash, Roy should also write one to her for a like amount. "Write one to me for, say, three or four hundred. Small bites. Then we'll go to another branch and try it again. Take what we can."

It was a plan, and it meant that Roy and Lydia would be together again, and that was more than fine with Roy And with Satan, who was of course monitoring the situation. Satan smiled with what might well have been mistaken for benevolence when Lydia allowed Roy to spend the night with her.

The next morning, Roy approached the teller's window with his check made out to "Cash" for $500. He hadn't written a check that size for... well, quite some time, at least not one that he would have dared present in person. The Teller checked his account... and then said to him, "How would you like that?"

"Huh?" said Roy.

"How would you like that? Hundreds?"

Roy nodded, not daring to speak. Five one hundred dollar bills. And while all this was going on, Lydia was at another window cashing her check, made out to her by Roy against the fifty thousand. Everything went much as it had for Roy, except that Lydia didn't say, "Huh".

Back in Roy's car, in the parking lot, there was a moment when Roy thought Lydia was reluctant to hand over the cash she'd collected. She reminded him that some of what he had borrowed from her in the past had really come from Buddy, and she wanted to pay him back. But she gave Roy the money after he told her what the bookie had in store for him. And she didn't want to fight with him, because they had other branches to go to. She'd even picked up a brochure which listed all the other local branches.

Another branch, another couple of checks cashed. And another and another. Sometimes, things do go your way. And they really were accomplishing all this on their own. Satan didn't have to do a thing to assist them. Of course, the bank would want its money back but that was a minor problem in light of the benefit of paying off the bookie. The bank, as Roy pointed out, wouldn't rip his lungs out or anything like that.

Roy was close, getting closer - he owed his violence-prone creditor just ten thousand, even with the accumulated charges - and then he had it and a chunk more, a total of nearly eleven thousand. He could pay the bookie. He was free.

Lydia didn't see it that way. She didn't want to give all that money to some bookie. She wasn't the one who bet on games. Why should she have to give any of it up?

Of course, she didn't put it quite this way to Roy. She did suggest that this windfall could mean the resumption of a plan they had once had, it seemed so long ago, that somehow they could have a life together.

Tempted though he was, deeply tempted, Roy had enough sense of animal self survival to realize that the first order of business was to pay off the bookie. Anything else they collected, that could be put toward this new life. And so, on they went. They stopped at banks in Hollywood, downtown LA, Glendale. Pasadena was next. Pasadena was where things went awry.

"There's an activity alert on the account." A Teller at the Pasadena branch told them this, and then a Supervisor. It seemed the bank's computer had a template which spotted patterns like this. And once the account was frozen, it couldn't be unfrozen until someone had looked into the matter and that wouldn't happen until that evening at the earliest. Lydia took over and was charming - she didn't think seductive would be relevant with this particular Supervisor even though he was a man - but to no avail. The account was frozen pending a routine check, and that would certainly lead to discovery of the original mistaken deposit.

Once again, Lydia resumed her campaign for Roy not to give the money to the bookie, and once again Roy resisted. She suggested they leave town.

"And go where?" asked Roy.

"You have family in Philadelphia."

"You wouldn't like Philly". He had lots of reasons not to want to go back to Philadelphia. To tell them all would have meant making bad jokes about how it isn't really the City of Brotherly Love.

"Some place else then. Florida or some place like that."

"Florida? Where in Florida? Who do we know there? What would we do?"

And so it went between them, Roy anxious to get the bookie off his back and Lydia determined they - well, perhaps she was thinking more of just herself - keep it.

And then Roy had his brainstorm. After all, they were already on their way. They'd been drifting east and north. If they just kept going, in a few hours they'd be in Las Vegas.

Las Vegas!

Roy promised to be responsible. His idea of being responsible was to put aside the money he owed the bookie, not to gamble with that and to bet only with the excess, nearly a thousand. He might run that up to… up to.. ten thousand. It happened all the time.

Lydia almost gave up right then and there. If Roy had the self restraint to bet only the money he could afford to lose (what an odd concept, she thought, one of a slew of thoughts racing through her mind), then he wouldn't be in a jam. And yes, running a thousand up to ten thousand… well, sure it happened all the time. That's why there were so many rich gamblers and poverty stricken hotels on the Strip. But she said nothing, knew there was no point in arguing with him, this idiot, this fool sitting there with more money than he'd had his hands on in a long time or was likely to ever have again. Oh, wait a minute, she thought.

Lydia was silent. Roy was hopeful, always hopeful.

And then she spoke. She said, "Las Vegas. Why not?"

Roy, mistakenly believing the way was now open to a wondrous future, could hardly believe his ears. "You're not mad at me?" he asked.

"No," she said, "I'm not mad." But she did want to eat something before they headed out. Could they stop at a coffee shop? After they ordered, she left the booth as though going to the bathroom, but what she really did was call Uncle Buddy. She told Buddy the amazing story and when she got to the part about going to Vegas, he started keening like an old man, "No, no, no" he wailed. She waited until he had finished with his lamentations, then she explained what she wanted, why she was calling. As things stood, there was no way Roy was going to hold on to the money, He'd lose it all in Vegas or give it to the bookie and of course sooner or later the bank would be on him. The only thing to do, she'd figured out, was to take it from him *before he got to the tables*.

Buddy was surprised but not astonished. "Are you suggesting what I think you are?"

She was. "You know people who do this kind of thing," she said.

"Are you sure you want to do this?"

"Yes. It's the cash, Uncle Bud. All that cash."

The details were quickly arranged. It would take maybe a couple of hours to get someone to Vegas from L.A. Buddy would call her when his man was in place. In the meantime, they both agreed, Lydia would do her best to keep Roy out of the casinos. That, thought Satan, should be about as easy as keeping flies from sugar. Satan was enjoying this more and more.

At the craps table where Lydia found herself all too soon, Roy was having a real run of luck, good luck for a change. You could probably train a pigeon to play craps and certainly a chimp could master the game, but with all those numbers and all those chips laid out, things look complicated and Roy was impressive as he made his bets on the Pass line and then backed them up "behind the line" as he explained to Lydia and laid money out on the Come line and then backed up those bets... And he kept winning. Lydia needed to stay with him, to find some opportunity to get him away before he started losing, but she also needed to call Uncle Buddy and make sure the plan was underway.

Buddy told her that a guy named Vincent was in Vegas now and where was she?

"Bally's"

"Do you have a room there?"

"Yeah."

"You got to get Roy up to the room. When you do, call Vincent on his cell." The plan was for Vincent to knock on the door, for Lydia to let him in. He'd show them a gun, tie them both up, take Roy's money.

"Tie us up?"

"He's got to do both of you, so Roy doesn't figure out you're behind it,"

"He's going to have a gun?"

"Vincent's a very steady guy. Peaceful guy. Roy doesn't carry a gun, does he?"

"No. Buddy, you know, I don't want Roy to get hurt."

"It'll be all right. If Roy had a gun it could get dangerous. He doesn't?"

"No."

"Okay, then, but you got to get him up to the room."

Lydia hurried back to the table, where Roy was, incredibly, still winning. When she suggested he take a break so they could treat themselves to a self-indulgent feast (via room service, of course), Roy said he couldn't possibly quit while he was on a winning streak. As long as he was winning, he wasn't budging from that table. And of course, as long as he stayed at the table, he couldn't be held up and his money taken and, in a way, saved.

Then he rolled a 7. His face fell. All the chips he had out, all his bets -the Stickman took them all.

"I thought seven was good," said Lydia.

"On the come out," said Roy bitterly. "When you're trying to make your point, seven is craps."

Oh. Whatever. Oh, well. Then Lydia got as bright as she could and said, "Maybe it's a sign you ought to take a break.

Roy did need to piss. They'll bring you drinks and sandwiches when you're at the tables, why not hook up a catheter or something? Maybe he could sell that idea to the casinos. Naw, probably not. He did agree to take a break and have coffee with Lydia. In the coffee shop. He wouldn't go up to the room. He had work to do.

"I have to get even," he said, as they waited for their coffee and pie.

"Even? How much have you lost?"

"Hmmm," said Roy. He fingered the chips in his pocket. He had a system - fives in one pocket, tens in another, quarters in… well, that pocket was empty, and a small fistful of shiny black hundreds. "Ummm. Six thousand plus… "

"You had eleven."

"Craps moves fast. I was up to twenty at one point."

"Six thousand. You had nearly eleven and now you have six? I thought you weren't going to risk any of the money you needed for the bookie."

"I'm not through yet."

"Great."

"There are battles to be fought and won, my Lady fair. I'm off." With that brand of reckless gallantry peculiar to the addict slamming his head against a wall, Roy lurched to his feet and headed back to the action. But he was determined to pace himself, to go a little slower this time, so he took a seat at roulette, where the action isn't nearly as fast as craps.

Lydia was lingering over her second rum and coke, trying to keep from chasing after Roy and cold cocking him with whatever she could lay her hands on and dragging him off, when a man who seemed as broad as he was tall approached with surprising gentleness. "Excuse me," he said. "Sorry to interrupt your thoughts… Do you happen to know Buddy?"

"He's my Uncle. You're…"

"I'm Vincent."

"Well, that's half the plan in place."

"Yeah. What's your room number?"

"Fifteen forty."

"Where's the guy?"

"In the casino. At the tables."

"You gotta get him up to the room."

"I know that."

"Then you call me and I come up. But you guys have to be there. He's gambling?"

"Yes."

"How's he doing?"

Lydia's grimace said it all.

"You gotta get him up to the room."

"I know, I know," said Lydia. "You know not to hurt him?"

Vincent nodded. He looked like he could handle Roy even without a gun, if Roy was dumb enough to take him on. And he did, after all, have a gun. But none of that would matter if Roy lost the rest of the money before he came up to the room to be robbed.

So Lydia set out to find Roy somewhere in the racket and bright light and forced smiles of the casino. Hope surged within her when she couldn't find him at any of the crap tables. Maybe he'd stopped, was looking for her in the coffee shop right now, or was on his way up to the room. And then she saw him sitting at the high stakes roulette wheel.

There was an empty seat next to him, She slipped into it, and as he played she said things to him about how this adventure had made her believe in him again, she was willing to try again for the life of quick money and daring, and how she wanted nothing more right now than to take him up to their room and fuck him for hours.

"Thirty two, Red," droned the croupier.

"I'm on that, Lydia!" Thirty two, straight up!"

The croupier pushed a small stack of high denomination plaques to Roy and as he was about to spin the wheel again, Lydia sensed a presence behind her, a player. More accurately a would-be player who wanted a seat at the table.

The croupier did his job, politely but very succinctly explaining to Lydia that she was welcome at the table if she played. Otherwise, would she please…

"I'm on my way back up," said Roy. He didn't mean to the room.

Disgusted with him and with her failure, Lydia relented, left the casino, went up to the room, turned on the television. Time passed. At the roulette table, the numbers began going against Roy and slowly but steadily the House edge began to tell against his pile of chips. He was tired. This was a stupid game. He decided to take a break, wound up at one of those small open bars right on the floor with the video poker machines built into the counter top, where he had one of those encounters which Satan finds so exquisitely ironic. He sat down next to Vincent, the man whose fate was so entwined with his, although neither knew it at the time. Each thought the other was just a gambler hoping for a turn in his luck, which, come to think of it, they both were.

Vincent, a perfectly agreeable guy when he wasn't putting on a face to do a job for Uncle Buddy, said to this man he did not know,

"How's it going."

"Up and down," said Roy.

"Maybe you ought to knock off." Vincent said this from a genuine concern, not because he knew who Roy was.

"People keep telling me that," said Roy, "but I've got work to do."

They both drank for a while in silence and then Roy was ready to return to the great contest. Vincent wished him good luck and Roy returned the good wish. Of course, there was no way they could both have good luck. Satan savored this encounter like an old man enjoying a sip of even older Port.

In their room, Lydia stirred from sleep and then woke as Roy entered. It was very late. It got abruptly later when Roy asked her if she had any money. Shock, confusion, despair. Anger. Yes, he was busted out, flat broke. Yes, he'd started with eleven thousand dollars (of which he had sworn to risk only one thousand) and it was all gone.

"But I know my luck's gonna turn."

Lydia actually, for a moment, tried to explain to Roy that... that... that for once in her life she had been close to a nice fat score and this... this.. oh, what was the point of trying to explain?

Again, Roy asked for whatever she had, a few hundred, something. He needed it so badly. The bookie might very well kill him if he didn't pay him when they returned to L.A., and the only way he had a chance of making any money was to bet, and to bet he needed...

Lydia threw the money at him, threw it on the floor and said something about how he was a loser and she was a loser for being mixed up with the likes of him and now she was giving up all hope of ever having anything worthwhile.

Quite possibly for the first time in his adult life, Roy felt a cold tide of shame sweep through him. Until then, he'd been afraid of being caught at this or that, but guilt was always a matter of definition and who was doing the defining; petty crime and swindling were games; gambling was heroic, a matching of his wit and his luck against the mysterious forces of the universe.

Now, the way it's supposed to happen in the lives of mystics and visionaries, he suddenly saw things altogether differently. He realized he had the power to make another human being happy, and he wanted to make Lydia happy. As a matter of immediate survival, he had to save himself but he made her a promise. He promised that if he could just win enough to pay off the bookie - he'd deal with the bank some other way - he would never gamble again. And then he disgusted her and astonished himself by dropping to his knees and praying, right there in Room 1540 of Bally's on the Strip in Las Vegas.

"God, please help me. Get me out of this and I swear to you I'm through with gambling, through with it. Please, God, help me."

"Fat chance, sucker," said Satan to himself. He knew God never helps gamblers.

But gamblers do get lucky and a gambler who has shed his arrogance might just walk away ahead, if it really is his last time at the table, ever.

Lydia had somehow fallen back to sleep and was furious at the pounding at the door. Some drunk trying to get into the wrong room. She almost called Security, then, needing to take out her accumulated rage on someone, went to the door, whipped it open. "What the fuck do you..." she was saying as she saw that it was just idiot Roy. Had he managed to lose the door card along with everything else?

No. He wanted to make this a dramatic moment. He stepped into the room with the strangest look on his face.

"Room service," he said as he closed the door behind him. That look on his face - it was happiness. How odd.

He was carrying a small canvas bag. He pulled a wad of cash out of it and threw the bills into the air. What the hell was going on? And then another bundle and another. Then he started pulling packages of bills out of his jacket, his pants. A magician of moolah. Money fluttering all over the room, like a scene in one of those old black and white comedies with lots of crazy people running around the room and feathers from a pillow and sometimes a duck or a horse or something. Of course, this was no comedy and this moment marked the beginning of the slide down to the final catastrophe.

"You should have been there, Lydia. You should have been there."

He chattered on as they collected up the cash he had thrown around the room like play money but it wasn't play money and as it accumulated back into bundles it emanated that irrefutable authority cash has, an authority unlike any other in the world.

Roy was anxious to get back to L.A. Lydia tried to stall him so she could contact Vincent and get the plan back on track. She suggested they stay for another day, indulge themselves here in Las Vegas in royal style, the style a winner like Roy deserved.

Roy was determined to keep the tragedy on course. No, they would return to L.A., he would repay the bookie and the bank, there was that much and some beyond that, and then he would settle down to something honest, make an honest life for them both. What had be been smoking?

Lydia did manage to get Roy to agree to take a shower, so she could have a few minutes to herself to try to get hold of Vincent.

Vincent's cell phone was ringing... had he gone back to L.A.? In any event, there wasn't time to pull off the hold up in the room. She was thinking this just as Vincent answered. He'd been asleep in a motel, a local motel. Quickly, they worked out the details.

Lydia made sure they dawdled over breakfast, several cups of coffee, and then she said she'd better drive. She told Roy this was because his driving really couldn't be trusted, him having been up all night. That was one reason.

Lydia went to get the car and be sure Vincent was in place while Roy checked them out of the room.

As Roy turned from the check out desk, he felt the pull of the casino right behind him. The hotels are designed that way. There's even a slight slope built into the floor so that if you were to faint at the front desk or one of the entrances, your body would roll into the playing area. And this is only one of a battery of features which can be dangerous for people like Roy. Despite his determination, his promise never to gamble again, he knew he was at risk, so with the cunning of Ulysses, he navigated a circuitous course around the casino's perimeter, until he dared the shortest direct route past the tables and the video poker machines to an island of safety where he could mark and seal his resolution not to gamble ever again. Like the drinker emptying his stash down the sink, he approached the Cashier.

He turned over all the money, all of it, to the Cashier in exchange for a Certified Check. Then back to the main desk and an envelope and a stamp, and he mailed the check to Lydia's address in L.A.

He went outside and found the car waiting with Lydia behind the wheel. Deeply contented with himself and the world, he climbed in next to her, and settled down for a nap.

As Lydia pulled out to begin the trip, she looked in the rear view mirror to be sure that Vincent, in the car he'd rented, was following.

About half an hour outside Vegas, Roy woke and wondered why they weren't on the I-15, the most direct route to L.A.

"It's prettier cutting through Lone Pine," said Lydia.

"Pretty? Okay," said Roy, amused male tolerating the sensibilities of the fairer sex. "Okay, wake me when we get to the pretty part."

So she drove on, taking one side rode and then another off that, Vincent all the time following them.

As Lydia slowed and stopped, Roy woke again. "Now what?"

Lydia said nothing and then out of the cloud of dust which the cars had stirred up appeared Vincent, gun in hand.

"Just stay calm," said Vincent. "This is just a stick up."

Roy remembered Vincent from the conversation at the bar. "I know you."

"No, you don't, but I know you won a lot. So hand it over, okay and everything will be fine. I won't hurt you if you just hand it over."

"I don't have any money."

"Yes, you do."

"No. You can search me. Search the car."

Well, this wasn't in the script. Vincent looked to Lydia for clarification.

Lydia was out of patience with both of these idiots. "Roy, goddamnit, give him the money." It struck Roy that she was irritated, not frightened.

"Lydia," said Roy, "what's going on?"

"Stop fooling around. Give him the money."

"I don't have it."

"How could you lose that much that fast? I didn't leave you alone for more..."

"I didn't lose it."

Vincent was so confused by all this that he lowered his weapon. Was Roy really going to talk his way out of this?

It happened fast. Lydia said, "I'll shoot you myself if you don't come across." She grabbed for Vincent's gun. Instinctively, he pulled it away from her and it went off. Everyone was shocked, as people so often are when guns do exactly what they're designed to do,

Lydia was lying on her side, a spreading red seeping out from just under her left breast. Vincent was babbling about how it was an accident, you saw what happened, it was an accident. Roy, kneeling by Lydia, was shouting at Vincent to call 911. Then, even though he knew she had betrayed him, Roy tried to buoy her, to keep her alive. He told her why he didn't have the money, that he had sent it to her because he didn't trust himself with it. And he had sent it to her, he said, because he wanted to show her how much he loved her and trusted her. And he forgave her and they could still be partners. The only merciful thing that happened to Lydia in those final moments was that she heard little of this as she died.

You might like this to be a story in which Satan is beaten, and some day I will tell you such a story, but this time Satan won. There was nothing accidental about how it all worked out. Roy hadn't been the challenge, there's no triumph in tempting a man whose life depends on getting some money. No, the challenge, the one Satan had been after all along and who could have so easily saved herself from this terrible fate, was Lydia.

Coury Turczyn

Among The Gods

1991

//

Coury Turczyn runs the infrequently updated pop-culture webzine
popcultmag.com. He is also available for assignments.

I'm sitting in the back this time, inhaling a steady diet of cigarette smoke, bathed in the purple light of sin and pounded by a stale disco beat. My table is right up against the stage so I can get a close view, but the dancer isn't very good. She twists her thick body in an absentminded grind, vacantly staring at a wall while squeezing her tits. I sip my warm beer, study her pelvis, and ponder the fact that I can't manage even the slightest erection.

Two chairs down, a drunk in a bad sport coat howls and prepares to launch a crisp dollar bill into the dancer's g-string. She squats down, thrusting her hips out, and lets him rub her mound as he slides in the note. Finally, he drops his face into her crotch, and she locks her legs around his head for a moment before standing up. He screams in ecstasy, pounding the stage with his fists, shaking his head like a dog. I haven't had sex in over a year.

Meanwhile, at the door, the bouncer strokes his goatee and considers admitting a couple of Latino new jacks too cocky to even bother with fake ID's. They slap him a twenty, flash their gold teeth, and strut in to join us, we the deprived. The Monte Carlo gets all types. But the one thing we have in common is that we have nowhere else to go.

Like the others here, I've come seeking help. There is something definitely wrong with me, but I'm not sure which problem to blame first. The psyche is the obvious choice, sun-warped yet wobbly spinning 'round, playing its distorted melodies. Then again, it may simply be a matter of a disconnected synapse or two, rendering me a bile-filled misanthrope unable to communicate with any type of normal human being. Or maybe I'm just really very shy.

My health-it must be the culprit. If only I could feel *good*. My skin feels like wet tissue, torn at a touch, wrapping matchstick bones and jellyfish muscles. My head throbs with a pulse of its own, permanently drumming offbeat. My eyes won't stop burning and the left eyelid has developed a new twitch. Sometimes I think I should start smoking.

The dancer finishes her performance with a final attempt at erotic enthusiasm, jutting out her tongue as she strokes her patchwork thighs. She gives me what I take to be a lust-filled smile, causing a fearful thought: *It's finally happened! A stripper wants me.* Fortunately, she turns and jiggles off the stage before my lack of interest is apparent. The DJ decides to enliven the small crowd.

"YEAH! THAT WAS KASHMERE! SO SOFT, SO SWEEET!

HEY-YOU GUYS HORNY? YOU WANNA GET SOME ASS TONIGHT? THEN GET THE FUCK OUTTA HERE! BUT IF YOU WANNA SEE SOME HOT BODIES, STICK AROUND! 'CAUSE COMIN' UP ISSS… CRYSTALLL!"

Right about now my self-disgust approaches. This usually happens when I'm in public, faced with my inability to need, when I can't quite work up the effort required to assimilate my surroundings. It likes me best this way.

My disgust settles down beside me, disdainfully sniffs my beer, and quickly orders three shots of tequila. I drink the first one, willing my self-loathing to get lost. It just snickers. I drink the next one and order the sonofabitch to leave. It challenges me instead: feel something else, why don't you? Anything-hope, fear, desire, greed, faith, despair, whatever. Give it a shot. So I try, panning for the remains of my ambitions, hoping to recall some stray sense of what I was before I came to this sparkling oasis of myth, this legend, Hollywood, California… but all I feel is the hatred for what I am now.

"HEY BOO-YA HEAD, WHA'S UP?"

I look up, and to my horror I discover it is Lenny Martinez, the Mack Daddy King. His glistening black hair is swept into an immaculate bi-level pomp, gold hoops sparkling from each ear, a trimmed shadow of beard bristling his white smile. I grip his moist hand in a clumsy shake.

"Not much. Take a seat."

He sits down, dunks the remaining shot of tequila, and whistles at the dancer in a single blur of motion. Lenny is a man of the night, my skulky guide to all that I dislike about Los Angeles. He knows which clubs to attend on what night, and which neighborhoods offer what goods. He lives to enjoy himself in whatever manner becomes available. Detestable.

"So what're you doing here?" I ask, hoping he's on his way to a date, hoping I won't be sucked in to another endless search for a connection.

"Hey, sometimes I like to get a little dirty!" His laughs bellow across the table. If this place was dirty, then Lenny had entered the monastic life. "Ahh, this is a warm-up for the night to come, a little lubrication. You wanna beer?" He orders me two before I answer.

The dancer is a redhead this time, shimmering satin red. She turns her back to us, and then slides into the splits, spreading her legs wider than I ever thought humanly possible. The tattoo on her thigh looks like a butterfly, but as she stands up it retracts into a death's head underlined by two crossed bones. She looks at us with disgust.

"Man, the bitches here get nastier every time I come in," Lenny muses in wide-eyed wonder. He pitches a dollar onto the stage. "Here! Get yer voodoo ass offa the stage! *Shiit!*" Lenny slaps the table and guffaws. His arms are permanently bent into an impossible twist, deep scars running along their undersides; I never asked. The dancer spits at him before taking the dollar, then moves on to other, more appreciative patrons.

"So what's on your agenda tonight?" I ask.

"What?"

"What're you gonna do, dumbfuck?"

"Oh! I got plans, you know I always got plans." Lenny shoots me a sly, wet smile. "You wanna join me? You got any money?"

I consider my options. I have no interest in going with him, but I have no desire to do anything else, either. And there's always the chance that something might go right; perhaps this is the night I'll find my redemption. Impossible. Another fantasy. Stupid.

"I got some bills. Let's go."

We down our beers one after the other, and I follow Lenny out into the cool California night, casting myself into the moonlit eddies of hell and heavy traffic.

My compatriot and I attack the night like conquistadors into the New World, boldly gunning Lenny's lime-green Duster through the heart of Sunset Boulevard, our laughter chilling the hearts of all those who hear it. Lenny the Banderillero whips the ungodly beast through the midnight traffic, cutting off honking cruisers, a crazed look of death gleaming from his moon-sized pupils. He has bared the dragon tattoo on his right bicep and has prepared his soul for whatever the evening may bring.

"Let's get fucked up," he cackles, teeth gleaming. "Let's get really, really fucked up. I never seen you fucked up yet."

And I'm thinking: is this me? Am I truly fated to spend this night running Hollywood with a wide Puerto Rican, jamming to Gothic synth-pop on KROQ? Is this my life?

"C'mon man, you gotta loosen up-you're always so tight, like an old woman, worry, worry."

He's right, but I knew that long ago; I am relentlessly aware of my dissatisfaction. It beats like a heart, over and over: *You're failing, you're failing, you're failing.* Wherever I go, whatever I do, the voice throbs in my head. I'm convinced it's an inevitable part of life for me, like arthritis or rectal cancer.

"You lead the way, cholo. This is your part of town, show me its worst."

I talk brave, but am entirely resigned to my fate. I don't care what happens. I have already convinced myself that there will be no new beginnings tonight-only variations of self-abuse. We will buy our drinks, stare at sexually immaculate women, ignore and be ignored. Love won't suddenly fill me, nor even lust. There will only be a vacant desire for something I cannot name. I will make my jokes, prop up my ego, and totter off to another waiting place. And on and on.

The whining locust-drone of a pack of Geezers envelops us. Suddenly, we are surrounded: gangsters perched on their new Suzuki GSX-R's, slashing between the stand-still cars, their girlfriends clinging to their backs. The sportbikes whoop and growl like angry panthers aching to take chase.

"Look at that ASS!" Lenny shouts. "OhmygodwhattaBUTT!" One girl wears a pair of cut-offs slashed to the hips, her ass a perfect, smooth curve as she leans over her boyfriend. Lenny sticks his head out to catch the final view of the receding ass. "Jesus, what I could do that culo! I'd make her a happy woman!"

"This traffic's never going to end. Let's get the fuck out of here."

"Hey, hey, relax. This is what you do on a Saturday night. You cruise, you kick back."

"You die of carbon monoxide poisoning. Which is at least quicker than dying of boredom."

"You want excitement? Here."

Lenny ruthlessly yanks the ancient Plymouth into the oncoming traffic, cutting across two lanes of screeching cars, popping the opposite curb, and slamming into a Von's parking lot. Then he smokes the rear tires, braying like an enraged Kodiak bear. The onlookers in the lot applaud and whistle. I start to feel better.

"There, bitch! Happy now? Things more exciting?"

I reply with a sniff.

"That's it?"

Lenny growls, muttering Latin oaths, and slams the gas pedal down. We spin out to a stop next to a group of homeboys watching their friends perform: dropped pick-up trucks whose beds rear into the night sky like trumpeting mastodons, gyrating on hydraulic lifts for no particular reason other than awesome spectacle. Lenny blares his horn.

"Hey!" he yells. "Your truck smells like pussy! Or is that you?"

Hands are thrust under seats.

Lenny peels out. I slinker down below windshield level. Laughing insanely, we hump over a few parking barriers and head toward freedom. Five cars line up to get out ahead of us. We detour over the supermarket's sidewalk, mercilessly crushing several watermelons, and make it to the exit. Somebody thumps the trunk. The rear window cracks.

We hit the side street. Providence smiles upon us: a clear lane to the next block. Lenny guns the engine. Behind us, the trucks honk, trying to get out in time; but their finishes are too fine and their suspensions too low to risk ATV maneuvers.

"*AaaaiiiiHAAA!*" Lenny screams into the subdivision, wailing on his horn, pushing the engine to a rasping 70, the conquering savage.

I feel a slight tingling in the loins.

"On to the bloodbath," I command. "I am ready."

Lenny sweats out whatever drug he took earlier and replies with the smile of a carnivore.

We park on the street across from the club, wedging the Duster between a neon-pink Camaro and a Bug with tires the size of breakfast tables. A steady train of people with unnaturally stiff hair head toward the entrance of a featureless white warehouse.

"Circus," Lenny whispers. "It's Latin night. You're not gonna believe it. Looka that!" He clutches my shoulder in a spastic grip. Two chubby girls of 16 walk by in sheaths of what looks to be food wrap, their hair-do's arching skyward in a frozen frenzy of Final Net. "Owowowowow*Ouch.*"

"Is this a teen club?"

"No, no! Though I do know a few places where it'd be easy to-"

"Forget it. If I'm going to catch a disease, let it be from an adult so I won't get arrested for it, too."

"Whatever you want, you'll find it here. Trust me!"

We shuttle past the line to the door. I'm hoping Lenny's ersatz clout is enough to get us past the doormen. It usually doesn't work.

"Hey hey hey! Look who's still got a job!"

The pony-tailed doorman doesn't smile back at Lenny, the glaze of brain-death covering his bulky features. He turns his scrutiny to me, and I briefly wonder if I look acceptably decadent. I've got jeans, boots, and a $12 thrift-store sportcoat that I've yet to have dry-cleaned, the smoke of 30 years following me like a dark cloud. The hair is overlong and the eyes overdrawn. I hope this lends me sufficient panache.

"So wha's up?" Lenny oozes. "Been workin' out? You look yoked, man, fully."

The doorman grunts and lets us in, as if acting on some bothersome obligation he'd rather not think about. Lenny flashes me a look of victory. I give him the thumbs-up to make him feel good: *Way to go!*

We weave our way through the obstacle course of hangers-on and stride onto the main dance floor like soldiers of a conquering army; whatever we survey is ours-we're the motherfuckers. The warehouse is one big floor of compressed humans pretending to dance to the relentless sputter and throb of Euro-house-techno-acid-blah-blah-blah, a soulless beat-box repetition meant to live a week, maybe two. Lights flash, heat rises, deals are struck. The place is no different from any other dance club, no more personality, no more interesting-except that it's popular this month.

"We're gonna make you Latino tonight, man," Lenny screams into my ear. "Then ALL the women'll want you!"

"Is that right."

"Why do you think they call us Latin lovers? We know what we're doing-not like you white boys."

He had me there. I wasn't sure what I was doing this very moment, in fact.

"I'll go snag us some drinks-why don't you pick us up a couple of Betties? Use that educated charm of yours! HA HA!"

Lenny threads his way to the bar. It'll take a good 20 minutes to get us drinks. Meanwhile, I have to look as if I belong here. I feel impossibly Caucasian, as white as a glossy china plate at Norm's Diner. The boys here wear chains of gold beneath unbuttoned shirts, bristling with wispy mustaches, slick hair, and tall boots. The girls wear big floofy-shoulder dresses that stretch down to their thighs, and hang sparkly baubles from their ears. I look for anyone to look back, but there's nothing. This is not my element, I decide.

There are two large go-go cages on the floor. I huff my way to the nearest one. Inside, well out of reach, is a perfect sexual creature, a writhing Amazon-woman, wielding her flawlessness like a sharpened ax. She can't possibly have human worries or weaknesses. I glimpse a cold shark-eye, and I wonder: What does she do for fun?

"Hey dummy! Time to go!"

Lenny clutches a woman on either side of him like bundles of faded flowers. One is tall and skinny with eyes that flitter and dart, her complexion sweet browned butter. The other is shorter with a soft bare midriff and dark eyes that were sultry once, but now worn and lined. One of them shines purple from an old bruise.

"This is Rebecca and this is Letti, old friends of mine. We're leavin'. Wanna come?"

Rebecca giggles and Letti gives me a lazy smirk. I tell myself that there's a residue of compassion in that smile, as if she might have actually felt the emotion once, and may remember how to again someday.

"What are we waiting for?" I yell over the din of electronic combustion, and apply a rigor mortis smile.

We're in the Duster, making our run down Santa Monica Boulevard to Lenny's little hovel in Silverlake. There are fewer cars here so we cruise right along, hesitating only at the sporadic cop sighting. I'm sitting in the back with Letti, my ass perched over loose tools and crushed beer cans. She squeezes my knee. On the back of her hand is a self-inflicted tattoo of three intersecting lines crowned with three dots, blue like the ink from a Bic pen.

"Lenny says you're a movie writer. What've you written?"

Lenny never shuts up. He talks and talks and talks.

"Many, many important things. I can't list them all, there're so many."

"Well tell me just one. What's your most famous movie?"

"Hmmm-the *most* famous? That's hard... you know the commercial where the margarine tub talks? 'Butter!'"

"Uh-huh."

"That's mine."

"You wrote that commercial?"

"No, not all of it. Just that one word. *'Butter!'*"

Letti giggles.

"You're weird! Lenny, your friend is weird!"

"You should see him in his underwear!" Lenny bellows, triumphant.

The girls laugh. We pass a row of dark little bars without signs, and a small parade of transvestites struts down the sidewalk in a show of regal pride, hair perfect, hot pants tight and sparkling. They eye us as we drive past, as if waiting with expectation and dread for the car to stop.

"They're so pretty!" Rebecca coos. "I wanna take one home with me."

"Believe me, they're better looking in the dark," Lenny comments. "Once you turn on the light and get a close look-oof! Forget it! You lose all interest."

"Sounds like you know what you're talkin' about, Lenny," says Letti.

"Hey, what can I say? It's the '90s! Things happen!"

The girls squeal in delight. We zip past Vermont Avenue and a half-mile later turn into Lenny's neighborhood. He lives on the top of a hill in a little one-room "bungalow" behind a house-his low-rent love hut. No one knows why it exists, unless the builder of the main house once had delusions of live-in servants. Silverlake is not Bel Air, and I doubt if it ever was.

"Gotta make a run," Lenny mutters, and we scuttle past his house, down a few blocks, left here, right there. We stop at a corner and a darty short man comes to the window. He looks like a mailman gone to seed, still making his deliveries.

"Watcha got?"

"The best, only the best. The motherlode."

"Sounds good to me!" Lenny passes him the money and takes a plastic bag in return. Letti stares at the little package like a mother to her first-born. "Have a nice night!"

"You too, man. See you soon."

We pull away. It took less than a minute.

"Let me hold it, Lenny," Rebecca whispers.

"WHAT'RE YOU WHISPERIN' FOR? THINK THE COPS GOT US BUGGED?"

The girls collapse in giggles.

"Gimme that!" Letti snatches the baggy away from the front

seat. She fingers it lovingly, eyeing me. "We're gonna have so much fun tonight. You ready?"

"Yes, ma'am," I reply, and wonder when this evening will end.

Lenny pulls up to the house, shutting off his car then racing outside to jam a cinder block behind the tire. Letti and I extract ourselves from the rear seat and climb the steps to Lenny's one-room mansion. We walk past the main house to the rear, ignoring the next-door neighbor's lunging Doberman, and make it inside without being arrested, killed, or bitten.

Lenny locks the door, then scoops up the two women into his arms for a hug. "Ladies, ladies, ladies... am I not the Great Provider? Hmmm?"

The three of them huddle together near the sink, breaking out their equipment. Lenny brandishes a small propane torch that looks like a miniature flame-thrower. "Here it comes, girls-THE TERMINATOR!"

He fires up the rock and they share its smoke. I turn on the TV and catch the last few minutes of a *Saturday Night Live* rerun. I'm not sure which is worse.

Letti peers at me through red slits.

"Hey, aren't you gonna join us?"

Lenny coughs up a few pieces of his lungs then answers for me. "No, no, he ain't into this shit. He's straight, straight, straight. But STILL totally fucked up! HA HA!"

Letti shakes her head in puzzlement, then fills her brain with the smoke until there's no room left for thoughts. Lenny and Rebecca share a kiss and trade the exhaust of their acrid high. I flip channels, trying to find wrestling.

A few minutes later, Lenny and Rebecca walk into the bathroom together, pulling the partition shut. Letti sits down next to me and finds a pack of cards.

"Let me tell you your fortune," she says. She starts shuffling the deck.

"So you're a Gypsy woman, then."

"No way-my mom taught me this. She's from Brazil."

"So she's a Gypsy and she taught you her ways of Gypsy magic."

"No, no, no. She's a bank teller in Reseda."

"So who's the Gypsy then?"

"NOBODY! Christ, you're so confusing."

She stops dealing and tries to study the cards facing up.

"What do you see?"

"…Either you're dead… or… I'm too fucked up to do this right."

"I trust you with my life. What do you do for a living?"

"Oh, I'm a teacher. Grade school kiddies."

"Yeah? Where at? Compton? Watts?"

"Fuck no! Brentwood. I teach at a private school. The best."

Rebecca comes out pulling Lenny in by the arm.

"Lennyyy… c'mon. Are you sure you don't have any more?"

"Sure I'm sure! You crackheads sucked me dry."

"What about the carpet? Did we drop any?"

Rebecca crawls around on the floor, trying to discern between the year-old crumbs and any remains of the crack.

"Lenny, get us some more," Letti commands.

"Hey, am I your sugar daddy or something? Shell out the didge, woman-you make more money than any of us. Besides, you two are the ones jonesin', not me."

Letti sighs and then digs into her purse.

"I don't have that much left. Lisa is making me pay rent to stay with her. Here." She passes the money to Lenny. "Rebecca, get off the floor!"

"Oh!"

"Yeah, c'mon with me," says Lenny. "Let the lovebirds alone for a while."

They snort and giggle then go off to score. Letti gives me a little smile, and gathers up the cards.

"What games do you know? Wanna play poker?"

"I'm not sure how."

"Five card stud?"

"Never played it before. Why is Lisa making you pay the rent?"

Her smile fades a bit.

"I've been there two weeks now, so…"

"Where do you usually live?"

"With my boyfriend."

"Who…"

"Who hit me two weeks ago. Strange coincidence, huh?"

"Why did he do that?"

She stares at the cards while she deals them.

"Because he's a big man, and big men have this thing about

proving they're big."

"You should find one that doesn't."

"The ones that don't are gay. And besides, I don't want some-one else."

"You still..."

"I think I'm going to move back in next week. If he'll let me."

"That's fucking ridiculous."

"Well, maybe you can help me stop missing him... "

Letti strokes my inner thigh, as if in question. My mind races: an actual sexual advance. I think this woman is *attracted* to me. She doesn't see whatever it is the others see when they pass me on the street or glance at me in a bar. She is not disinterested. What are you supposed to do when this happens?

I look into her eyes and see something friendly there. Why? No one else here looks that way. Least of all me. I slip my hand onto her hip and kiss her. She squeezes my cock and makes a gentle probe with her tongue. A thought flutters through my head: Will I be able to get it up? She kisses my cheeks and my eyelids. Maybe it won't matter...

"GOT THE SHIT!"

Lenny bursts in with the goods. Letti leaps up and tries to snatch the baggy from him.

"About fucking time! What took so long?"

As they fire up the pipe, I slip outside, walking back past the main house. The neighbor's Doberman doesn't growl; I doubt if it even notices me.

Down on the street, I ponder my options on how to get home. I head toward Santa Monica Boulevard, making a silent prayer that no one stops me. It is cool and dark here in the neighborhood, no lights. You can't see anyone, but beneath the overhead rustle of palm trees in the cool Pacific breeze, you hear them talking, laughing. More deals being struck.

I make it to the boulevard on rubber legs and start looking for a bus stop. There are people here. Bright fluorescent light spills out from the door of an adult bookstore onto the sidewalk, a static-filled radio blaring out Whitney Houston's paeans to love. Men stand out-side and stare at me as I pass, their packages tightly gripped, wait-ing. Further down, leaning against a wall, a Mae West in pink span-dex blows me a kiss and licks his lips in promise.

I keep going. A bar door is open, and the dim glow of its juke-box makes a blue and red halo of invitation; two men stand next to it kissing each other. It's playing Patsy Cline, and it makes me think of another bar in another town so very far away. I wonder if they're playing that same song right now, and if anyone I know is listening to it.

A couple of buildings down lies an underground nightclub, just opening its doors as others close theirs. A line of people in studded collars and fishnet stockings and black tattoos wait at the entrance.

"I think it's blood-letting night," someone says, "isn't it?"

At the corner is a taco stand. The bean and cheese burritos are a dollar, and it's hard to fuck them up. I order one with onions and salsa. The sweaty man with the flat face behind the counter scowls and swears with every move, clearly hating his job, his desperation, his life. Why is he here doing this shit at this time of night? The question consumes his brain like a cancer.

I take my hate-filled burrito and sit down at the graffiti-scarred bus stop. I'm not even sure which bus to take, or if they even run this late. It doesn't matter. I'm here at the whims of some very strange and twisted gods, and there's no real direction home.

Rob Neighbors
Hank, and Diane
April 2001 (approx.)

//

Rob Neighbors was born and raised in Sheridan, Wyoming, just south of the Montana border, and fifty miles from the Little Bighorn River where Custer's last stand took place. From an early age, California was pulling him like a magnet, away from his landlocked home. Swimming pools, movie stars.

Rob moved to Los Angeles the day after he graduated from Montana State University. Like thousands of fools and dreamers before him, he had big plans. Luckier than most, not as lucky as others, he's had limited success as a screenwriter, writing B-movies. He's had as many failures as successes, and has paid a big price for his dream, but is still plugging away. From the mean streets of Van Nuys, to the Strand on Hermosa, Rob has experienced a wide cross section of life in Los Angeles. He loves writing and reading short stories, especially literate realism, and is currently writing a book of short stories loosely based on his experiences.

Hank put five dollars worth of gas in his car and bought a can of Coke and a Slim Jim, leaving him two bucks to his name. He hadn't been eating right lately and he knew it, but times would get better as they always did. He had been living on the edge for a long time now, and was comfortable with it, but near poverty allowed him his freedom he thought - freedom from the stifling monotony of a career, a marriage, and the prodding eyes of his family who were all twelve hundred miles and a time zone away. He was alone most of the time and that's the way he liked it he guessed. He could deal with the solitude, though it was eating alone that killed him. Sitting in restaurants by himself waiting for his food and watching groups of people at other tables interacting with each other, and remembering the times when he had eaten and laughed with friends, his wife, and his family. His ex-wife had predicted to him aloud one day he "would be a very lonely man", and now he saw very clearly her prediction fulfilled.

He climbed back into his eleven year old Pontiac and accelerated onto the 405 freeway heading south from LAX. He was going to see Diane, the girl from Orange County he had met at the airport. He had been seeing her for a few months now and she quelled his loneliness in the late night hours and he gladly made the forty-mile trip across the LA basin to see her. Each such journey was a head trip as well, because he would zone out in his memories as the vastness of Los Angeles as the ribbons of its freeways unfolded in front of him.

He would think of the other girls before her and songs on the radio would remind him of them. Hank could not complain, he had had many such relationships since his divorce, and he gained something each time, even as he lost. He never started these things knowing that they were doomed from the get go, because the women he chose, or who chose him were incapable of having lasting, meaningful relationships; or maybe it was he who was incapable. He wasn't quite sure, but he gave it a lot of thought. He only knew that it was a pattern with him. He would meet a woman, usually a very flawed, lonely and needy person like himself, and they would come together for a few quick months, and then it would be over as quickly as it started. They each would move on, looking for their next victim.

This one, Diane, lived in a bland suburb on the L.A./Orange County border. She was a stripper and Hank was okay with it because, after all, he was the one getting the trim at the end of the night, not all of those fools who paid for lap dances. She was incredibly good looking, but dense. She was thirty-five, had been married twice, and had a son whom she saw sometimes. Hank had his baggage too.

He stopped in front of her apartment building and sat in his car on the street, delaying his appearance for one reason or another. He was anxious to see her, but nervous at the same time. A nagging feeling inside of him told him that this would be the last time. He sat quietly in his car and listened to the music coming from her second story apartment. She always had her stereo blaring and tuned into KROQ. It became an irritating drone after awhile. Many things about Diane irritated him - but she had some good qualities, most of all a killer body.

He got out of his car and walked underneath her balcony, calling to her. She appeared on the balcony like Juliette and smiled at him. He walked up and she greeted him at the door, giving him a hug and a light kiss on the lips.

"You got here fast, dude. We gotta' go to the store for some laundry detergent."

He followed her in and she continued sorting her stripper costumes for wash. This was the routine with them; he would show up and help her with her domestic chores, then they would fuck.

"So, how was your day?" she asked, not looking at him as she messed with the clothes.

"Okay," he said, not elaborating.

She elaborated about hers, "It sucked at the club. Nothing but cheap men in tonight. None of my regulars showed up. I've gotta' pay the rent, dude."

He looked in the refrigerator; it was empty except for half a twelve pack of Coors Light. He grabbed one for himself. Diane glanced at him.

"Grab me one."

He did and went and sat next to her. He rubbed her shoulders as she continued sorting the dirty laundry. "I've gotta' get money for my yoga certification, so I can teach, you know?" Hank nodded and sipped his beer. "I've got to call that guy about starting my web site too," she said, "We've got mailers to send out dude, the envelopes and labels are over there."

Hank glanced at the envelopes on the coffee table. Herbalife.

She hadn't sold one package, but she sure was busy sending out those mailers. He didn't have the heart to tell her it was in vain, and he helped her each time she did it without a complaint.

She fished for some money in her purse and handed it to him, "Get the liquid detergent, okay, dude?" She smiled and batted her eyes. This was the price he paid for pussy, and he would be well rewarded later, so he put up with it.

He went out to his car and was thinking the whole way what a *pussy* he had become. He never lifted a finger to help his wife around the house when he was married, well... look where that got him. He would do his duty and then Diane would do hers, that's the way it worked and they both knew it. Besides, he admired her for her tenacity. She was a survivor - she never seemed to give up, no matter how futile it all was. She was a stripper, and she maybe turned a trick now and then when necessary, but at least she paid her own rent and wasn't looking for some sugar daddy to do it for her. Those were the girls Hank really despised - the leggy blondes who ended up with sixty-year old sugar daddies, fucking and sucking for a free ride. Of course, he hoped he would have one when he was sixty.

He pulled into the 7-11and a Los Alamitos police cruiser was parked out front. He thought about going somewhere else, but he figured what the hell, I'm not doing anything wrong, and walked in. The clerks here all knew Hank and Diane well - they bought everything here, even though it was twice as expensive, but Hank guessed it was her money and easy come easy go. As if grinding your ass into some three hundred pound forklift operator's crotch is easy money. Two of Los Alamitos' finest were at the counter buying coffee. The Sri Lankan behind the counter was being extra friendly and nodded and smiled as Hank walked in. The cops gave Hank the once over, then bade the clerk farewell and left. Hank got the $6.95 liquid detergent and walked to the counter where he bought two chocolate covered cherries, Diane's favorite.

"How are you, boss," the clerk asked. Hank smiled and said, "Good." Just fine.

When Hank got back Diane squealed with delight over the chocolate covered cherries and they moved into the bathroom where she began hand washing her costumes in the sink and he sat on the toilet seat watching her and drinking his beer.

She chatted on and on as she lathered up each nylon g-string,

"When are we going to write that script, "Hank and Diane?", she asked him.

It was an idea for a screenplay she had based on he and her. She saw it as a comedy; he knew it was a tragedy. He played along with her and gave her excuses about how he would have to complete other projects first, but yes, indeed they would eventually do it. He knew they never would, but that was one of his ways to keep her holding on. They laughed and were happy with their charade for a few moments when her roommate showed up.

The roommate was another stripper, Alexis, who was rarely there, had a bunch of her costumes hanging in the living room, and mostly stayed with some boyfriend. After months of hearing about her, this was the first time Hank had ever seen her. She was a short, punk looking blonde much younger than Diane. Diane introduced them and Hank got a little charge, wondering if this would be the night of his fantasy; a threesome. Alexis didn't seem impressed though, and she had a hard cynical way about her. She was not the sweet clueless type like Diane. Diane repeated the whole run down to Alexis: the cheap guys in the club, the yoga instruction, the mailers, the web site, etc.

"Hanks a writer you know, we're going to write a movie together called 'Hank and Diane.'" Alexis glanced at Hank, knowing he was full of shit for letting Diane believe that.

Alexis went into her own problems, a fight with a boyfriend, an impounded car, etc. Hank excused himself to get more beer, knowing full well the threesome was not happening that night.

Hank stood at the sink thinking about how simple Diane actually was sexually. Diane really only loved it one way, missionary, and that's the only way she could get off. She didn't like to give head, nor was she good at it, so Hank didn't ask for it. She had a great pussy though. He remembered that first night together, at the Hilton in Palm Springs. She was working a club over there, and he had driven out there on the spur of the moment to see her, as she had invited him to do when he met her at LAX. He didn't get there until after ten o'clock, and he wandered around the club looking for her for two hours. Just as he was about to give up, she appeared like a vision in a dream - long legged, long black hair, a white g-string and top. To Hank, she was the hottest one in there and she was his. Possibly... Hank approached her and called out her name.

She recoiled, "Who are you?"

"I'm Hank, remember, from the airport?" he said, wondering if she was the wrong girl.

"Oh, yes! How you doing dude?" she said, "Lets go get a table." She was drunk already, but she led him to a table and a waitress brought more drinks.

Later, they drove around looking for a motel. Everything was full. They ended up at the Hilton downtown which was way over Hank's budget, but what the fuck he thought as he shelled out $250 for the night. The room was a suite with a balcony overlooking downtown Palm Springs and Diane was impressed. Hank was in the large bathroom brushing his teeth, when Diane walked in, pulled down her pants and proceeded to take a dump. He'd never seen a girl with such a lack of modesty, but Hank liked it. It was honest, there was something pure about it as he smelled her shit drop into the toilet. She was talking to him the whole time, telling him about her web site, etc. She wiped her ass and stood, then, pulled all of her clothes off and walked gloriously naked into the bedroom. Hank felt his cock growing hard and he took all of his clothes off, but walked into the bedroom with modesty and apprehension.

She was lying under the covers flicking through the television channels with the remote. "I'm too tired to fuck you tonight, but we will in the morning, okay, baby?" she said.

He crawled into bed with her, disappointed, but not completely.

"Just hold me," she said, and Hank did, and within moments, she was fast asleep in his arms. He laid there with her unable to sleep and sexually charged. She was sawing logs, oblivious to the world. She felt good in his arms.

The next morning Hank got up first and made coffee with the in-room coffee maker. Diane awoke and smiled at him from the bed, mascara caked around her eyes.

"How do you like it?" Hank asked her.

"With cream and sugar," she said, "Extra sugar."

He brought her coffee too her, thereby establishing his subservient role. She sat up naked to drink her coffee and Hank stood by the bed just admiring her. She drank it down quickly, then shot out of bed.

"I've gotta' pee, then we'll fuck, dude," she said as she ran to the bathroom.

Hank's moment had arrived. He slipped his underwear off and

laid on the bed waiting for her. She came back and they kissed for several minutes. Hank went down on her and she pulled his hair and thrust her shaved pelvis into his face. She came in his mouth. Then she made Hank put on a condom and she guided him in. He started stoking into her when she suddenly stopped him.

"Take the condom off," she said, "Just don't cum inside me."

Hank thought about it a moment, imagining potentially hundreds of her past partners, yanked the rubber off and dove in anyway. Her pussy squeezed his cock like a vice and she dug her fingernails into his back. There was a big wet spot underneath them. Hank looked into her face and thought he could see the spirit of an ancient Samurai warrior and it unnerved him. Diane was his first Asian girl.

"Fuck me harder," she screamed, and he pounded her for all he was worth. When Hank pulled out he sprayed her stomach and tits with cum. It had been awhile for him.

So that's how it started, and they had been seeing each other for six months now. Hank couldn't believe it was still going. Hank heard Alexis telling Diane something in the bathroom. Something about her getting fired because a jealous boyfriend kept stalking her at the club.

"That sucks, girl," Diane said.

"I'm splitting to Vegas," Alexis said. "I've got go pick up a few more things at his place, then I'm leaving in the morning."

"Do you need any help?" Diane asked.

"No," Alexis said, "I can handle it." Alexis put her jacket on and walked toward the door. "See ya later," she said to Hank.

"Yeah, nice meeting you," Hank said.

Alexis left and Diane walked into the room and grabbed a stack of envelopes, "Time to do mailers," she said, handing a stack to Hank. He got right to work.

Hank awoke the next morning with a raging hard on. Diane was snoring next to him. He looked across the room and could see Alexis sleeping under a blanket on the floor. She must have returned sometime during the night and he hadn't heard her. He laid there watching her sleeping form. Soon, Diane awoke and she pulled Hank to her. They started kissing and Diane threw the covers off the bed. Hank was thrilled that Alexis was in the room and knowing that Diane didn't give a damn. Diane guided him in as she always did and he started slamming her. Hank watched Alexis, who was playing possum.

"Fuck me hard, dude," Diane said with extra emphasis. This went on for probably half an hour. They were putting on a show for Alexis, but she wasn't watching, pretending to be asleep.

After Hank came all over Diane's stomach, she said, "Go make the coffee, dude, and get me a glass of water." Hank did so, walking past Alexis with a glistening hard on. When he walked back Diane was smoking a cigarette. Hank lit one for himself and sat next to her, naked on the bed.

"I'll go put on my makeup and we'll go get breakfast, okay, baby?" she said.

"You don't need makeup, baby, you're so beautiful," Hank told her.

"I know, baby, but makeup enhances a woman's beauty," she said very seriously. Diane smashed her cigarette out and went into the bathroom. Hank laid back down watching Alexis as Diane spent an hour applying her "mask" as she always did.

At Denny's, Diane was eating her cream of wheat with fruit bowl on the side like always. Hank was working on his two eggs over easy with hash browns and English muffin like always. There were several moments of silence between them, when Diane finally placed her hand on top of his. "I've got to jam up to Vegas for awhile, dude," she said. Hank couldn't hide his disappointment and hurt, and this seemed to irritate her. "I'm not making any money here, dude," she said, squeezing his hand. "I've gotta' go to where the money is. It's not like you're supporting me, dude."

"Yeah, yeah, yeah," Hank said, not wanting her to continue. Then, after a long silence, "How long will you be gone?" he asked, his voice stammering.

"I don't know. Can you follow me to the gas station and check my oil?" Diane pulled some money out of her purse to pay the bill. Hank dropped his last two bucks on the table for the tip.

Diane sat in her bright red Honda Prelude while Hank checked her oil. She was two quarts low and when Hank told her she handed him the money through the window, "Get me a bottle of Evian too." Hank walked into the gas station feeling like a chump. He walked back and handed her the water, then put the oil in.

"Okay, I guess you're ready," he said. Their eyes met briefly, then she slipped her shades on. "Are you going with Alexis?" he asked her like a sad little boy.

"Yes," she said. Hank stood there awkwardly, waiting for her to get out of the car or something, but she didn't. He leaned down into the window and she pecked him on the lips. "Take care of yourself, dude. See you when I see you."

"Yeah, you be careful up there. Call me," he said.

"I will," she said. She started her car and Hank stepped out of her way watching her drive out of the lot. Without looking back she turned onto the boulevard and took off like a bat out of hell. Hank stood there a moment feeling numb. He climbed into his car and headed for the freeway behind a big line of cars building up to the on ramp.

Deidre Woollard
Fender Bender
2002

//

Though Boston-bred, Deidre throws her allegiance to LA in all areas except baseball (go Red Sox). Her stories have appeared in various literary journals including Sojourn and Words and Images. Other stories and strange mutterings can be found on her website at www.thefictive.com.

Alice comes into my apartment swinging a large tote bag behind her. Her hair is pulled into a bun but looping tendrils of hair have escaped. "I need to check my messages," she says, pulling a cell phone from the depths of her bag. She perches on my sofa with her legs folded beneath her. I like to watch the way her face shifts as she nods or grimaces at the phone, like she is listening to music that only she can hear. She pulls a bottle of water out of her bag and drinks hungrily letting a bit of the water run down her chin. She is heedless with me; I think I like that most of all. After all, here she is on a Thursday afternoon, wearing what are obviously her workout clothes. She trusts me or perhaps she despises me. Either way, she is comfortable.

"I don't have much time, Peter," she says, "and I'll need to use your shower. I'm due to meet Seth for the ballet at 6:30."

Seth. The boyfriend. I don't begrudge her the boyfriends; they have a way of not lasting. But good old Seth has been around longer than most. I suspect it has something to do with his pedigree, and the fact that he owns the hottest restaurant in town. I've seen pictures of the two of them in the society pages of local magazines. The museum curator and the restaurateur-they are one of the "it" couples that Boston seems to dote on. I assume she is very careful with him, she doesn't get drunk; she doesn't let him see her in anything but ideal conditions.

Alice helps herself to a drink. I always keep her favorite Stoli Vanilla Vodka in the freezer. She goes into the kitchen and comes back with the glass cradled against her throat.

"I'm a little sweaty. The teacher in my yoga class keeps the room overheated. It's supposed to loosen your muscles."

"I like you sweaty. Come here."

She walks across the room, drinking as she moves. When she reaches me, she sets the empty glass on the coffee table and sits on the floor in front of me, staring up with those big green eyes of hers. Without any prelude, she reaches forward, unzips my pants and takes me into her mouth. I'm already hard. She sucks and licks and swirls her tongue around me. I wish I could make it take longer but within minutes I'm moaning and moving my hips and although I try to think about baseball statistics and state capitals I still end up in ecstasy, grunting in pleasure as my orgasm fills her mouth.

"I'm off to the showers," she says, picking up her bag and heading for the bathroom. Before I can argue, I hear the water running.

I am not allowed in there. Although she has seen me naked count-less times, she has a very strict no-nakedness policy with me. That way it isn't cheating. So she says.

She comes out not more than twenty minutes later. It could be a whole other girl. Her royal blue wrap dress displays without flaunting. That crazy-wild hair of hers has been slicked into obedi-ence and her makeup is a perfect mask.

"Nice dress."

"Can I talk to you for a second?" There is a slight flutter in her voice that I feel answered with a twitch of anxiety inside me. We sit on the couch.

She takes one of my hands in hers and it is then that I see the ring. Glittering, gigantic, perfect diamond, marquise-cut, perched like an insect on her third finger.

"I gather you wish to make a change to our arrangement," I say it in, what I hope, is an offhand voice. He asked, she said yes. I should have guessed this would happen eventually.

"It's been three years. I was thinking maybe we could stop this."

"I never said you had to do it. This was your choice, too. I call, you answer. You don't have to answer."

"You know that I felt obligated. And now it needs to end."

"Because you are getting married."

"Come on, Peter, did you really think I was going to keep giv-ing you blow jobs for the rest of your life because you witnessed my accident?"

"I was your passenger. You could have killed me!"

"But I didn't. It was a long time ago. I don't drive drunk any-more, it wasn't even a big accident."

"Big enough for you to run away."

"Three years ago, Peter."

I just stare at her. I know she has probably already scripted out this argument in her head. There is no way I can convince her right now.

"You've got a date in twenty minutes," I remind her, "let's talk about this another time."

She raises an eyebrow. "I know you're just delaying me, but you happen to be right. We'll talk later." She kisses me on the cheek and disappears out the door.

My apartment is quiet in the absence of her. Usually that doesn't bother me. I like it after she goes most days, she doesn't fill my thoughts. I'm not supposed to think about her romantically, so I don't. I walk her to the door and then I switch on my Bang and Olufson stereo and I get a few hours of work done before I even notice the time. I've done my best designs in the past three years and I know that part of that is because I have focus. I haven't dated much nor haunted endless bars, I have a few close friends and I have her. My world feels seamless, complete.

But now, she wants to go. And I think back to the beginning, when I first met her and I was going out all the time, constantly looking to score. The idea of returning to that makes me very tired. And I can't sit here now in this house where her perfume lingers in the air.

At the Griffin Grill I can always get a nice rare burger and a cold glass of India Pale Ale. Sonia, my favorite bartender, knows to give me a side of mayonnaise and a thick slice of onion for my burger. These things comfort me. Burgers from the Griffin, salads from Green Harvest, sushi from Village Fish-I have lived in this town long enough to have figured out where to get the best of everything I require. And of course that's what Alice is too, the best.

I hold off on calling Alice for a week. I work, I see movies and I even answer a personal ad. That was a waste of time, a whole night of listening to a girl who clearly models her life on old episodes of *Ally McBeal*. I sipped my wine, cut my food into small bites and thought of Alice. I don't think Alice owns a television. She sees movies, lots of movies, foreign films certainly, but teenage exploitation movies, karate movies, even horror. Whenever her work at the museum stresses her out too much, she ducks into a theater for an afternoon and watches whatever's on.

If I had dated Alice traditionally she would have dumped me in a few dates. I can imagine that she might have humored me, sat through a dinner or two, but a woman like her needs a trophy guy. Even the night we met I knew she was out of my league. She gave me her number because she didn't care whether I called or not. Our first date, that abortive adventure that set all of this in motion, was sandwiched between a gallery opening and an after-hours party she never ended up making it to.

That night, we had agreed to meet at Griffin Grill and when I arrived she was already there and already loaded. I could tell by the slight wobble of her body and the hazy smile with which she greeted me that the drink she was holding was by no means her first. She was drinking martinis made with vanilla vodka and I must confess I supplied her with the final one that pushed her over the edge. But I wasn't exactly sober myself at that point either. When, a half hour later, she leaned up to whisper in my ear that she wanted to leave, who was I to disagree?

She drove one of those fancy Lexus convertibles, which she left unlocked. She slid in behind the wheel and put the top down and the stereo up. I never offered to drive. She just put the car in gear and off we went.

Two turns later, flying down a double-parked side street, she ran a stop sign and crashed straight into a Lincoln Continental in the middle of the intersection. The front of her car crumpled like a used tissue. I couldn't see the damage on the Lincoln but it pulled over to the side of the street. I waited for her to do the same but instead she flung the gearshift into reverse, spun around and drove off. One of her tires had been damaged, I could smell burned rubber as she left a trail of smoke.

"I can't get caught. This would kill my family. I can't get caught."

"It's a pretty distinctive car, they're probably going to find you anyway. Maybe it's better if we go back now."

Alice didn't answer; she concentrated on steering the car, which was now listing heavily to the left. When we arrived at her townhouse, she put the car in the garage and we went upstairs. To her credit, it wasn't until we were safely inside the house that she began to break down. She collapsed onto her leather couch, her shoulders shaking with the release of fear. I sat down beside her and awkwardly stroked her shoulders.

"Do you need a glass of water?"

"That would be nice. The glasses are in the cabinet above the sink."

I walked to the kitchen, fumbled for the light, and then poured two glasses of water. When I went to the refrigerator, I read the newspaper clippings on the door, and I began to understand why she was so afraid. She wasn't just Alice Randall; she was State Senator Randall's daughter.

I brought the glasses back to the living room. We drank in silence. She was still pale but at least she had stopped shaking.

"You should stay here tonight," she said.

"I could take a cab home if you want to be alone."

"No, not tonight. Tomorrow, I'll have to deal with all of this. Tonight, let's just go to bed."

I followed her upstairs to her loft bedroom with its massive white bed and the view of the city outside. We undressed and got into bed, side-by-side, awkward. I didn't know if I should touch her or not but she rolled over and curled up against me so I wrapped both arms around her.

After the night of the accident, when we both sobered up in her bed the next morning, I never wanted to see her again. You don't start off a relationship with a drunk-driving accident, no matter how beautiful the woman is. A week after her accident, I was called away to design and install a sound system for a new theater in Vancouver. I was gone for four months.

When I got back, in an unseasonably sweltering October, I decided to move to a new apartment. I made some money in the Vancouver deal, enough to buy a condo in a sunlit restored warehouse. A slip of paper on which her number was written fluttered out of one of my numerous boxes. I picked it up off the floor and looked at it for a moment. On a whim, I dialed her number. She answered. Next thing you know, she swung by in her convertible to come and get me.

"You got the car fixed," I said as I slid in.

"My family found me a mechanic that would fix it without asking any questions."

"Must have been expensive."

"So, did you like Vancouver?"

"It's a very clean city."

She maneuvered the car out onto the highway and shifted it into fifth gear. Her hair was whipping around her face and she grabbed a ponytail holder off the gearshift and took both hands off the wheel to fasten her hair back. When she wasn't looking, I surreptitiously fastened my seat belt.

"This is my favorite beach," she said as she pushed her little Lexus around the twisted curves of the roadside. The road was pitch dark and I couldn't see the ocean anywhere nearby but then we popped around a corner and it spread out before us-the wine-dark sea and a thin ribbon of white sand gleaming in the moonlight.

"It's beautiful here. Are you sure we are allowed to go on the beach at night?"

"Allowed?"

I looked over at her aristocratic profile and realized it never occurred to her that she would not be allowed anything she wanted to do. I wondered if the accident was the first thing in life that didn't go her way. And after all, even that did, here she was, not in jail, not on probation, her car still looking brand new and her driving record intact.

She led me through the sand dunes and out onto the beach. She took off her shoes and rolled up her pants, so I did the same. We trailed along the water's edge, up to where rounded rocks formed the beginnings of a jetty.

"Here's the best part," she said "see, this rock is just like a chair." She positioned herself between two stones and stretched her long jean-clad legs onto another rock. "It's even got an ottoman. You have to try it."

She got up and I sat tentatively between the rocks. She sat opposite me on the ottoman rock. I leaned forward to kiss her, twining one hand in her thick, curling ponytail, and using the other one to trace the curves of her body. She stiffened, holding her herself away from me slightly when I shoved my hand up her shirt. And that's when I made the fateful move that started this whole thing in motion. Using her ponytail as leverage, I pushed her head in the direction of my crotch. She hesitated for a moment but then she went right to it.

The thing is, without the accident between us I would never have had the confidence to treat her so cavalierly. But I was a witness to her deepest secret, her most shameful moment. And I took full advantage. Now I'm paying for it with goodbye.

On Tuesday night, I eat dinner at Seth's restaurant. I hate new places so I invite the Ally-McBeal chick from the personal ads as my date. Her name is Katherine but she insists I call her Kiki. I can tell she thinks it's a cute affectation that makes her seem tiny and wacky. I can't imagine taking anyone named Kiki seriously and wonder if she doesn't inspire fits of laughter behind her everywhere she turns. *I have a package for Kiki. And the winner is - Kiki. Do you Kiki, take Peter to be your lawful wedded husband?*

Later, I'll come to Seth's restaurant and sit alone at the bar, maybe I'll even become a regular, but for this first night I need my

Kiki-camouflage. For her part, Kiki seems to think I'm wildly sophisticated for choosing this place and she definitely sees this dinner as a positive step in the right direction. I wouldn't know these things, except for the fact that Kiki confides them to me as she strokes my forearm across the table.

I nod my head and smile in what I hope is an encouraging yet distant manner. Kiki's ability to rattle on, lost in her own butterfly thoughts would make her very annoying forever but makes her just perfect for tonight. I scan the room looking for Seth, Mr. Restaurateur, Mr. Ballet, Mr. Theatre, Mr. Charity Functions, Mr. My Picture is in Boston Magazine Every Damn Month. He doesn't disappoint, soon he comes gliding into the room as if he is actually floating on the adulation that comes from the diners whose heads swivel to follow him. Normal conversations turn hushed as he stops at various tables, bestowing his grace like a benevolent king.

"Oooo, is that Seth Lowry," whispers Kiki, "I saw his picture in the Improper Bostonian last week. He's a hunk. Of course, he's taken. He just got engaged to some blue-blooded museum chick. Old money sticks together I guess."

I look up at Kiki and for a moment I glare at her so hard that she nearly drops her wine glass. "What'd I say?"

"Nothing. Do you know what you want to eat?"

"Oh I'll just have a salad."

Best restaurant in town, specializing in heavy Italian peasant food and she orders a salad. Typical. Me, I want to order everything and nothing. I want to chew through the Tuscan flank steak as if I was chewing out his heart, and I also want to leave before his food touches my mouth. I shouldn't have come here. He is shiny with happiness; it's vile. But Kiki is staring at me expectantly and so I look down at the menu and choose my meal.

Later, I rush Kiki through dinner and drop her off at her door with a quick kiss. She says she appreciates how much of a gentleman I am. Me, a gentleman? That's the great cosmic laugh of all time. A gentleman who is using her to spy on the boyfriend (no, fiancé) of the girl he has been blackmailing into blowjobs for three years.

I get home early to call Alice, while Seth is still at the restaurant. She answers and I launch into my pitch.

"Alice, I'm sorry. I didn't mean to pressure you into anything. But maybe you should think about it before you marry that guy."

"Peter, I'm not sure where this is going but just stop."

"Please, I need you to hear me out. Meet me here tomorrow afternoon."

"I told you I don't want to do that anymore."

"No sex, I promise. I just want to talk to you."

"No, Peter."

"Things don't just end when you decide they do. Nothing has changed except your engagement to Old Snobby Pants Restaurant Owner."

Alice laughs. "You're a real jerk, sometimes."

"Please come over tomorrow."

"On my lunch hour. You better feed me, real food. No jokes about liquid lunches or protein shakes." Her laughter is quick and embarassed.

"See, you can't be raunchy like that around Seth now can you?"

"Don't push it Peter. I already said I'll see you tomorrow."

Any businessman knows when to leave the table. I say goodnight to her and plan my strategy.

She's in full business attire when she comes to my apartment and I already feel at a disadvantage. I should have dressed up instead of hanging out in my usual jeans and T-shirts. I own suits, nice suits in fact, it's just that most of my time is spent alone or in warehouses and so I don't often need to wear them.

"So, where's my lunch?"

"And hello to you too, Alice." I lead her to the table where I have spread out the lunch I ordered, baby back ribs and all the fixings from Dixie BBQ.

"It looks great but I can't eat that in this outfit."

"You can wear an old T-shirt of mine."

She flashes me a look but she nods and soon we are sitting down to a home-style Southern feast.

"This is fantastic," she says, licking crumbs of cornbread off her lips, "of course I am going to be ready for a nap in about an hour."

"Alice, aren't you going to miss this?"

"Seth lets me eat ribs."

"You know what I mean."

"Peter, it's not that we haven't had fun, it's just that I am trying to be an adult now and do what's right."

"What's expected of you."

"Yes, but also, what I expect from myself. The one good thing about that accident was that it forced me to grow up and make some changes and live as an adult."

"That's bullshit."

She shrugs and keeps eating. She's unflappable, which worries me more than anything.

"I can make you not marry him." She pauses mid-bite. "Say it."

"Alice, I think it's obvious."

"Go ahead, you know, you've never really said it. Three years of implications and pauses and little veiled threats. Go on Peter, let it out."

And she's daring me, taunting me, her sparking eyes challenging me. "Fine. If you don't agree to continue seeing me I will tell the authorities about your hit and run accident. I'll tell them you were drunk and you left the scene and you illegally had your car fixed." It feels completely shitty to say it all out loud; I immediately want to hit the delete key.

"Ha," she yells triumphantly, "you can't prove any of it. And the other car involved, they never reported it, so my lawyer said it's my word against yours."

"And the media? I could cause quite a scandal."

"Would you really do that to me?"

She looks so small sitting there in my Boston College Rugby shirt, her little pointed chin jerking up at me. And she knows I would never hurt her. She has called my bluff, I am sunk.

"Alice, I am going to miss you, doesn't that count for anything?"

"Peter, I really have to leave," she says quietly.

I should have let it go at that point. Most guys would have, they would end it with the goodbye scene at the door, the warm hug, her strong-shoulder silhouette walking away down the street. They might think they got off easy, no pun intended. But I still wasn't convinced that she was really in love with this Seth guy. Maybe it was just some bid for parental acceptance, perhaps there was an inheritance involved. She never did tell me she loved him. Now that might have been forgetfulness, but it might have been something more.

I started haunting Seth's restaurant like the ghost of Christmas

Past. Mostly I went solo but sometimes I brought Kiki, who finally beginning to get bored with the house salad. One momentous night, sitting at the bar alone, eating my tuna pomodoro, I even had a conversation with Seth. He seemed like a nice enough guy, optimistic about the Red Sox, concerned about the stock market-I wanted to strangle him. When I told him what I did for a living, he asked about the sound system in the restaurant. I hadn't paid much attention to it before but when I cocked my head to listen, I could hear the places where the noise was getting funneled in all the wrong directions. Next thing you know he's trying to offer me a job to fix the sound system and to create a design for a new nightclub he wants to open. This would infuriate Alice. I said yes instantly, captivated by the imagined vision of her shocked face.

Unfortunately, I never had the pleasure of seeing Alice walk into the restaurant to catch Seth and I hard at work, our heads bent over layouts and brochures. Before we could even get that far, she called my house.

"I don't know what you think you are doing?"

"Who is this?"

"You know damn well who it is. Seth told me about this great new guy he met who's going to design his sound system. Stay out of his restaurant, Peter."

"Or what?"

She growled with frustration and hung up the phone. I figured I truly had her over a barrel this time. She'd never tell Seth.

Of course, I was wrong on that count, too. Shows what I know about women. The next Friday night I came into the restaurant all innocence and smiles, and walked right into Seth's fist. He gave me a nice blue-black shiner. I don't know if she gave him all the details but certainly enough to take me off the guest list permanently.

Today is the day of Alice's wedding. I imagine that all of Boston society has been buzzing about it all week. I tried to forget but even before I opened my eyes this morning I felt that sickly pit-of-my-stomach ache. If this were a movie, I'd be waiting for her in that church and she would stop halfway down the aisle, look at my face and rush into my arms. Or perhaps she would get to the altar and the sight of her there would cause me to roar to my feet with mad declarations of love. But no, life is full of minor drama, words unsaid and the irredeemable. Instead, I roll over and kiss Kiki good morning.

Kevin Rogers

Closure

1997-2002

//

Kevin Rogers was born in Southern California, then moved to Oregon, then to Taiwan, from there back to Southern California, and on to San Francisco, then back to Taiwan, only to return to Southern California where he currently may or may not be holed up in an underground bunker with a few good men and enough canned provisions to make it through the next year. At any rate, *Closure* and the stories that came before and after it were written before he came back to Southern California the last time. The voices told him it should be this way.

There was a pistol in my backpack and extra clips in my pocket. Half-drunk, and lying in the shade of a tree. I was ready to kill someone, but I wasn't sure who deserved it most.

There was an illusive logic behind my feelings, but whenever I tried to translate it into actual words inside my head, this logic seemed more shoddy than illusive.

As of yet, I had committed no wrong, but I was ready to change that.

I opened the backpack, took out an apple, and ate it. Backpack still open, I removed the pistol and examined it. It felt solid in my hand, as if it could do what it was designed to do.

I zipped up the bag, tucked the pistol under my belt, and buttoned my coat. I walked down to the diner and ordered breakfast after buying a paper.

I opened to the funny pages looking for clues. These clues were to be found at the bottom of the page.

CANCER: Your life is full of problems right now, but luckily, the answers are right in front of you. Do what you feel is right and things will go smoothly. Pisces is flirtatious.

I could have interpreted this message in a million different ways, but I chose to ignore them all. After leaving a three dollar tip on the table, I walked to the phone booth outside the restaurant and dialed up April (the woman who had cheated on me with Charles I), acting distressed. After five minutes of telephone screaming, I pulled the trigger.

The patrons of the restaurant were confused. Occasionally, you would hear gunfire in this part of town. But confronted with something like this, they didn't know how to react. I gave them the thumbs up sign to signal I was okay. Then, leaving the receiver dangling, I walked back to my apartment, dialed Angel (the woman who I had cheated on Charles II with), and pulled the trigger again.

As for Charles I, he'd have his own problems. He was in love with a woman who'd recently fallen back in love with a man she assumed was dead.

At the time, the only person in this whole incident I felt sorry for was Charles II. In time, I would regret it more than anything else I had ever done in my life.

I hadn't smoked in years, but I was smoking now. Waiting for the bus, about to leave my past behind me, it seemed like a good habit to pick up again.

Smoking's a social activity. It's also a game of solitaire, love gone bad, a passive way to give offense, and a million other things that had a glorious feel to them at the time.

The bus was going south and I was on it. We stopped every few hours, to piss, refuel, eat, or change drivers.

I had bought a ticket to San Diego, but I stepped off in Los Angeles. There was a guy with dreadlocks and green overcoat sleeping outside the station. He was wearing a T-shirt that read, "Home is where the heart is." Only instead of the word "Heart" it had a big, red heart where the word could have been. It was then that I knew I had found my new home. Hell, it was spelled out on a T-shirt.

It was a bit of a hassle to get the driver to give me my bags.

He protested, "But you're ticket says San Diego."

"I know, but I decided to go to Los Angeles instead."

"You're in Los Angeles."

"Yeah."

"So," he said, "Technically, you'd be staying in Los Angeles, not going to Los Angeles."

"Good point," I responded.

He twirled the toothpick in his mouth.

I pushed the question, "So, can I get my bags?"

"Yeah, why not? L.A.'s a fine city."

So there I stayed.

Sleeping with Snakes
Notes from the Los Angeles Underbelly

*You don't need to flirt with the waitress because she is the actress
you slept with two years ago...*

In a town made up of transplants and implants, where devils never
sleep and a drug score is like a trip to the ATM, one would assume
that everyone has as story to tell. Well, within that thick layer of
guilt that LA holds above her - call it smog, call it sin - something
ain't right and good or bad, real or fad, you'll read about the rotting souls that live among the streets that are paved with gold.

Truth and fiction become a blur in this collection of 32 Los
Angeles based authors - including an early 80s commentary by the
late Charles Bukowski. All of these authors have placed their own
spin onto the culture that is so uniquely LA. From sinfully delicious tales of murder to porn and drugs to love and lust, you'll
read everything you ever thought you never wanted to know about
this town.

Put your plastic surgeon on hold, fire up the Range Rover and
become a part of this capitalist, commercial, celebrity obsessed,
self-indulgent community that we all call home.

Ron Sievers [anthologist]